D0378563

Chapter 1

"…AND ANY COUPLE THAT SPENDS THE NIGHT IN THE CHRISTMAS Cottage shall have love everlasting."

Lacey Quinn stifled a groan as she listened to her best friend and bride-to-be retell her family's fairy tale of a house that was the key to a successful and happy marriage. Lacey had been hearing the story her entire life; the Quinns and the Callahans had been friends long before Lacey and Ava were born. The story wasn't anything new. What was new was that Ava was the one getting married in seven short weeks and would get to experience the fairy tale for herself.

If Lacey didn't strangle her first.

"Yes, yes, love everlasting, blah, blah, blah." Lacey sighed as she reached for the last Chinese dumpling. "Honestly, don't you ever get tired of saying it?"

"Never," Ava replied adamantly. Standing, Ava took the clip out of her long blond hair and shook it out as she went to stand in front of the full-length mirror by her front door. "I'm thinking of wearing my hair up." Doing a quick twist, she turned and faced Lacey. "What do you think?"

A quick gulp of wine fortified Lacey for the conversation they'd had at least a dozen times before. "You know your hair looks fabulous in an up-sweep. Plus, with the tiara you picked out, it will look stunning. Positively princess-like," she added just to stroke Ava's bridal ego.

"Of course, if I wear it long and loose, I can have some fabulous curls done. Mason loves it when my hair is down."

There wasn't enough wine in the universe to make Lacey want to continue this conversation. "Then you should wear it down," she said as she stood and took the now-empty wine bottle to the kitchen and prepared to make an exit and head home.

"Well, which is it, Lacey? Up or down?" Lacey didn't have to see her friend to know Ava was pouting; it was there in the tone of her voice. Taking her time to rinse her glass and place it on the drain board, she silently counted to ten before heading back into the living room.

"You will look beautiful no matter how you wear your hair. Mason is going to be the luckiest man in the world, and it won't matter one bit about your hair. We'll see how you feel on your wedding day." There, that sounded comforting and diplomatic, didn't it?

"I know you're right," Ava said, sighing with relief as she released her hair and turned to face Lacey. "Before you go, there's one last bit of the wedding details I need to talk to you about."

So close, Lacey thought to herself as she looked longingly at the door. What more could there possibly be to discuss? The weddings in the Callahan family were traditional; no one strayed from the formula. They owned a massive ranch outside Asheville, North Carolina, where the family spent every Christmas. Lacey loved the old ranch and had spent many a Christmas there herself. The weddings were almost always done on Christmas Eve with the entire family in attendance. Then, the beaming bride and groom would head to the guest cottage,

SACRAMENTO PUBLIC LIBRARY
828 "I" Street
Sacramento, CA 95814
01/16

The CHRISTMAS COTTAGE

EVER AFTER

SAMANTHA CHASE

sourcebooks
casablanca

The Christmas Cottage copyright © 2012, 2015 by Samantha Chase
Ever After copyright © 2013, 2015 by Samantha Chase
Cover and internal design © 2015 by Sourcebooks, Inc.
Cover design by Dawn Adams/Sourcebooks, Inc.
Cover images © Getty Images

Sourcebooks and the colophon are registered trademarks of Sourcebooks, Inc.

All rights reserved. No part of this book may be reproduced in any form or by any electronic or mechanical means including information storage and retrieval systems—except in the case of brief quotations embodied in critical articles or reviews—without permission in writing from its publisher, Sourcebooks, Inc.

The characters and events portrayed in this book are fictitious or are used fictitiously. Any similarity to real persons, living or dead, is purely coincidental and not intended by the author.

Published by Sourcebooks Casablanca, an imprint of Sourcebooks, Inc.
P.O. Box 4410, Naperville, Illinois 60567-4410
(630) 961-3900
Fax: (630) 961-2168
www.sourcebooks.com

Printed and bound in Canada.
MBP 10 9 8 7 6 5 4 3 2 1

Contents

The CHRISTMAS COTTAGE

tucked a discreet distance farther up the mountain, for their wedding night.

The Callahans had been having wedding celebrations like this since the Depression. From the pictures Lacey'd seen, the cottage was a cross between a gingerbread house and a house you'd see on Christmas cards. Charming and inviting—those were the words that always came to mind when the pictures were brought out. But even charming old houses need to be renovated from time to time.

Ava had been distraught over the thought of the cottage being "wrecked" before it was her turn to stay in it. Luckily, most of the work seemed to have to do with bringing the wiring and plumbing up to date and some minor cosmetic changes. Everyone had assured Ava that none of the cottage's charm or "magic" had been tampered with.

Noticing that Ava was still standing there looking anxious, Lacey realized she'd let her mind wander for a moment. What were they talking about again? Oh yes, more wedding details.

Oh joy.

For the life of her, Lacey couldn't imagine what else in the world there was to cover. The wedding ceremony would be held in the Callahan home, the caterer had been booked, their dresses had been ordered, and all of the fittings were done. Invitations had been sent and all of the RSVPs had been received. Flowers had been ordered, bouquets designed, and the groom and his groomsmen had been taken care of as well. As far as Lacey could tell, all that was left was for the darn day to finally get here so she could get some peace.

"Right, details," Lacey said. "What's up?"

"Well, there is this one last little tradition that needs to be taken care of," Ava began, practically bouncing on the balls of her feet.

"Okay, shoot. What is it?"

"As my maid of honor, it is up to you and Mason's best man to take care of getting the cottage ready for us."

That was it? Score! Easy-peasy. "No problem," she responded, anxious to get home. "I'm sure we'll have time to slip out during the reception and light some candles, sprinkle some rose petals, and whatnot. No worries, Ava, I'm on it!"

"No!" Ava cried, despair written all over her face. "This is no ordinary honeymoon suite, Lace. You have to get the cottage ready for us, and not just with that silly, clichéd romantic stuff."

Of course not. Why had Lacey even thought for one second that this was going to be easy? "Okay then, what is it exactly that I'm supposed to do?"

With that, Ava grabbed both of Lacey's hands and dragged her back over to the couch. "Well, I have a *bunch* of ideas."

Of course she does. Before Lacey even had the opportunity to ask what they were, Ava reached down next to the sofa and pulled out a large three-ring binder and placed it in Lacey's lap with a big grin.

"All of this is about the cottage?"

"Yes."

What have I gotten myself into? "Am I re-siding the cottage? Putting on a new roof? I mean, look at the size of this binder, Ava!"

"I know it looks big, but if you would just open it, you'll see what I want to do."

Not trusting a single word Ava just said, Lacey sat back and opened the binder and hoped that her jaw hitting the floor was not noticeable. Re-siding the house and putting on a new roof would have been easier than what was detailed in this mammoth book.

There were notes, descriptions, pictures, drawings…on and on it went for seventeen divided sections. "Seventeen sections, Ava? The cottage isn't all that big, how in the world do you expect to have all of this done?"

"You're focusing far too much on the number of pages in the book and not enough on what's on them." Taking the binder from Lacey, Ava began to describe the "perfect" setting for her wedding night.

"First of all, there needs to be the right lighting. I want to make sure the lighting is soft, and yes, I know I said it was clichéd, but I do want candles. Lots and lots of white candles. There's a fireplace as well, so there will need to be enough wood stocked to keep the fire burning all night."

"Didn't they just update…"

"Yes, yes, they did, but a roaring fire would be so much more romantic." She sighed. "I'll want flowers—poinsettias—and greens, the kind that are particularly associated with Christmas—holly and mistletoe," she began, scanning the flower section of the binder. "There's a Christmas cactus that I would *love* to have here, and there's even a Christmas rose, or the snow rose I'm sure a florist can help you find."

"You're only going to be there for one or two nights, Ava. Don't you think…?"

"I know we'll have eaten at my parents' place, but food will need to be stocked. Champagne, chocolates, strawberries, whipped cream—the real stuff, not the stuff in the tub—and then maybe some 'normal' stuff like a fruit and cheese platter, some oysters on the half shell, an assortment of cookies, and then something for breakfast." More flipping through the binder quickly followed.

"Why don't I have a chef hang out on the front porch just waiting to take your order?" Lacey said dryly.

Ava shot her a sharp glance. "A girl only gets married *once*," she said emphatically before adding, "Hopefully." At Lacey's arched brow, Ava quickly rambled on. "There is nothing wrong with wanting my wedding night to be perfect. It has to be perfect, Lacey!" she cried as she reached over and grabbed her friend's hand.

"What has gotten into you?" Lacey asked cautiously. "I have known you my whole life, and you have never been like this. I understand that it's your wedding, but honestly, you're about to enter the bridezilla zone and it's starting to worry me."

Lacey had been friends with Ava her whole life, and she knew something wasn't right. Looking at Ava now, Lacey was concerned that something was clearly wrong. "What's going on, Ava? Are you having second thoughts?"

Gently closing the binder, Ava placed it on the coffee table and turned to face Lacey, her big blue eyes filling with tears. "Not exactly. It's just that, as the time gets closer and Mason and I start talking about the future, well, we're just not…you know, on the same page on some things."

"Like what?"

"Well, he wants to have kids right away. He's hoping for me to get pregnant on our honeymoon! I want kids,

Lace, you know I do, but I just don't want them right away. I want to settle into being married and have the time to adjust to living together before we have kids. Is that so wrong?"

"No, no, sweetie, of course it's not. What did Mason say when you told him?"

Ava pulled her hands away and looked at them as she clasped them in her lap. "I kind of mentioned it and he said I was just nervous and it was all going to be okay."

"That's it? That's all he said? So basically he thinks the issue is settled, but it's not?"

Ava nodded.

"You have to tell him the truth. This isn't a disagreement over something trivial, this is a major life-changing situation."

"Don't you think I know that? But that's why it's so important that everything at the cottage be perfect. If it is, then everything's going to be okay."

"I know you drank just as much wine as I did and I have to tell you that you are making no sense whatsoever. How is the way the cottage is decorated going to fix the fact that Mason wants to have a baby right away and you don't?"

"Don't you see? Sheesh, you've been complaining about me rambling on and on about the legend of the cottage and yet you still don't get it? Any couple who spends the night in the cottage…"

"…will have love everlasting. Um, yeah, got it. I hear it in my sleep. That still doesn't answer my question."

Ava gave a long-suffering sigh before looking at Lacey as if she were a child. "Once we spend the night in the most perfect cottage ever, we'll be guaranteed to have love everlasting. We'll agree on the right time to have a baby…and some other things…"

The last few words were added in a mumble, but Lacey caught them just the same. "You mean there's more? What else are you not in agreement about?"

"Well, the baby is the *main* issue, but then there's my job."

"What about it?"

"Mason thinks it's a ridiculous job and that maybe I should quit and focus on helping him build his business."

"But you love working at the bookstore! Plus you get a discount on your tuition! How else are you supposed to finish school?"

Ava stared at her hopelessly.

Now Lacey was mad. "So let me get this straight. Mason wants you to quit school, quit your job, and help him with his business until you have a baby."

Ava merely nodded.

"That's ridiculous! Why is this all just coming up now?"

"To be honest, we moved up the wedding because I wanted the whole Christmas Cottage thing. Our original plan had been to wait until late summer or next fall, but the thought of finally having my turn at the cottage was too tempting to miss!"

"Then wait until next Christmas and take this next year to get to know one another better and iron out all of these issues."

"Mason doesn't want to wait. He's thirty-two, and apparently *his* biological clock is ticking. His law firm is starting to grow, and he feels that, at this point in his life, he needs to be married and having children to cement his image."

"You're joking, right?"

Ava didn't answer. Reaching over, she picked up the binder and handed it to Lacey. "Please, Lace. I really need your help with this. I know it's a little hard for you to understand the fairy tale, but I've seen it happen for generations and now it's my turn. I know that if Mason and I stay there, all of this other stuff is going to work out. It has to!"

"You're putting an awful lot of hope in a fairy tale, Ava."

"I know, but you know I've always been a dreamer. I believe in happily ever after. I wish you did."

"I haven't had a whole lot of reason to believe in it."

It sounded more dramatic than the reality, but Lacey was just more practical than Ava. Always had been. Where love was concerned, Ava led with her heart. Lacey lost count of all the great loves of Ava's life and had initially thought Mason was just one in a line of many. Something about him stuck, however, and it left Lacey scratching her head because the two were as opposite as could be. Sure, she knew the old adage "opposites attract," but this was more than opposites; it was like Mason didn't even *know* Ava, and that was a shame because Ava would give him the world and he wouldn't appreciate it.

"You have plenty of reasons to believe in it," Ava interrupted her thoughts. "Your parents have been married for over thirty years! Your grandparents have been married for fifty-five years! I know your family well enough to know they are not simply tolerating one another—they are still in love. That, my friend, is happily ever after."

"Oh please! Do you hear yourself? My parents fight plenty. They've struggled and yelled and screamed, and my grandparents are no different. It's not a matter of happily ever after. After a while, you settle into something comfortable and that's your life."

"You make me sad."

Lacey glared at her. "I'm not sad, Ava. I'm practical. There's a difference."

"Not really."

"Look, can we just agree to disagree and move on?" She took the blasted binder from Ava's hands and began to scan through it again. It all seemed ridiculous. "I can follow every instruction, re-create every diagram in this book, Ava, but until you and Mason *talk,* nothing is going to change. A magical cottage in the woods of North Carolina is not suddenly going to make Mason *not* want kids right away or make you be okay with quitting school. It's not possible!"

"Well, I think it is! I have to believe it!" Ava fell to the couch sobbing, and Lacey felt like crap for pushing her. She eased down beside her and pulled her into an embrace.

"Why can't you just believe?"

"I want to believe, for your sake, but I also don't want you to settle for someone who doesn't get how amazing you are," Lacey said. "I don't want you to make a mistake."

Ava straightened. "You think marrying Mason is a mistake?"

Open mouth, insert foot. Lacey thought for a moment and chose her words very carefully. "I wouldn't say that. I just think you need to be more honest with him about how you feel. If he loves you, then he will see that this relationship is not only about him and his feelings."

Ava seemed to consider the words. "I'm sure it's going to all be okay. The cottage has never let anyone down. It has a one hundred percent success rate!" Straightening, she wiped her stray tears and once again looked at her friend. "You mean the world to me, Lace. I wish you would find someone amazing who loves you and treats you like a princess, too. I don't understand why you don't date more! You're beautiful! How could men *not* be asking you out?"

"They do." *Just not the one I want.* "But this isn't about me, this is about your cottage and getting it ready. I have a little more than a month to plan and prepare." She gave another hesitant glance at the giant binder. "This is an awful lot for one person, you know."

"No, it's not just your, or rather the maid of honor's, job. The best man helps, too!"

Lacey wracked her brain for a moment to remember who Mason had chosen for his best man. Bill? Ben? Brian? *Brian!* "That's, um, Brian, right? His best friend from college?"

"Well, it *was,* but they had some kind of falling-out recently. Mason won't talk about it, but it was serious enough that not only is Brian *not* going to be his best man, he's not coming to the wedding at all!"

"Wow! That definitely sounds serious. And he won't tell you what it was about?"

"Mason didn't want to upset me with his silly problems."

Lacey had her doubts on that one but decided to keep them to herself. "So who's the best man going to be?"

"Ean."

Everything in Lacey went still for the barest of moments before the room seemed to tilt. "I...um...I thought Ean wasn't going to be able to come home for the wedding."

"Please, *as if* my mom would allow my brother to miss not only Christmas but his baby sister's wedding! That was not going to happen. Anyway, he announced he was coming home the same day Mason announced that Brian wasn't going to be his best man, and it seemed like the perfect solution."

Lacey wanted to speak, she truly did, but her throat had gone bone-dry and her tongue seemed to be the size of her fist. Ean? Ean Callahan was not only coming home for Christmas, but she was going to have to work with him on this ridiculous cottage decorating plan? Clearly the universe hated her.

"Anyway, I figure that should make your job way easier since you and Ean know each other so well and are practically family, so it saves you from having to work with a stranger. Plus, Ean is familiar with the cottage and the area up in Asheville, so he'll be a big help getting all the supplies you'll need."

Her jaw moved; Lacey could feel herself willing it to move, and yet no sound came out. Ava didn't seem to notice; she kept the conversation going for the both of them.

"I'm not sure exactly when he'll be arriving home, but I'll have him call you and the two of you can work out arrangements for getting it all done. You should probably go up there and see it all as it is. Take the binder and go and shop for the stuff you'll need. Then, you'll want to work out how you'll get it done Christmas week so everything will be fresh for Christmas Eve."

For once, Lacey wished Ava would just stop talking.

She wished her friend could, for once, see *her* inner turmoil and focus on someone other than herself. Work with Ean? Spend time decorating a romantic getaway cottage with Ean?

Since she was twelve, Lacey had been in love with Ean Callahan, but he'd never seen her as more than an extension of his baby sister. She'd tried everything to get him to notice her, to no avail. Ean was not the typical guy most girls got dreamy over. He wasn't the class jock or the town heartthrob. He was studious and intelligent, with just a hint of computer geek. His wire-rimmed glasses were usually falling down his nose, and he'd been painfully shy throughout high school. But to Lacey, he was everything.

When Ean graduated high school and their families had gotten together to celebrate, Lacey decided enough was enough. Sure, looking back she knew that at fourteen there was no way anyone was going to fall for her—least of all an eighteen-year-old heading to college—but at the time, her confidence made up for her inability to see the situation for what it was.

It had been late, after eleven at night, and the party was winding down. Lacey's parents had given her the fifteen-minute warning that they were leaving. She and Ava had tried to swindle a sleepover out of the night, but neither set of parents had agreed. Noticing Ean going into the house, Lacey followed.

She tiptoed down the basement stairs and into the rec room, certain she could be the next Bond girl with her stealth mode. Quietly, she watched as Ean sat down on the large sectional sofa and turned on the TV. He took his glasses off and rubbed his eyes as he lay back and relaxed. She slipped in beside him before he even realized she was there.

"Hi, Ean," she said breathlessly, thinking she sounded sexy.

"Oh, hey, Lacey." He looked around nervously. "Where's Ava?" His black hair was longer than she'd ever seen him wear it, and it looked good on him. He was always so neat and tidy and polished that it was nice to see him a little disheveled.

"She's still outside talking with your grandparents."

Ean nodded and then looked at her expectantly. She knew he was probably wondering why she was here alone with him in the basement. They were never alone, and she'd certainly never sought him out for conversation.

"So are you excited about college?"

"Sure. I'm ready to move out and move on." There was a long pause, and Lacey inched just a little bit closer on the couch. Ean cleared his throat and shifted a little farther away. "We'll finish packing tomorrow and then my folks are driving me up to Massachusetts. The summer semester starts next Monday."

"What?" she cried. "You're leaving tomorrow? I thought you'd be home all summer!"

He looked at her like she was crazy. "No, I wanted to start right away. I can't wait to get away from this town and start working toward getting my own company started. That's certainly not going to happen if I sit around here all summer long."

She was crushed. Ean, the great love of her life, her reason for living, was leaving. Worse, he didn't even seem to realize he was slowly killing her. "Oh, well, that's great. Ava didn't mention it," she mumbled. Taking a deep breath, Lacey realized it was now or never. "Listen, Ean, I think you're amazing. You're so smart and so talented, and I think you are going to be the absolute best at…"—she had completely forgotten what he was going to major in—"…whatever it is you choose to do!"

Ean gave her a genuine smile, and in that moment, Lacey was sure he understood her feelings. How could he not? She believed in him! She was encouraging him! Certainly now, finally, she could make her move. With more enthusiasm than finesse, Lacy leaned over and kissed him. Her lips had barely touched his when he grabbed her by the upper arms and shoved her away.

"Geez, Lacey, what are you doing?"

Her green eyes went wide with shock.

"Are you crazy? Why would you do that?" There was a hint of annoyance in his tone, but first and foremost was confusion.

Lacey forced herself to speak. "Wh… Why?" she stammered. "Because I wanted to, because you're amazing, and because I love you!"

Now it was Ean's turn for his eyes to widen. "Love me? *Love me?*" Pushing his glasses up on his nose, he stood and looked down at her on the couch. "Are you insane? You're like, what, fourteen? I'm going off to college! You're like family, like a sister! You're Ava's best friend!" He was pacing, and by the time he finally stopped and looked at Lacey, he had essentially shattered what had been her dream of happily ever after.

Lacey had run from the basement as if the hounds of hell were after her, and went to wait for her parents by their car, refusing to interact with anyone else at the party. All she wanted was to go home, lock herself in her room, and cry until she was numb. When her parents found her and asked why she'd been waiting by the car and not saying good night to everyone, she pleaded a headache and climbed into the backseat.

The whole way home, she cursed herself for being so stupid. Of course a college guy like Ean wouldn't be interested in her. No one would be. She was an idiot for even trying. Luckily, Ean's visits home would be few and far between. No one would know about their basement conversation, and if she lived to be one hundred, she'd never speak of it. If she'd learned one thing from this night, it was never to trust her instincts where boys were concerned. Her heart was broken, and Lacey never wanted to feel like that again. Ever.

For years, she had managed to avoid seeing Ean. It wasn't hard to do. The Callahans always went to visit him, and on his longer breaks, he took internships overseas to help with his degree. Yes, avoiding Ean Callahan had been a relative breeze for almost twelve years.

Until now.

Until this stupid wedding and the Christmas Cottage that was quickly becoming a thorn in Lacey's side.

"I can't wait to see Ean," Ava was saying. Who knows if she had been saying anything else, so lost in her own misery had Lacey been. "I can't even remember the last time he was home for more than a weekend, can you?"

"No."

Her flat response went over Ava's head completely. "When was the last time you two even saw each other? What was it, his graduation, right?"

Lacey closed her eyes and counted to ten. "I don't remember, Ava, okay?"

Clearly *that* response got Ava's attention. "What's the matter? Don't you want to work with Ean on this for me?"

"It's not that, it's just…"

"Oh gosh, is this because you used to have a massive crush on him?"

"*WHAT?*"

"Please, you were never good at hiding your emotions, and for years I watched you watching him. Then after he left for school, you were always asking about him. I never could understand it because, basically, Ean is a major geek, but hey, if that's what floats your boat…"

"Ean does *not* float my boat, and you have no idea what you're talking about," Lacey said defensively, searching the apartment for her purse and keys so she could finally get out of there and process all of the things that had happened here today.

"Look, it's no big deal to me. For a while I thought he had a thing for you, too. He always asks about you, but you know, he went away to school and all that, and you never came around when he was home and it was sort of 'out of sight, out of mind' for me. So is that what has your bitch factor on right now?"

"I don't have a bitch factor…"

"Oh please, you *so* have a bitch factor going on right now. You forget, Lacey Quinn, you and I are closer than sisters and I know everything about you. You may think you hid your tracks well, but you didn't. You had a crush on my brother. So what? He's here for my wedding, he's Mason's best man, and if it's all no big deal to you, then working with him should be a breeze, right?"

For a moment, Lacey wanted to hit something and Ava was handy. But rather than risking a friendship, she merely shrugged. "Of course I don't have a problem working with Ean on the cottage," Lacey said grudgingly. "When he gets into town, give him my number and we'll coordinate our schedules. He's probably not going to be around for long, so I'll most likely end up doing the shopping and prepping on my own. It's no big deal."

"Mmm-hmm," Ava purred. "That's what I thought."

Lacey rolled her eyes and grabbed Ava for a hug. "I've got my assignment, Captain, and I'm prepared to take it on. Your Christmas Cottage is going to be a living, breathing dream come to life! Ean and I will make sure of it."

Ava held on tight. "You are my best friend in the whole wide world, and I knew I could count on you." When she finally let go, she looked Lacey in the eye. "It means the world to me that you and Ean are going to work on this together. You are the two people I trust most in this world. I love you."

"Love you too."

Lacey stepped off the porch and headed out into the cool night air. She turned once and gave a quick wave to Ava. For her friend's sake, she'd do everything in her power to make this cottage look the way she wanted, but there was no way she would do it with Ean. No, by the time Ean Callahan decided to stroll into town, everything would be done, and though she'd make sure he got some of the credit, anything he was going to do, he'd be doing on his own.

This time, she'd be the one dismissing him.

Chapter 2

EAN CALLAHAN WAS HOME. WELL, NOT HOME, exactly, but at his family's mountain home—or the ranch, as it was normally called. He'd get to Raleigh eventually, but right now he needed a break from his hectic pace. Right now there was no place more peaceful than the mountains of North Carolina.

The weather was crisp and cool, and even though logic had dictated that he fly home, the thought of driving to see the fall foliage had been impossible to resist. With no schedule to adhere to, he'd left his home in Boston bright and early Monday morning and spread the fifteen-hour drive out over two days. Having no one but himself for company, he had found the quiet very unusual. He spent most of his days surrounded by people wanting something from him, or more accurately, demanding something from him. His time was never his own anymore, and of that, Ean had grown weary.

Ava's wedding could not have come at a more perfect time. This time of year, most of his employees were distracted with the holidays and shopping and partying and celebrating. He couldn't get a decent workday out of half of them. When his mother had called and inquired if he was truly sure he wouldn't be home for his baby sister's wedding, he'd decided to throw caution to the wind and take a much-needed vacation.

That's not to say he wouldn't be working. With a

quick glance at the luggage he had just hauled into the house, Ean knew he had everything here to make a decent home office. The main benefit was that he would actually be able to hear himself think.

Work at his software company had never bothered Ean before, but lately it wasn't enough. He'd accomplished so many things over the eight years since he'd graduated from college, and even if he were being modest, he could say with great certainty that he'd done everything he'd set out to do. Unfortunately, there were no great challenges ahead, no mountains to climb, metaphorically speaking. His career was in maintenance mode, and while that was a good thing and kept him financially secure, Ean couldn't help but wonder what to do with himself next.

Well, first up was getting unpacked, and then it was off to town to stock up on some food so he could truly settle in. Ean had thought of letting someone know he was coming here, but then his much-needed quiet time would have been a distant dream. He felt a little guilty for keeping his family in the dark about arriving early in Asheville, but he knew that by doing things this way, he'd be much better company when they were all together for what promised to be a long, festive Christmas week.

Ean had been anxious to get to the ranch. It had been years since he'd been here, and he knew it had recently been renovated, so he wanted to see firsthand what had been done. Plus, checking out the pantry would help him determine what supplies he'd need.

Once his unpacking was done and he was settled into his old room, Ean moved to his father's office and set up his own equipment. The temptation to check emails and make calls was strong, but his growling stomach proved to be the stronger pull. Work could wait; his hunger could not.

The drive into town was uneventful, and once at the store, it was nice to be able to pick out exactly what he wanted. Back in Boston, he had a housekeeper who shopped for him and cleaned his town house once a week. He ordered out a lot, or used a personal chef to cook up meals and freeze them so all he had to do was defrost and microwave his dinners. The novelty of walking through the supermarket and choosing foods at whim was more pleasant than Ean would've thought possible.

Looking around, he noticed the store was particularly crowded. When he saw a harried stock boy quickly tossing canned goods onto a shelf, he let his curiosity get the better of him. "Is there some sort of sale going on that I'm missing?" he asked lightly.

The boy, who had to be maybe sixteen, turned to him, eyes wide. "No, sir, everyone's stocking up because of the snow."

"Snow?" Ean asked incredulously. "It's only the second week of November."

"Yes, sir. I know that and you know that, but it seems Mother Nature doesn't care. The weatherman's predicting almost a foot of snow tonight!" And with that bombshell, the boy turned back to the task at hand.

Snow? Well, he'd certainly be getting the peace and quiet he'd been looking for. He just hoped he had the electricity to complement it. Ean made his way around the store, buying everything he could think of that he'd need. Snow wouldn't be a problem for him. He'd stop and get gas for the generator, he had snow boots at the house, and he knew where his father kept the shovels and snowblower. No, sir, this storm was not going to ruin the first day of his vacation.

The checkout line seemed to be a mile long. There were easily a dozen lanes open and each was about ten people deep. With nothing left to do but people-watch, he scanned the crowd. There were several mothers with children who were practically dancing on their toes at the thought of snow. He heard many "Will we build a snowman?" and "Can we have snowball fights?" The questions made him smile because he remembered feeling that exact same way when he was a boy.

Looking around, he saw people like himself who, judging by their business attire and the annoyed looks on their faces, were clearly here on their way home from work. No doubt they were just as anxious as he was to get their groceries and get home before the weather turned.

The lines moved slowly, and a quick glance out the window showed the first snowflakes starting to fall. He pulled out his iPhone and was about to check the weather when a flash of cobalt blue caught his eye two lanes over to the left. The woman had long, wavy auburn hair, and although the noise level in the store made it nearly impossible to hear himself think, he heard her laugh and felt a tightening in his gut he hadn't felt in a long time.

Ean strained to get a better look at the woman. The color of her hair reminded him of home—of Lacey. He was sure they'd see each other for the wedding, especially since she was Ava's maid of honor.

It had been twelve years since he'd seen or talked to her. Not that he hadn't wanted to. Over the years he'd thought about the last time they'd seen each other—probably more than he should have. Ean had known immediately that he'd handled it wrong and hurt Lacey's feelings, and it had never sat well with him. Maybe he should have made an effort, one of the times he'd been home to visit his family, to seek Lacey out and apologize. Or maybe he should have called or written or…something.

He'd always liked Lacey. She was younger. She was his little sister's best friend. If she had been older and had approached him, Ean knew his reaction would have been completely different.

He would have kissed her back.

He would have kept in touch and maybe come home to visit a little bit more.

It was all ancient history though, right? There was no way he could change the past or what he'd said and done. Ean just wished he could erase the memory of the look of devastation on Lacey's face. Even thinking about it now caused a slight clench in his stomach. It was so long ago and yet…

Would she still look the same? Well, not the same, but familiar? The woman two lanes over had the same color hair, and it had him wondering if Lacey wore hers long or short now. It had been somewhere in between all those years ago, but that didn't mean anything.

The woman turned and he saw her fix her cobalt-blue wool coat, flip an emerald-green scarf around her neck—*the same color as Lacey's eyes*, he thought absently—and he waited, with breath held, to see if she'd turn his way. A glimpse of her profile was all he could see: ivory skin, a straight, pert nose, and rosy cheeks, all surrounded by that mane of auburn hair.

Damn.

Clearly he was just feeling nostalgic because of being home. It couldn't possibly be Lacey. From what he knew from his mother, Lacey still lived in Raleigh and was working for an interior design firm. So it couldn't be Lacey, could it? No, that would be too much of a weird coincidence for Lacey Quinn to be shopping in the same small-town grocery store as him in a town neither of them lived in with the wedding still more than a month away.

Too weird.

Too coincidental.

Totally impossible.

Ean realized the cashier was looking at him expectantly. Somehow he had managed to lose track of the fact that he was currently having his groceries checked out and bagged. He smiled apologetically and paid for his stuff, all the while looking out the front window for the woman in the cobalt-blue coat. The cashier thanked him and wished him safe travel, and Ean walked out into the lightly falling snow.

If he could be thankful for a small miracle, it would be for the fact that the snowstorm was taking its time in hitting the area. He'd have some time to get to the gas station and then home before the roads got particularly treacherous. With the last bag safely placed in the back of his SUV, he turned and saw the woman climbing into her own SUV at the end of the row he was parked in. Without conscious thought, Ean started to head toward her, but she pulled out and away before he was even halfway there.

It was all for the best. What was he going to say to her? "Hey, I've been staring at you for several minutes and you remind me of a girl I grew up with. Do you want to get a drink?" Geez, he was out of practice with the art of approaching women. Wait, who was he kidding, he'd never had the art of the approach. Work and school had been his life. He never dated much, and when he did, it was with like-minded women—ones who were too involved in their jobs to want to get into a serious relationship. He met most of them through mutual acquaintances, and after a couple of dates, they'd each moved on.

He sighed at an opportunity lost, then headed back to his car and continued to finish his errands so he'd be home before dark.

The ride back to the ranch took a little longer than Ean was comfortable with. The roads were already getting slick and treacherous. He was used to the snow up in Boston, but he wasn't used to driving up a mountain in it. There was quite a difference. He hurried into the house with his groceries, and then went back out to grab the gas cans and put them in the garage near the generator, just in case he needed them. Once his task was complete, Ean headed back to the kitchen and looked at the time. Four o'clock. A little late for lunch, a little early for dinner, so he opted for a sandwich to tide him over until he felt like making something more substantial.

The sandwich he made looked very promising, and Ean was lifting it, anticipating how good it was going to taste, when a flash of headlights on the far end of the property caught his attention through the full wall of windows at the back of the house. Who in the world would opt to drive up here in the snow when it was getting dark, he wondered? Thinking that whoever it was may be a neighbor he didn't know about, he went back to his sandwich.

Twenty minutes later, with a somewhat full belly, Ean went into the office to check his emails and see how business had gone that day without him. He was about to close the plantation shutters when he noticed a soft light off in the distance. Now, he knew he hadn't been up to the ranch in many, many years, but if he wasn't mistaken, that was the guest cottage with all the lights on. Who in the world would be up there? His parents didn't rent the place out, and the renovations were done.

Trespasser? Squatter? Ean had no idea, and now he had no choice but to find out. Dammit, this was not part of his plan! He was here to relax; he was here to unwind. He was *not* here to have to fight off some would-be trespasser at his family's guest cottage. Grumbling the entire way, Ean went to the mudroom and found a pair of snow boots, a coat, gloves, and a hat before grabbing his keys and heading out into the dusk.

His first thought had been to drive his SUV up to the cottage; it would be faster and it would give him a better way to give chase should he need to, but he didn't want to alert whoever was up there that he was coming. Locking the house up, he trudged up the path leading to the cottage.

The snow was starting to stick to the cold ground, and though it was still flurrying, Ean had no doubt that this path would not be easily maneuvered in a couple of hours. He hoped whoever was up in the cottage would take his warning seriously and leave the premises promptly. It didn't take long to realize the cottage was farther away than he remembered and that his breath was a little ragged, and he cursed. He went to the gym regularly; how could he be out of breath? *Clearly because there's a big difference between walking up a mountain in the snow and jogging on a stationary treadmill*, a snarky inner voice mocked.

Well, he'd be damned if he was going to stop and catch his breath. The sooner this intruder was gone, the sooner he'd be safely back at the ranch in front of a fire enjoying a steak dinner. Reaching into his pocket, Ean fished out his phone and checked to make sure he had reception in the dense woods. Seeing three bars, he felt confident that, should this person give him any trouble, he'd be able to call for backup without any problem.

Almost there. The words even sounded winded in his head. He could only hope that the brides and grooms who used this blasted cottage drove up here and didn't find it "magical" to climb the mountain together as part of the experience.

As he stepped into the clearing, the first things he noticed were a black SUV parked in the driveway and smoke coming from the chimney. *Made yourself at home, did you?* Approaching the cottage, Ean decided to walk the perimeter and see if he could get a good look at how many people he was dealing with. No one was visible through the front window, and a quick jog to the left had him remembering there were no windows on this side. As he carefully made his way through the trees and toward the back of the cottage, he saw a shadow of a person behind the blinds.

Holding his breath, Ean realized it was definitely the silhouette of a woman. He shuffled through the trees some more and had a full view of the rear of the house, but all of the windows were covered. *Dammit!* With one last hope, he walked around to the last side and finally had an unobstructed view through a window. At six feet tall he should have been able to see right in, but the window was just about a head higher. Looking around for something to stand on, Ean reached for one of the deck chairs closest to him and positioned it under the window.

Hoping it was sturdy enough to hold him, he took his chances and balanced on it to get a better look inside. He saw shadows, but no actual person. Craning his neck for a better view, he heard music playing, saw flames in the fireplace, and if he wasn't crazy, he smelled something cooking on the stove. He'd barely managed to make and eat a sandwich, and this person had settled in, made a fire, and had food cooking on the stove already?

Cursing the cold, the snow, and the fact that he was acting like a Peeping Tom on his own property, he was just about to climb down when the mystery woman stepped into view. She turned toward him and, like a deer caught in headlights, all Ean could do was stare. The woman let out a bloodcurdling scream as Ean fell off the chair and flat onto his back in the snow.

Several thoughts hit him at once. First, he was going to have one hell of a headache in a few hours. Second, his back wasn't doing much better. And third, the intruder was coming toward him; he could hear her footsteps approaching.

"Oh my God, are you all right?"

Ean heard the voice, but his eyes hadn't refocused just yet. He shook his head gingerly, and when his vision cleared, he stared up in complete shock. It was the woman from the grocery store. He forced himself to study her more closely and felt that familiar punch in the gut again.

It was Lacey.

Chapter 3

EAN TRIED TO SIT UP, BUT EVERYTHING BEGAN TO SPIN.

"Easy," she said softly. "You must've banged your head pretty good when you fell." Without asking permission, Lacey reached around and felt his head for any bumps or bleeding. She knew she'd found a tender spot when he winced. "Sorry."

The snow started to fall more heavily, and now that her heart rate had returned to normal, she finally took a moment to look at him.

Ean.

Sure, he had changed a lot in the last twelve years, but she'd know him anywhere. The black hair, the blue eyes, the square jaw... There wasn't a man alive who compared to him in her mind, and she mentally kicked herself for still getting all tingly at the sight of him. While her first instinct was to nurture and make sure he was okay, Lacey knew that would be giving him a foothold into her life where she didn't want him; so she went with her defense mechanism.

"Ean Callahan, you scared me half to death! What the hell do you think you're doing prowling around in the woods peering into windows?"

Lacey's tone was enough to snap Ean out of his stupor. "What am I doing? What are *you* doing?" he demanded. "What do you think you're doing up here in the cottage? The damn wedding is over a month away!"

He struggled to his feet, and though things were still spinning, it was like the ride was finally coming to an end. He braced his hands on the side of the house and took a couple of deep breaths.

"I know when the wedding is, Ean," she said sarcastically. "Ava has a list a mile long of all the things she wants done to the place for her wedding night. I decided to take some time to come up here and scope it out." She stared at him and dared him to argue.

"In a snowstorm?"

"Well, in my defense, I didn't know about the snow until I was halfway here, and at that point, I didn't feel like turning around and heading back home. I don't have a problem with it. A little snow doesn't scare me."

"They're calling for over a foot," he reminded her and felt a small wave of satisfaction when her expression fell a little. She recovered quickly.

"As I said, I don't have a problem with it."

"You will if you want to go home tonight."

He had her there. Her plan had been to come up, look at the cottage, and get a hotel room for the night, but with the storm blowing in, she knew she'd be stuck here at the cottage. It wasn't a hardship, or at least it hadn't been until Ean had shown up and scared her to death!

"I had planned to grab a room in town, but I'll just stay here tonight. I'm sure the roads will be fine in the morning. They're used to snow up here. The plows will be working all night. Plus it will give me time to do some work here. Your sister certainly has some very specific ideas on what she wants."

"I'll bet," he murmured. Ava always tended to have very strong ideas and plans on what she wanted and how she was going to get them, so he had no doubt that this list Lacey mentioned was going to be a nightmare. Moving away from the side of the cottage, Ean took a tentative step and was relieved that he felt steady.

"C'mon inside and let's get a better look at your head." Lacey didn't wait to see if he'd follow, she just knew he would. Why? Because what she really wanted right now was for Ean to leave. To go back down the mountain and leave her alone to deal with the maelstrom of feelings just the sight of him had caused.

Back in the cottage, Lacey made up a small ice pack, and when she turned, she found Ean sitting on an ottoman in front of the fire and darn it if he didn't look good there. Reminding herself of all the reasons why she wanted him gone, she strode over and handed him the ice. "You've got a small bump, but the ice should help. By the time you drive back down to the ranch, the swelling should be gone."

"I didn't drive up, I walked."

"What? Why?" she asked. "It's snowing out, it's dark, and you thought the best way to go about stopping a potential burglar was to *walk* up the mountain?"

Ean shot her a sharp glance. It had seemed sensible at the time, but hearing Lacey say it made him realize how poor his decision was. Now it was pitch black out, his head was pounding, his back didn't feel too hot if he was being honest, and he had to walk all the way back down. It didn't take a genius to realize that the path was covered in snow, and in the dark, there would be no way to tell if he was staying on it.

"I'll drive you back down," Lacey said quickly,

knowing she'd do whatever it took to get him out of the cottage. It was too small, too cozy, and too intimate to share this space with him for a minute longer. A quick look around had her finding her keys, and she walked to the door. "Are you ready?"

Clearly he wasn't. "What's the rush, Lace? I mean, can't we take a minute and say a proper hello and how are you before you throw me out of my own place?"

Her first instinct was to tell him she didn't care to have a proper hello with him and she didn't want him here, but no matter how she worked the words in her head, they sounded petty and childish. She sighed with resignation, closed the front door, and took off her coat. She didn't need to see Ean to know he was watching her. It should have thrilled her; instead it made her feel self-conscious. What did he see when he looked at her? She was no longer that fourteen-year-old girl who professed her love to him, but a woman who was irritated with the situation they were currently in.

Trying to put space between them without being too obvious about it, Lacey chose the sofa on the other side of the fireplace. She looked at him expectantly, hoping Ean would be the first to break the awkward silence. When minutes passed and he still said nothing, just simply sat looking at her, a small grin on his face, Lacey decided she'd had enough.

"Ava didn't mention that you'd be here," she said finally.

"That's because I didn't tell anyone I was going to be here."

"Why?" she asked, puzzled that he would come home and not tell anyone. Well, it was also puzzling that Ean chose to come to the mountains rather than to Raleigh, but she didn't want to seem too curious.

"I needed a little bit of a break and I knew that once I went home, I wouldn't get much time to myself. I need to ease into the whole family-togetherness thing."

"You wouldn't need to ease into it if you came home more often," she quipped.

"Been talking to my mom, have you?" He smirked.

"Just stating the obvious."

There was another long pause, and this time Ean was the one to break it. "So how've you been, Lacey? It's been a long time. What have you been up to?"

Not thinking about you! was what she wanted to snap at him, but lying had never been her thing. "I'm doing well, thank you. I graduated top of my class at Meredith College and started work immediately at the design firm I'm with now. I've been there for four years."

"So you're still in Raleigh?"

She nodded. "And you? How have you been?" God, this was ridiculous! Sitting here making small talk was tedious and there was so much Lacey wanted to get done. Why wouldn't he just let her drive him home and let her be? She didn't want to know how he'd been! She'd learned enough about his life over the years through the family grapevine, so nothing he could tell her right now would be new information to her.

"I've missed you."

Well, almost nothing.

Lacey took a deep breath and waited for him to continue.

"Don't you have anything to say to that?"

"What would you have me say, Ean? We grew

up together, I'm sure I'd miss my siblings if they moved away."

"You could say that you missed me, too," he answered honestly.

"It was a little weird at first when you left, the empty seat at the table and all that when Ava and I hung out. But other than that, I don't think I gave it too much thought." Her breath hitched on the last word. And *that's* why she never lied—she was not a convincing liar. Thankfully, Ean didn't call her on it or didn't notice. He gave a curt nod and stood.

"I guess I should let you get me home before the snow gets worse. The trip down won't be too bad, but getting back up here could be dangerous and I don't want you to have a problem."

Lacey appreciated his consideration and murmured a word of thanks as she walked back over to the door and retrieved her coat and keys. Ean walked past her as he made his way out the door, a little too close for Lacey's comfort. She was able to smell his cologne, feel the heat radiating from his body, and for one split second, she almost reached out and grabbed his coat to pull him closer. Luckily, by the time that thought registered, he was outside and heading toward her car.

She joined him and they got settled into the SUV. She used the wipers to clear the snow from the front and rear windshields; it was still light and fluffy enough that it was easily wiped away. The snow on the ground, however, was not as cooperative.

Lacey maneuvered the vehicle through a three-point turn so she could head down the steep hill, but found she had little to no traction. A cry of despair escaped her lips as the car skidded precariously close to a tree. They were angled off the road and she made several unsuccessful attempts to get back on track.

"Let me try," Ean suggested. "We get a lot of snow in Boston, so I'm more used to driving in it than you are." His tone wasn't condescending or offensive, he was merely stating a fact. She climbed out and stood to the side while he tried to get her car out of the rut in the side of the road, with no success.

"Great," she mumbled as he made one last try. "Now my car is stuck in the snow, on a hill, and we *both* have to trudge through the snow back to the houses. Fabulous." The look on Lacey's face was one of complete despair.

Ean climbed out and apologized. "City snow driving is a lot different from mountain snow driving." Though the snow was really to blame, he couldn't help but feel a little guilty. His SUV was better equipped for this kind of thing, and if he'd just driven up here, none of this would be happening.

"Well, there's nothing I can do about it tonight, right? If the plows don't come up here by lunchtime tomorrow, I'll call the auto club and have them tow me out so I can get into town and then head home." They stood and stared again, each not knowing what to say. "So, um, I guess I'll see you around." Lacey turned a little too quickly, forgetting how slick the road was, and nearly lost her balance. She was not wearing snow boots; her boots were more of the everyday variety. Great for a walk around town. The snow? Not so much. Ean quickly stepped forward to catch her.

"You need to be careful," he said gently, moving closer to her, "and watch for the slick spots. Otherwise you'll fall and get hurt."

"The entire road is one giant slick spot, Ean. What am I supposed to do? Stand here in the snow all night and not move? Is that what you're suggesting?" she snapped. She just wanted him to go! How much worse could this get?

Stupid question.

Ean moved in closer and wrapped his arm tightly around her waist. Lacey jumped at the contact. "What are you doing?"

"Look, Lace, this is a crappy situation, but the weather is getting worse. We'll hold on to each other and slowly make our way back up the road. I've at least got snow boots on. The cottage is way closer than the ranch. We'll just have to stay there tonight. You've got food, right?"

"You can't stay there tonight!" she cried in dismay.

"Why not? It's my damn house!" he said, but her mind was too busy reeling from the realization that she wasn't getting rid of him any time soon.

"Like you said, you have snow boots on and get traction or whatever. You see where the road is, you can easily walk down it. The snow's not that bad and it's only a quarter mile or so."

"Only a quarter…?" he started and then stopped himself. "I have already fallen off a chair, banged my head, and slammed my back pretty good. If you think I'm going to try walking down that steep hill in the snow and risk doing that again, you're crazy." They were nearing the porch of the cottage, and he reluctantly pulled his arm from her waist. "You know, Lace, if I didn't know any better, I'd swear you were trying to get rid of me. Now what gives?"

She wanted nothing more than to tell him exactly what gives. He turned her world upside down! He'd ruined her whole plan of getting the cottage ready without having to spend any time with him, and now she was going to be snowed in for the night with him! Where did she begin?

"Look, Ean, it's been a long day and I was looking forward to the time alone. Your showing up here just threw me for a loop. I'm a very organized person. I make lists, I check things off, and I don't like surprises. You being here threw off my list, that's all." She sounded cool and flippant and was actually pretty darn proud of herself. Turning, more carefully this time, she made her way up the porch steps, opened the door to the cottage, and walked inside.

Ean stood there looking at the open doorway. He threw off her list? What the hell was that? How was it that seeing her had thrown him completely down for the count and Lacey was so blasé about it? He knew they hadn't left things on the best of terms twelve years ago, but she couldn't possibly have held a grudge all this time, could she?

Feeling the snow seeping into his clothes, Ean trudged up the steps and into the cottage, closing the door behind him. Within minutes Lacey had everything coming to life. The roaring fire, the smell of something simmering on the stove, and Lacey standing in stocking feet made quite a picture, and for an instant, all Ean could think was *home*. It had been a long time since he'd come home at the end of the day to someone preparing a meal for him. True, it was usually his mother because he never got that deeply involved with a woman to the point of her waiting for him after work.

But this? This scene before him was almost achingly right. Lacey turned and looked at him expectantly. "I stopped at the grocery store on the way up here. I planned on staying at a hotel tonight, but I get tired of takeout so I was whipping up some chili and a quick bread. I hope that's okay."

Okay? "That sounds a little bit like heaven, Lacey, thank you."

She gave him a shy smile and turned back to stirring the chili. "You should probably take off that wet hat and coat, maybe hang them by the fire and get yourself warmed up."

She didn't need to tell him twice. Within minutes, Ean was back to sitting in front of the fire and soon felt like himself again. He turned toward the kitchen as Lacey was taking the bread from the oven. She had set the small table that was snug against the wall in the kitchen.

"There's not much to choose from to drink, unfortunately," she said apologetically as Ean walked toward her. "I brought a couple of colas with me and there's coffee and tea if you want something hot."

"I think that's enough of a variety," he said, noticing for the first time that Lacey was fidgeting. She wouldn't meet his eyes, and she was clearly fluttering around the kitchen trying to keep busy.

"There's no beer," she said quickly and then went back to stirring the chili.

"That's okay, I don't normally drink it."

"Oh, okay." Lacey didn't need to turn to know that Ean was close behind her. She could sense him. How was it possible for him to have this effect on her after all these years? It wasn't fair! And of all the people in the world to be trapped in a snowstorm with, why did it have to be him?

"It smells wonderful, Lace," Ean said from right over her left shoulder. "You always did love to cook."

That he remembered a small detail about her gave Lacey that fluttery feeling in her tummy again. "Well, the whole family is full of budding chefs. It's no wonder I feel comfortable in the kitchen." She was yammering and she knew it. Why wouldn't he move away? "Um, I think we could use another log on the fire and then dinner will be ready."

Ean took the hint and did what she asked. True to her word, by the time he had the fire settled, she was placing two bowls on the table. He walked across the room and noticed the mammoth binder on the counter. Curiosity got the better of him and he picked it up on his way to the table. "What's this?"

Lacey let out a small laugh. "That," she began, "is your sister's dream of what this cottage should look like for her wedding night."

Ean opened it and looked at the labeled tabs. "Food… flowers…lighting…" He looked at Lacey. "How many categories are there?"

"Seventeen."

His eyes bugged out a little on that one. "Are you supposed to completely remodel this place? Does this say furniture placement?" he asked incredulously. "How does she expect you to do all of this alone?"

"Oh, you mean you didn't get the memo?" Lacey asked, ready to witness on Ean's face the same exact expression she'd had when Ava told her the news.

"What memo?" he asked slowly, not liking the look of mischief on her face.

"As best man and maid of honor, it is *our* job to get this place ready for the newlyweds."

"*What?*"

"You heard me. You and I get the great honor of setting the scene for your sister's wedding-night sex."

Ean dropped the binder to the floor as if it had burned him and glared at Lacey as she laughed. Her face was full of merriment and innocence, and she was the most beautiful woman he'd ever seen. Lacey had been a pretty girl, and even in the awkward teen years it was possible to see the woman she would become, yet none of that prepared him for the woman sitting across from him. She simply took his breath away, and right now, when she finally let her guard down, he felt like he was looking at the sun.

"I am not facilitating my sister's sex life," he began.

"Oh, lighten up. She'll be married and she wants the cottage and her wedding night to be perfect. There are diagrams…"

"Please tell me they're of the floor plan and not anything…else." His appetite was slowly fading at that disturbing thought, but then Lacey laughed again.

"The floor plan, color schemes, foods… She's clipped things out of magazines, she's very organized. Part of me loves her for it and another part of me wants to beat her with the binder. She's fixated on this place." Lacey nodded toward his bowl. "Eat, please, before it gets cold."

Ean took a spoonful and felt the flavors burst to life on his tongue. This simple, quickly thrown together chili was a culinary delight. "This is amazing," he said finally. "I can't believe you just whipped this up."

Blushing at his compliment, she took her own first spoonful, realizing that she'd waited for him to taste it first, anxious for his opinion. He hadn't disappointed. "Cooking is second nature, but back to Ava. She's turned into a bit of a bridezilla."

"Mom's told me," he said around another mouthful of chili. "She was the last person I'd thought would be that way."

"I guess you don't know until it's your turn."

"What about you, Lace? Any trip down the aisle in your future?"

Her blush this time was out of embarrassment. "No," she said. "So now that you know you need to be a part of this, I guess we can go through the book and divide and conquer." The change of subject was swift and luckily well-received.

Ean merely nodded, wondering why someone as beautiful as Lacey wasn't attached. Was she just getting over a breakup? Was she jealous of Ava? He dismissed that thought before it even took hold. Lacey wasn't the jealous type; she had no reason to be. Ean loved his sister dearly, but she lacked the confidence Lacey had always had. Truth be known, he had been a little dismayed that Ava and Mason were marrying so quickly, but he knew his sister had always been a little obsessed with the idea of following the family tradition and marrying on Christmas Eve. "True, she could wait until next Christmas…"

He didn't realize he'd spoken that last part out loud until Lacey dropped her spoon and said, "Exactly! Why does it have to be *this* Christmas? What harm could waiting another year cause?"

"So you think this was a little rushed, too," he urged.

"I do! I asked her about it, and it seems Mason is just anxious to get himself settled with his law firm, and having a wife and baby would make him extremely happy. Add that to the fact that Ava wants nothing more than to be part of the Callahan Christmas wedding tradition and it's like a feeding frenzy."

Ean stood so quickly that his chair fell over. "Wait a minute, wait a minute," he snapped. "Are you telling me Ava's pregnant? Do my parents know?"

Oh boy. Awkward. "Ean, sit down. Your sister is not pregnant." Lacey explained to him the conversation she'd had with Ava a week ago. Part of her felt that maybe she was betraying Ava's confidence, but hey, this was Ean. He was Ava's brother and maybe he was the key to helping Lacey figure out how to convince her friend to do some serious soul-searching before the wedding.

"So he wants Ava to give up everything and do exactly what he wants?" Ean was pacing the kitchen, his dinner momentarily forgotten. "I'll kill him! There's no way my sister is going to…"

Lacey stood and placed a hand gently on his arm to stop him. "You're not going to kill Mason. That would be ridiculous."

"He can't force Ava to get pregnant and drop out of school, Lacey. I won't allow it!"

She sighed. He was obviously thinking along the same lines she was. She was really worried about Ava's decision. "It just seems like they need to have an honest heart-to-heart conversation. I think Ava is scared to rock the boat because she wants this wedding so badly. She believes in the fairy tale of this house and feels that if they spend their wedding night here, their marriage will be perfect and all of their issues will be resolved."

Ean looked at her like she'd grown a second head. "Well, that explains it. We need to get her checked into a psych ward because clearly, she's crazy!"

"Why? Because she believes in love conquering all?"

"Oh for crying out loud, Lacey, don't you go spewing that crap, too! This house isn't magical or anything. It's a house. It does not have the power to guarantee a lifetime of happiness!" Ean shook her hand off and went back to pacing. He walked over to the fire and stared into it for a moment before turning to her again. "All of those marriages lasted because, back in my grandparents' and great-grandparents' day, you stayed married. Yes, they were blessed with good marriages, but they had their struggles, too."

"Does Ava realize that?"

"She should! We grew up in the same house, we have all of the same relatives, and I can tell you we've witnessed our share of family disagreements."

"But it's not just the older generations. You've had cousins who have gotten married here and…"

"That's true, but ten years or so of marriage does not equal love everlasting, and I am pretty sure none of them started out their marriages with a list of demands that one of them change their entire life to suit the other. This is a recipe for disaster, Lacey, I'm telling you. Ava has got to call this wedding off!"

Lacey knew she should be agreeing with everything Ean was saying, but for some reason, she found herself getting angry with his words. "You cannot tell Ava to call off the wedding, Ean."

"Why the hell not? It's a mistake. She'll regret it as soon as the honeymoon's over."

"It's her decision to make. Look, you've been gone for a long time, and you have no real idea who your sister even is anymore. She's a dreamer, she's whimsical, and she has her heart set on this wedding and following in the Callahan family tradition. If you push her on this, the only thing you are going to accomplish is pushing her away and losing the fraction of a relationship you have now."

With a look of defeat, Ean collapsed down on the ottoman beside the fire. He ran a weary hand over his face before looking up at Lacey standing before him. "What am I supposed to do, Lace?" he asked gruffly. "She's my sister. I don't agree with a lot of the things she does, but at the same time I wouldn't want her to change one bit."

"Well, it sounds like you kind of do," she said cautiously and took a step back when Ean's fierce gaze met hers. "You want her to call off the wedding, not to believe in fairy tales…but that's who your sister is."

"So, what am I supposed to do?"

Against her better judgment, Lacey sat down beside him, the fire warm at her side. "Talk to her, express your concerns with love, not anger. You have to listen to her side of the story and not judge her or try to force her to change her mind. Ava does not like to be pushed, and if you try, she's going to go through with this wedding and to hell with the consequences."

Turning his head to look at her, Ean was struck with

just how amazing this woman was. The fire reflecting off her hair, the fierce love for her friend showing in her eyes, and her sweet, gentle voice were almost his undoing. At this moment he'd promise her anything to make sure she was happy.

"I doubt she'd listen to me no matter what I had to say. I haven't been the best brother since I moved away."

Lacey reached over and took one of his hands in hers. "Ava is an independent spirit, Ean. She rarely listens to anyone's advice. She's so proud of you, and you have been a wonderful example to her that you can be whatever you want to be." She paused. "I guess that's one of the things that bothered me most about this situation—the fact that she's been working so hard to get her degree, and now one comment from Mason has her ready to give it all up."

Looking at their fingers twined together, Ean gave a gentle squeeze. "Thank you for saying that—about how she's proud of me. I've been selfish with my time— cut all of my ties, or as many as I could, and went on to be what I wanted without thinking of the ones I left behind." He stared purposefully into Lacey's eyes. "It was never my intention to hurt anyone."

They were no longer talking about Ava or his family. Lacey knew what he was trying to say, and she was uncomfortable with the memory. She tried to tug her hand free, but Ean wouldn't let her.

"At first I was just anxious to get away, have my independence. Then it was about proving I could make the grade and be at the top of my class. It was easy to get a job, and then the next one, and they were time-consuming. I saw those visits with my family as intrusions into the life I was trying to make for myself, but now I realize they were what was keeping me strong and pushing me to keep going even when I felt overwhelmed." He swallowed the lump in his throat. "I don't think I could've made it this far with my business if not for them having my back."

Lacey smiled. "They have always been so proud of you. You could've worked in the mail room and they still would have been proud of you."

They sat in silence for a long moment before Lacey glanced over to their forgotten dinner. "C'mon, let's finish our meal. I can heat it back up in the microwave, and we'll get to work on this binder of your sister's and we'll come up with a realistic plan to get her and Mason to sit down and work through some of their problems before the wedding. I think between the two of us; we should be able to multitask and figure it out."

They stood and Ean smiled down at her. "We always were the more levelheaded ones anyway, right?" Lacey nodded and they walked back over to the kitchen to reheat their dinner.

Chapter 4

"Flannel sheets."

"But the book clearly says silk."

"I'm telling you, it's going to be cold. Flannel sheets are more practical!"

"It's their wedding night, Ean. Practical isn't what they're looking for!"

They had made it through dinner and cleanup and the first ten sections of the binder. The divide-and-conquer plan had worked out perfectly. Ean was ordering flowers; Lacey was handling the food. Ean was looking into switching out the lightbulbs to give the place the soft glow Ava wanted, along with making sure the cottage would be well stocked with wood.

Lacey agreed to see to the music selections, and made plans to order one hundred white pillar candles. With her connections at the design firm, she'd get a great deal on them *and* have them delivered.

They agreed to have a cleaning service come in a few days before Christmas and give the whole place a thorough cleaning rather than taking on the task themselves. There was a list of Christmas decorations in the closet that they would have to go through at some point as well, but currently they were battling over the pros and cons of the bedding selection.

"Silk is not the kind of bedding you want when it's below freezing outside, Lacey. Be realistic!"

She rolled her eyes at his comments. "I keep telling you, a wedding night is not *about* practical and realistic. There will be heat, a blazing fire in the fireplace, and they will have each other to stay warm. Do I need to draw you a picture?" she snapped. "If anything, the flannel sheets will be overkill!"

"So we should just turn this place into a bordello, is that what you're saying?" he snapped back. "Maybe we can get some red or black satin sheets, drape some silk scarves over the lights, and hang a disco ball from the ceiling, along with some mirrors…"

The look she gave him proved how unamused she was. "If you're not going to be serious…"

"I'm being totally serious! This list is what can't be serious. Who has the kind of spare time in which they can even create a book like this? What is she going to school for if she has this kind of time on her hands?"

He was infuriating. There was no other way Lacey could describe him. He had an opinion on everything and no sense of the romantic at all. While she herself had balked at a lot of what Ava had in the binder, hearing Ean mock it all was beginning to grate on her nerves.

"Look, no one is asking you to sleep in the damn bed with the silk sheets. I'll buy them so you don't have to even *look* at them, but you are going to have to lighten up here a bit because you are making me crazy!" She hadn't meant to add that last part, but it just slipped out.

"Me? What have I done?"

It didn't take long for Lacey to rattle off a list of every snarky comment he'd made that evening about Ava's binder. "Well, you have to admit," he said in his own defense, "some of it seems a little over the top."

"Oh, believe me, I agree, but it's her wedding night and this is what she wants. Luckily neither of us has to spend the night in it, but as the bride, Ava gets to call the shots on this." She scanned through the pages and stopped when she saw Ean sit down on the sofa and look at her quizzically.

"What?" she asked.

"You've made an interesting statement."

"I have?" Lacey stopped and thought about what she'd said. She didn't think any of it bore further conversation. "What did I say?"

"You said neither of us has to spend the night in it. So let me ask you this, if you had your choice, what would you do with this place?"

It was like opening Pandora's box. For a decorator, this place was like a wonderland. Placing the binder down on the coffee table, Lacey began to wander the room. "Well, let's start with the outside. There would be white twinkly lights outlining the roof and the windows. I would want a giant wreath with a big red bow for the front door and smaller versions on the two front windows. We'd need evergreen garland for the porch railings and candles in the windows." She turned to Ean to get his reaction.

"Sounds like a typical house at Christmas. What else have you got?"

Lacey should have been offended, but she noticed the slight upturn of his lips as he spoke. "Once inside, the fire would be roaring, of course, and there would be another large wreath hung over the fireplace and candles on the mantel. Champagne would be chilling in a silver ice bucket next to the bed. The bedding would be all white…"

"Flannel or silk?" he teased.

"Hmm…good question. I think I'd want the silk because it would feel fabulous and decadent and I would deserve that on my wedding night."

Ean nodded. "Go on." He was leaning forward with his elbows resting on his knees as he watched Lacey tour the large one-room floor plan that was the cottage.

"The Christmas tree—done in white lights—would be over here, in front of the window. Wedding gifts would be piled high around it." She took the two steps up to the tiny kitchen area. "I'd move the table away from the wall like this," she said as she moved it, "and it would be covered in a red tablecloth. Candles would be lit and there'd be a tray of some light snacks—cheese, fruit, and crackers—and an enormous floral arrangement of lilies."

"No holly? No mistletoe? No Christmas cactus?" he interrupted and Lacey laughed.

"The mistletoe would be hanging in the front entrance. After all, once I'm carried over the threshold and I see how magnificent it looked in here, we would of course kiss under it."

"We?" he asked suggestively.

"Well, yes, if this is my wedding night…"

"I didn't say it was your wedding night. I just asked if you, as a decorator, had to plan all this out without a silly binder, what would you do?"

Suddenly she was fourteen all over again and realized she had gotten sucked into a fantasy and embarrassed herself in front of Ean again. She instantly looked away from him and walked over to the binder and began flipping through the pages.

"Well, luckily I don't have to think about that since I do have this silly binder." Her voice sounded shaky, and Lacey felt as if her whole body had gone hot and then cold. She turned toward the nearest chair and sat down, feigning interest in something Ava had written.

"Did I say something wrong?" Ean asked, thoroughly confused by Lacey's abrupt end to her vision for the cottage. "I was enjoying your description."

She spared him a glance. "It doesn't matter what my vision is for the cottage. We're preparing Ava's wedding night and I have to stick with her plan." Looking around the room, Lacey made some mental notes about window coverings. The place might look like Christmas on steroids, but—as she tried to remember when dealing with a difficult client—the customer was always right. It didn't mean they had good taste, but they were always right.

"Look, clearly I said something to upset you. Whatever it was, I'm sorry. It wasn't my intention for you to stop," Ean pleaded.

"I get caught up in my projects sometimes and have to catch myself before I try to force my ideas on my clients."

"We were just pretending, Lace. There was no need for you to stop." He suddenly noticed she was far less animated than she had been just moments ago. "You want to know what I'd do if this were about me?" Ean jumped up from his chair and came to stand in front of Lacey.

"Sure, why not," she said, forcing a smile.

"Well, I agree with you on the outside. It's a classic look for a reason, right?" When she nodded, he headed to the entryway. "The mistletoe was a great idea, too.

Then when we step into the room here, the fire would be roaring, the tree would be in front of the window… all that stuff sounded great. However…" He left that dangling as he looked over at Lacey, who was watching him intently with a more relaxed smile on her face.

"However?"

"Cheese and crackers and fruit?" Ean made a tsking sound before walking over to the refrigerator. "That's not enough to build up any real energy for a wedding night. There would need to be a cooler full of Gatorade, maybe some pizza, and a platter of grilled hamburgers and hot dogs. Man food."

"Man food? Is there something you're trying to tell me here, Ean?" she teased.

He laughed when he realized what she was saying. It was a hearty laugh and Lacey couldn't help but join in. "I guess there could be some of that cheese and cracker stuff for the bride, but after spending the day dealing with the family and doing the picture thing, I would like to know that I'm coming here to actually eat something I want and to be able to relax and fuel up for the night ahead."

Such a guy, she thought to herself. *Not a romantic bone in his body.* "And what about the rest of the room?"

"What? The decorating?" Lacey nodded. "What difference does it make? We'd have food, we'd have heat, and a bed. What more could a newlywed couple want on their wedding night?"

He did have a point. While atmosphere was important, Lacey thought, when it's your wedding night it should be about being with the person you love most in the world and not about the material trappings around you. If only his sister shared the same ideals.

"Well, that's all neither here nor there because this particular client is all about setting the scene." Lacey reached forward and grabbed for the binder again. "Wardrobe?" she mumbled. "Is she kidding me with this?"

"Let me see that." Ean took the binder from Lacey's hands. "I absolutely draw the line at buying my sister and her husband sexy underwear. Pass! That one's all yours, Lace." He paused for a moment and laughed.

"What's so funny?"

"Lingerie? Lace? C'mon, that's good."

Lacey wanted to keep a straight face but she couldn't. Seeing Ean like this, so relaxed and carefree, was something new to her. It had been so long since they'd been in each other's company and it felt nice to be able to sit and laugh together. He looked much more at ease than he had earlier in the evening, and Lacey was sure she looked more comfortable as well. She studied his face as he continued to ramble off a list of things he refused to buy for the newlyweds, most of which were luckily not on any list of Ava's.

His hair was still as dark as always and right now was mussed up just enough to make one wonder if he was some sort of tech genius businessman or a carpenter. He filled in the faded Levi's perfectly, and his flannel shirt was unbuttoned enough to show the plain white T-shirt he wore underneath. A five o'clock shadow was barely there, but she would bet good money that if she touched his face right now it would feel deliciously scratchy.

She was just about to interrupt his tirade on edible underwear when she realized what was missing. "Your glasses," she said.

"What?"

"Your glasses. You used to wear glasses."

"I still wear them from time to time, but they were a nuisance so I had Lasik treatment done a couple of years ago. It's made life a lot easier."

She nodded, but had to admit she'd always liked his glasses. Who knew she would miss something so ridiculous. She stared at him until she realized how crazy she must look and then took a glance at her watch. "Oh my gosh! It's after eleven! Did you realize it was so late?"

"No, I had no idea." He honestly hadn't. Spending time with Lacey, talking with her, had him giving no thought to the time. He was simply enjoying her company and didn't want the night to end. He'd waited twelve years to see her and talk to her again, and now that they had finally crossed over those first few awkward moments together, Ean had to admit they got along better than they ever had.

"Oh no!" she cried suddenly.

"What? Now what's the matter?" He was hoping she wasn't such a planner to the point that losing track of time was going to upset her that much.

"I need to grab my overnight bag from the car. But it's down the hill. All of my stuff is in there. I completely forgot about it when we left it earlier. Dammit." Reaching for her boots, she sighed with frustration. "I'll be right back." Lacey turned to head for the door but Ean stopped her.

"You cannot go back outside in this weather. Like I told you earlier, you'll break your neck. Give me your keys and I'll run down and get your stuff." He opened the door and stopped dead in his tracks. "Um, Lace?"

"Yeah?" Something in Ean's tone made Lacey

worried about what she was going to see. She stepped up beside him in the open doorway and froze. Not because of the cold, but because of the scene in front of them.

"How much snow were we supposed to get?" he asked.

"Only a foot!" she cried. "This is clearly more than a foot and it's still coming down! How long were we in here?" She was starting to become hysterical and Ean wrapped an arm around her and led her back to the couch and sat her down before going back and closing the door. "I'm going to need my stuff, Ean!"

"You'll have to do without it tonight, sweetheart. I'm not going out in that mess and digging out your car to get to your bag and neither are you. There is most likely a big variety of everything you'll need right here. It's a guest cottage after all, and if I know my mother, she keeps it well stocked."

That was little comfort to Lacey. She didn't want to use someone else's stuff, she wanted her own. She was just about to voice that concern when she turned and saw Ean going through a chest of drawers beside the bed.

"There are clean flannel sheets for the bed." He tossed them onto the king-sized mattress and opened the next drawer. "There's a pair of men's pajamas—again, in flannel. You take the shirt and I'll take the pants."

"Ean, seriously, I want my…"

He slammed the drawer with a little more force than necessary and headed over to the closet next to the bathroom. "Here are towels." He tossed several onto the bathroom vanity. "There are new toothbrushes, toothpaste, and a variety of soaps and shampoos," he said as he dug through the shelves. "We have extra pillows and blankets in the hope chest," he added as he shut the closet door, "and plenty of wood for the fire. Now unless you have some sort of medical emergency, there should be nothing you need from your car."

"Slippers," she blurted out. "The floors are going to be cold and I would really like my slippers."

He arched a dark brow at her. "Seriously? You want me to go out and wade through eighteen inches of fast-falling snow in freezing temperatures just to dig out your car for a pair of slippers? No way. I said medical emergency, and from what I can see, Lacey Quinn, you are the picture of health." Before she could say another word, Ean walked back to the chest of drawers and searched around until he found a pair of thick wool socks. He tossed them her way. "There. Now you won't have cold feet."

Dammit, Lacey thought, *he's covered everything and we are seriously snowed in together for the night.* There was no getting rid of him now.

But did she even want to?

"Let's get this bed made up and then I'll go get some more wood from out back for the fire," Ean suggested.

"Um, how are we going to do this?"

"Well, I don't know about you, but I tend to put the fitted sheet on first and then the flat one, and then there's a blanket and a comforter. We don't have to use both, but if you wanted to…"

"I'm not sharing a bed with you, Ean," she said adamantly.

"It's not *really* sharing a bed, Lacey. I mean, come on. Where am I supposed to sleep? That is a two-seater couch. I can't lie down on it, and after falling off that damn chair earlier I certainly don't want to sleep on the floor."

"Well, whose fault is it that you fell off that *damn* chair? Certainly not mine!"

Ean looked at her in complete shock. Was she serious? "Lacey, no one was supposed to be up here. I saw the lights on and thought someone was breaking into the house. I had to come up and investigate!"

She snorted with disbelief. "You could have called the police to come and check it out. You could have driven up the hill and knocked on the door like a normal person!"

"Seriously?" he asked. "That's what normal people do? Knock on the door of a house they suspect is being broken into and wait for the intruder to kindly invite them in?"

"Don't be ridiculous, Ean! I wasn't an intruder!"

"But I didn't know that when I saw the lights on and decided to come up here!" he shouted. It was the most ridiculous argument he'd ever had. "Why are you making such a big deal out of this?"

"Because…" she trailed off and looked at the bed.

He made all valid points, Lacey conceded, but it had been an emotional enough day seeing Ean again after all this time. Lacey didn't think she'd be able to handle sharing a bed with him, knowing it was the first time in over fourteen months since she'd shared a bed with a man, and it was a platonic sleepover. A girl could only handle so much rejection!

When she didn't respond, Ean threw down the pillow he had been putting a case on and stalked over to where Lacey stood. "Be reasonable! I'm not some stranger you've never met before! We've known each other our entire lives, we've camped together, you've slept at my

house as much as your own, and it's a big enough bed
so there will be plenty of space between us. You don't
have to worry, I'm not going to touch you."

If he had slapped her in the face, it wouldn't have
been a worse insult. She felt her face get hot and her
hands get clammy. "I don't see that it's necessary to
share a bed. There are plenty of blankets and pillows
you can use to make a perfectly fine bed on the floor.
That's what a gentleman would do."

He wanted to argue with her, but the exhaustion of
the day was finally catching up. "Fine. Take the bed
for yourself. I'll sleep on the floor. You can make
the whole damn thing by yourself, princess, while I
fetch the wood." He stormed across the room and out
the back door, slamming it with such force that the
walls shook.

She refused to cry. So what that after all this time,
Ean Callahan still didn't want her? She would survive.
Rejection hurt no matter who was doling it out, though.
With a shaky breath, Lacey took on the task of making
up the bed, and when she was done, she prepared an area
in front of the fire for Ean. It wasn't a perfect arrangement, but she'd layered enough blankets and quilts on
the floor in hopes that it wouldn't hurt Ean's back any
further. It was bad enough that he'd fallen and hurt himself; she didn't need to add to it by making him sleep on
hard wood with no padding.

Fifteen minutes later, when he hadn't come back in,
she started to get worried. What was taking so long?
The wood closet was right out the back door, he should
have come right back in. She was just about to open the
door to check on him when he came in, his arms full of

wood. Ean stalked past her and placed the wood next to the fire. "Hopefully it won't be too wet and will burn fine through the night," he said flatly.

"Thank you, Ean," she said softly. "I appreciate you going out and getting that. I don't know what I would have done if I were here by myself." She'd have been out of luck if the electricity and heat went out due to the storm, that was for sure.

With nothing left to say, she grabbed the socks and the flannel pajama top and headed into the bathroom, not once meeting Ean's gaze.

When she emerged ten minutes later, she felt slightly more at ease. She'd washed up, brushed her teeth, and found the pajama top to be almost comically large, covering her to mid-thigh. Combined with the thick socks, she had no doubt she'd be warm through the night. It wasn't fashionable, but it was practical. Besides, she didn't need to look fashionable for Ean. He'd made it abundantly clear, yet again, that he wasn't attracted to her. Although, in his defense, they hadn't seen each other in over a decade, so what did she expect? That he'd throw himself at her feet at just the sight of her and say he'd been wrong to reject her all those years ago? That he'd never stopped thinking about her?

Actually, she thought with a grin, that would have been perfect!

The room was dark except for the fire, and Ean was already in his makeshift bed with his back to her. Lacey took a look around and noticed that everything was put away, and there was nothing left to do but go to sleep. She'd brought a book with her to read to help her fall asleep, but it was out in her car. Sighing with resignation,

she quietly walked over to the bed and climbed in. Ean
didn't make a move or look in her direction.

Lacey feared sleep would elude her. She had a night-
time ritual to guarantee falling asleep because she never
slept well in strange beds. Now without her book, in this
strange house with the man who'd haunted her dreams
for far too long, she was in for a long, sleepless night.

Remarkably, it wasn't hard to get comfortable in the
big bed. The mattress was the perfect level of firmness
she enjoyed, and the flannel sheets did feel perfect on a
cold winter's night.

"Good choice on the flannel sheets, Ean. They feel
much nicer than I thought they would," she called out,
hoping to extend the olive branch. He didn't respond
and Lacey wracked her brain for something to say to
draw Ean into conversation and to get them back to the
easy manner they'd shared earlier. "I'll mention the idea
to Ava and see if I can get her to change her mind."

Nothing.

"I'm sorry, Ean," she finally said wearily. "I didn't
mean to come off sounding so harsh. I guess this whole
night has put me out of sorts. I wasn't expecting to see
anyone while I was up here working on the cottage, least
of all you." She peered down to where he lay by the fire
and noticed he hadn't moved. Was he asleep already?

"A long time ago we were friends, practically family.
You've always been one of the good guys, and I guess
it just took me a little while to remember that. But in
my defense, it's been twelve years since we've seen one
another." She paused, hoping he'd speak, but he didn't.
"Anyway, I'm sorry for…holding stuff against you that
really wasn't your fault."

Again she waited, but after a solid minute of silence she gave up. *He must not be ready to forgive me*, was her first thought. Or maybe he truly was asleep. Lacey preferred to think he was asleep because otherwise it meant she'd blown it here with Ean. Again.

"I'm sorry, Lacey," he replied. "For everything."

His words were spoken so softly and yet with such deep emotion and regret that Lacey felt tears well in her eyes. She knew it wasn't about the sheets or the bed or this cottage. It was about the past.

That one simple statement erased twelve years of battered ego.

"Ean?" she whispered.

"Hmm?" Now he did turn to look at her.

"I missed you too."

Chapter 5

No words had ever sounded sweeter to Ean. He knew Lacey had a stubborn streak—she always had—and to hear her admit she had missed him, even after the way things had ended between them, made him smile.

"So we're okay then?" he asked hesitantly, and was relieved to see Lacey nod as she looked at him from the bed. "I'm glad, Lacey, I truly am. You have no idea how much it troubled me to think I'd caused you any pain over the years."

Lacey did not want to take this particular trip down memory lane right now. "It's no big deal, Ean. I was a kid. I'd rather just forget about it, okay?"

"No, I should have…I should have made more of an effort to apologize. To make things right between us. I've always regretted it."

"Thank you for saying that," she said quietly.

It was Ean's turn to nod, and he wished her a good night before rolling over to face the fire again. She couldn't help herself; she watched him as he clearly tried to get comfortable, and then felt a twinge of guilt. The bed was big enough for the both of them without feeling too intimate, and she was no longer that impulsive girl of fourteen; she was a grown woman who had mastered the art of self-control.

"Ean?"

"Hmm?"

"Um… I was being ridiculous earlier. It's crazy for you to sleep on the floor, especially since you hurt your back. There's plenty of room here in the bed and, like you said, we're both adults and…"

She never got to finish. Ean threw off the blankets, kicked them away from the fire, and was climbing in beside her in a flash of movement.

"Thank God," he said as he pulled the comforter up to his chin and turned to face Lacey. "I mean, it was toasty in front of the fire, but my back was killing me."

Oh, this is bad, she thought. Ean walking around the house or sitting on the ottoman or lying on the floor was one thing; Ean inches from her in the bed was quite another. All that bravado moments ago seemed to vanish. All thoughts of self-control were slowly fading. What harm could admitting to a little attraction do?

They were face-to-face, the only sounds in the room the crackling of the fire and their own breathing. Ean seemed to be memorizing her face, so intense was his expression as he looked at her. Lacey licked her lips unconsciously, willing him to close the distance between them and be the one to initiate a kiss. Her eyes felt heavy, slumberous, and if she just leaned forward a little bit…

"Well, good night, Lace," he said and turned his back to her.

That was it? *Again?* Oh, when was she going to learn? Why did it have to be this man who made her crazy? She flopped onto her back and stared at the ceiling, wondering what it was going to take to make her crazy crush on Ean Callahan go away! Wasn't twelve years enough?

Turning on her side, facing away from him, Lacey

stared into the fire. The bed was incredibly comfortable.
The cottage itself was warm and cozy, and if she could
just forget about the man lying beside her, all would be
right with the world.

---

*Everything was slightly blurry. She kept blinking to try
to see what was going on around her, but there was
some sort of white haze blocking her view.*

"It's time, Lacey."

Was that her dad's voice?

*Turning, she saw that her dad was dressed hand-
somely in his best suit, and he was smiling at her with
such tenderness that she wanted to cry. "Time? Time for
what?" she asked.*

*"Don't be silly, sweetheart. We don't want to keep
everyone waiting."*

*Lacey was confused. Who was here and why were
they waiting and why couldn't she see clearly?*

*A door opened and she saw a room full of people. She
couldn't make out most of their faces, but she knew they
were all smiling. Her father was holding her arm and
then they were moving, slowly walking toward the front
of the large room. That's when she noticed Ava standing
and smiling at her. Was this Ava's wedding? No, Ava
would be behind her if that was the case.*

*Panicked, Lacey looked down at herself and for the
first time noticed that she was wearing white. It wasn't
a haze in front of her, it was a veil! She was getting
married? What? To whom? She stopped and her father
turned to look at her. "You're absolutely beautiful,
Lacey. Mom and I are so proud of you." He prompted*

her slightly and they continued to walk to the front of the room. It hadn't looked that large and yet they kept walking and walking and walking.

Finally she could see a man dressed in a black tuxedo ahead. His back was to her. Was this him? Was he the man she was marrying? Who was he? Before she could give further thought to that question, she was beside him. Her father turned her toward him and whispered, "Be happy, sweetheart," before lifting her veil and kissing her on the cheek. She watched him walk toward her mother, who was wiping a tear from her cheek. They joined hands, and Lacey wondered what she was supposed to do now.

With no other choice, she turned to face the man in the tuxedo and nearly collapsed to the ground when he turned to take her hand.

It was Ean.

—————

Lacey woke with a start and tried to sit up, but there was a heavy weight keeping her pinned to the mattress. Her heart was racing and it took a moment for her to remember where she was.

"What the…?" she whispered, struggling to sit up.

"Are you okay?" a deep voice whispered from behind her.

A deep voice?

It was then that Lacey remembered she was in bed with Ean. Only they were no longer sleeping on opposite sides of the bed with their backs to each other—they were sharing the center of the bed, spooned together. She pushed his arm off her and sat up frantically, looking around the room for some sign that this was just a dream. The alarm clock next to the bed read 2:04.

Ean sat up beside her. "Lacey?"

She turned to look at him and shook her head to clear it. It was just a dream. She had not married him; it was all just a dream. Clearly she had weddings on the brain because of Ava and her binder and the fact that they were at the cottage. It was all no big deal.

"Um...yes. I'm fine. I just had a bad dream, and when I woke up I forgot where I was. Sorry I woke you." With that said, she moved a little bit away from him and settled back onto her side of the bed.

Ean watched as Lacey turned her back to him and settled down. She'd scared the hell out of him. With the blankets pooled around his waist and missing the heat of Lacey's body beside him, he felt chilled, so he climbed out of bed and walked over to the fireplace to put another couple of logs on the fire. He shivered as the flames rose again, and quickly got back into bed. "Cold out there," he whispered, and wished she'd roll back over and help him warm back up.

In all honesty, he'd had no idea how they'd gotten so entangled in their sleep. Last he remembered, they'd been on opposite sides of the bed and he had no recollection of moving, let alone shifting to the center of the bed with Lacey. Luckily, it seemed as if she had done the same. He'd have felt awful if they'd woken up and they were both on her side of the bed. She'd never trust him again if that had been the case. Maybe by morning she'd forget they'd slept spooned together for a couple of glorious hours.

Now he was wide awake and *thinking* about lying

all tangled up with Lacey. He looked toward her side of the bed. She had grown into such a beautiful woman. His heart lurched just thinking about her face. Lacey had always been pretty, that was never in doubt, but the woman lying beside him took his breath away. All those years ago she'd been a child. Her kiss had shocked him, not just because she was only fourteen, but because he'd actually enjoyed it.

She'd told him that she loved him. He wasn't foolish enough to take her seriously; after all, she was too young to understand what she was feeling. But right now, beside her in the dark, Ean found that he longed to hear her say it again. If she did, he knew that as a grown woman she'd be in full knowledge of what she felt and what she was saying, and the thought of hearing those words made him ache.

He'd never been the kind of man who looked for relationships or even felt comfortable in them. He was comfortable with his work, with his career. But with Lacey, a world of hope and possibilities came to mind. She knew him so well, he was comfortable around her, and he was wildly attracted to her. Ean thought about how she'd drawn him in from two lanes over in the supermarket earlier, and chuckled. Lacey Quinn owned a part of his heart that he was just now realizing had always belonged to her, and he had no idea what to do about it.

As quietly and unobtrusively as possible, he moved toward her. Lacey's breathing was slow and steady, and Ean was pretty sure she'd gone back to sleep. He was in the center of the bed on his back when she suddenly rolled over toward him. He waited, breath held, to see what she'd do next. Within minutes she was secured tightly at his side, their legs tangled together, her head on his shoulder, her hand on his heart.

The one that clearly belonged to her.

—⁓—

There were no more dreams to disturb Lacey's sleep, and when she finally awoke, the cottage was bathed in sunlight. She blinked the room into focus but felt far too comfortable to move. The fire was still going in the fireplace and had kept the place warm and toasty all night long. She moved to stretch, and that's when it hit her exactly why she had been so warm and toasty—she was practically lying on top of Ean!

Oh dear Lord, what had she done? Her subconscious must have gotten the best of her and that damn dream had wreaked more havoc than it should have. Trying hard to move without waking him, she untangled her legs from his and was about to roll away when his grip tightened around her.

"Going somewhere?" he whispered sleepily, placing a soft kiss on the top of her head.

Her heart melted. For so long she had dreamed of hearing him whisper such words to her and to be in his arms! "I didn't think you were awake," she said honestly. She reared back slightly and looked at his handsome face. There was a light stubble on his chin and, without conscious thought, she reached up and touched it. Scratchy, just as she'd thought. When she made to pull her hand away, Ean grabbed her wrist and held her steady. Slowly, his eyes never leaving hers, he placed a gentle kiss on her palm.

Lacey's heart began to pound frantically. What was

happening here? Ean wasn't attracted to her; he'd never been attracted to her. Was he even fully awake? "Ean?" she whispered when he released her wrist.

Everything happened in slow motion. He moved forward as Lacey rolled onto her back. Ean's eyes continued to scan her face, committing it to memory. "You're so beautiful, Lacey, do you know that?"

Unable to speak, she merely shook her head. Their connection was so deep, so powerful, she couldn't look away. "It's true, you are, and you always have been. I look at you and you take my breath away." No sooner were the words out of his mouth than he was leaning forward and placing his lips on hers, testing the waters with a sweet kiss.

Sensations overwhelmed her as Lacey let herself sink into the kiss. Ean's mouth was firm, but gentle; each touch of his lips was light and playful. When Lacey finally reached up and put her arms around him to pull Ean close, it took on a deeper feeling. Over and over his mouth slanted over hers, and it was as if they had always been lovers. He knew her every desire even as he was discovering it for the first time.

Lacey's hand wound up to tangle in Ean's hair and hold him to her, and she was rewarded with a growl of pleasure from him. It was madness; in her wildest dreams she'd never thought she'd wake in Ean's arms and be kissed as if she were essential to his survival.

Needing a moment to clear her head, she hesitantly drew back and was nearly overwhelmed with the look of raw desire on Ean's face. Their breathing was ragged and her hands stayed busy—touching his hair, his face, his shoulders.

Her touch was killing Ean. He'd kept his hands to himself, not trusting that he'd be able to stay in control. One hand was behind the pillow Lacey's head rested on, while the other was on top of the comforter near her hip. His skin tingled with the thought of actually touching her, being skin to skin. But if Ean knew anything, it was that he didn't want to rush this; after not seeing one another for so many years, this strong attraction came as something of a shock to him. He always knew he'd see Lacey again and had been pretty confident he'd still be attracted to her; it was the intensity of his attraction that scared him.

"How did this happen?" she whispered. "I thought you weren't interested in me."

Confusion marked Ean's face. "Why would you think that?"

A giggle escaped her lips before she could stop it. "Are you serious? The last time we were like this you pretty much threw me out the door! That's not the action of a man who's attracted to a woman."

Pulling back and sitting up, Ean looked down at her and let out a hearty laugh. "Sweetheart, we were never like this. The night of my graduation you were a child and I was a self-centered jerk who was only focused on getting out of town and being on my own."

"I was almost fifteen," she argued lightly, and Ean reached over and finally allowed himself to touch her face.

"At the time, it wouldn't have been appropriate for me to respond in any other way. I was eighteen—legally an adult. You were still technically a child. A beautiful one, yes, but still a child."

The transformation in her face was amazing. Ean was able to see all of Lacey's insecurities disappear. "You thought I was beautiful?" she asked shyly.

"Always." He leaned forward and began to kiss her again. "If you had been older, I might have skipped that summer semester and stayed home." He kissed her again, lingering. "I probably would have locked the basement door and kept you down there with me for the whole summer."

And with that statement, the past was forgotten, and Lacey pulled Ean back to her and showed him all the ways she would have entertained him that long-ago summer.

Chapter 6

IT WAS AFTER LUNCHTIME WHEN THEY FINALLY SURFACED from the bed. Ean was placing more wood on the fire while Lacey reheated the leftover chili for lunch. "I think we may have to be adventurous today and head down to the ranch," she said as she placed the warm bowls on the table. "I didn't plan on being here this long and we're almost out of food."

Lacey turned her back to reach for some silverware and let out a squeak of surprise when Ean grabbed her around the waist. He spun her around and gave her a very thorough kiss before pulling back. "I'll go down and bring some back. It may have stopped snowing, but you still can't maneuver through the snow in those boots."

She rolled her eyes and playfully swatted him away. "Are we back to that argument? I can *maneuver* in them just fine. I wear them all winter long. While no, it's not in eighteen inches of snow, I still do okay." Checking to make sure everything they needed was on the table, she nodded toward Ean to sit down.

"We'll try it your way, Lace, but if you slip and fall in the snow, I'm leaving you there," he teased. They laughed and dug into their lunch, hungry from the long night and their active morning in bed.

Lacey hated the thought of leaving the cottage but knew the real world was waiting for her beyond the front door. She had to find out when the plows were coming through, call the auto club, and call into work because she had been due back later today. There was no way that was going to happen, but she had to at least check in—a fact she shared with Ean.

"I'm sure the plows are already going strong," he said, "but we may need to make a call to get one up here. My dad used to have one here for the property, but I think he got rid of it a couple years ago. Said he was getting too old to do that for himself anymore. He'd rather pay someone."

"I certainly don't blame him one bit," Lacey admitted, "although it would definitely come in handy right now so I could get my car out."

"Anxious to leave?" he asked, his tone suddenly quiet, serious.

How could she possibly answer that? On one hand, Lacey never wanted to leave. The real world was cold and lonely. What she'd experienced here in the cottage in less than twenty-four hours had made her realize just how lonely she'd been. On the other hand, everything had happened so fast that she wanted some time alone, away from Ean, to collect her thoughts.

With a smile of reassurance, Lacey reached across the table and took one of Ean's hands in hers. "Not anxious, but I do have things I need to get back to. Unlike you, I'm not the boss." He smiled in return, but it didn't quite reach his eyes.

Ean recognized the hurdles that were suddenly in front of them. They'd just shared an amazing morning together and would hopefully share another full night before Lacey had to go back to work, but what happened after that? His life was in Boston while hers was in Raleigh. Would she consider relocating? Could he even ask her to do that?

Not wanting to ruin the lighthearted mood they'd created, Ean pushed the negative thoughts aside and put a smile on his face as he kissed Lacey's hand and they finished their lunch.

"I can't wait to talk to Ava and give her some ideas to tone the place down from her grand plan," Lacey said as she put dishes away. "I mean, I get what she's going for, but if we do everything she asked, it's going to look like Christmas threw up in here."

Ean laughed. "You know if you stray from the plan, she's going to have a fit. We'll do everything she asked for, just in moderation."

Lacey agreed but Ean could tell that she was mildly distracted. "What's going on?" he asked, taking her by the hand and leading her over to the sofa.

"I'm worried about her, Ean. I mean, I don't doubt that she loves Mason and he loves her, but I don't think either of them is doing this for the right reasons. Does that make sense?"

Nodding, Ean took a moment to respond. "Do you think my parents know what's going on?"

"No. I don't think Ava even wanted me to know; it just sort of came out. When I tried to talk to her about sitting down with Mason and talking about things, she accused me of not believing in love and fairy tales and all the crap that goes with them."

Ean chuckled. "So what you're saying is that fairy tales are crap? Did I get that right?"

Punching him on the arm, Lacey couldn't help but laugh too. "It's not that they're crap, it's just that life isn't a fairy tale. People have to actually *work* for their happily ever afters. It doesn't just appear because you spend your wedding night in a specific cottage. She and Mason are going to be starting off on the wrong foot if Ava isn't honest with him."

Standing, Ean walked to the front window and looked out at the acres of untouched snow. What Lacey was saying made perfect sense; the problem was his sister. Ava was single-minded when she was on a mission, and right now her mission was to get married. While he had been looking forward to a little more alone time before reconnecting with his family, he knew he wasn't going to get much rest with the impending nuptials weighing heavily on his mind.

"Maybe I'll head into Raleigh a little sooner than I planned and spend some time with both Ava and Mason—not together, but a little one-on-one time with each of them to sort of feel them out. What do you think?" he asked, turning to face Lacey again.

Standing, she went to join him by the window. "I think you are an amazing big brother and Ava is very lucky to have you." Lacey stood on her toes and planted a light kiss on Ean's cheek. Turning, she looked out the window and sighed. "That is an awful lot of snow. I can't even see my car."

"It's there and we'll get it out." He turned Lacey to face him and kissed her deeply, his hands anchored in her hair, loving the feel of it. "Later."

—⁂—

Proving Ean wrong had seemed like a good idea at the time, but the reality was that her sensible boots were in no way meant to be worn in a foot and a half of snow. When they'd finally left the cottage, he'd found an extra hat and gloves for her to wear, but no extra snow boots. Lacey'd put up the argument that it would not be hard to walk; the snow was deep enough that she wouldn't have the opportunity to slip. Ean had reluctantly agreed only because he was hungry again and they were out of food.

"We'll call the town when we get to the ranch and see about that plow and getting your car out," he called over his shoulder as they made it past where her car was snowed under.

Lacey sighed and trudged on, every step its own little slice of hell. If she lived to make it to the ranch, she was going to throw the boots into the fire!

"Oh, wait!" she called before Ean got too far ahead of her. "Since we're right here, can we get my bag out of the car? We can dust it off and get the door open if we try." She batted her lashes at him and her green eyes twinkled. How could the man possibly resist?

His sigh was long and dramatic, but Lacey could tell it was all in good fun. It didn't take long for them to move enough of the snow for her to open the door and grab her overnight bag. Relieved to have her essentials back in her possession, she was just about to say how she couldn't wait to change into dry clothes when a snowball hit her square in the chest.

"Ean!" she screeched, shocked that he would do such a thing. Now wasn't the time for playing; all she wanted to do was get to the ranch, change into dry clothes, and have something to eat. Obviously, Ean had other plans.

His laughter was contagious and within minutes they

had a full-blown war going on. Lacey used her car as a shield, but Ean didn't play fair. With no fear of running in the snow, he was able to pummel her from all sides and it didn't take long for Lacey to cry out in defeat.

She was brushing snow off her coat when Ean came forward and wrapped his arms around her and kissed her. She swatted him away, feigning annoyance, but Ean wasn't buying it. "Admit it, Lace, you had fun."

"No, I did not," she replied primly. "I'm soaked to the skin, this coat will never dry, and these boots are letting in more snow than they're keeping out!" That last admission hurt the most, but walking in her socks was starting to look appealing.

"Dammit, I knew I shouldn't have let you talk me into letting you walk to the ranch. C'mon, let's get going." Taking the overnight bag in one hand and reaching for one of Lacey's gloved hands with the other, they walked silently back to the Callahans' home.

By the time they were safely inside, Lacey's teeth were chattering. Ean helped her take her boots off and led her to the guest bathroom where he ordered her to take a hot shower while he made them something to eat. She didn't argue, and once she stepped under the steamy spray, all seemed right with the world.

Honestly, she could have stayed in there for hours, but the smell of whatever Ean was preparing was a big enough draw to lure her out. Drying off quickly and putting on clean clothes, Lacey slathered on some moisturizer and towel-dried her hair. With any other man she would have been horrified to be seen like this, but with Ean, it seemed perfectly natural—plus, having grown up together, he'd pretty much seen her at every phase of life; her not having makeup on wouldn't traumatize him too terribly.

There was a fire roaring in the massive stone fireplace that divided the kitchen and family room, and Ean had prepared steaks and baked potatoes for them. He smiled as Lacey entered the kitchen and held a chair out for her so she could sit.

"I made some calls," he said as he carried their plates to the table. "The plow will be out first thing in the morning. It's the local guy my father uses. When I told him about your car, he said he'd help us get it out of the rut and back onto the road, so I think we're set with that."

"Thank you. I really appreciate that, but it wouldn't have been any trouble to call the auto club."

"They're probably overworked right now. Why bother them when we can take care of it?"

Over the meal they talked about their careers and got caught up on each other's lives. The previous day and most of the morning had been spent talking about Mason, Ava, and the wedding; now they finally had time to focus more on themselves.

Lacey knew how successful Ean's career was; the Callahans bragged about him constantly. Ean traveled the world, and his software company was one of the most popular on the market today. Likewise, Ean had been kept up to date on Lacey's career with interior decorating. The difference now was talking to one another, getting personal, unbiased feedback on what it took to maintain their careers.

"I love the travel," Ean said, "but I feel like I have been going nonstop for eight years now and I'm starting to burn out. That's why I came up here before heading to Raleigh. I know being with my family isn't work, but I just needed some time to not be around people."

"And then I ruined it for you," she replied, pouting slightly.

Ean reached across the table and took her hand. "No, you didn't ruin anything for me, Lacey. It's been a long time since I relaxed and had a conversation that wasn't work related, and in the last twenty-four hours I've laughed more than I have in years." He lifted her hand to his lips and gave it a gentle kiss. "You were a most pleasant surprise."

"That's not what you were saying when you first saw me last night."

Letting go of her hand, he gave an exaggerated eye roll. "I had just fallen off a chair onto a hard deck and banged my head. I wasn't going to be pleasant to anyone right then."

"Excuses, excuses…"

They cleared the table and straightened the kitchen before heading into the family room to share a spot on the sofa in front of the fire. "I can't wait to talk to Ava about the cottage," Lacey said as she reclined against Ean, enjoying the warmth of both the fire and the man. "I still think some issues need to be resolved between her and Mason, but I'm not going to stress about it."

"Maybe if we approached her together…" Ean began.

"No!" she replied, a little too quickly for Ean's liking. "Why not?"

"Well, for starters, if she found out you were up here, your whole family would be upset. They have been talking about you coming home for weeks, and if they find out you came here first, they'll be very hurt, Ean."

"I can handle my family, Lace. That's not an issue."

What she had to say was not going to come out right no matter how she said it, but although it pained her, Lacey was never one to walk away from a challenge. Straightening from Ean's embrace, she turned and faced him. "I think it would be best if what happened here stayed here." She said the words slowly and winced at the expression on Ean's face.

"Like Vegas? Seriously?"

"No, not like Vegas. It's just that, well, think about it, Ean. Your life is up in Boston while mine is in Raleigh. You clearly have no desire to come back to North Carolina—"

"You don't know that…"

"I can count on one hand the number of times you've been back in the last twelve years! Are you telling me you'd move your company to Raleigh?"

His eyes bored into hers, his expression fierce, but he said nothing.

"Ean, what happened up here was a wonderful, exciting surprise. I never would have thought you'd see me as anything more than Ava's friend. You have no idea what you've done for me. You wiped away the humiliation I felt from that night and gave me a beautiful memory."

"Dammit, Lacey, it wasn't about atoning for that night!"

"No, no, I know that, Ean. I truly do. But once I leave here in the morning, it's back to reality. This has been a wonderful, magical break from the real world we both live in. I don't want to end it fighting with you." She leaned forward and kissed him softly on the lips. "Please, Ean," she whispered. "Tell me you understand."

The sad part was he did understand, but that didn't mean he had to like it. He'd already acknowledged to himself the hopelessness of their situation. Logistics just weren't on their side right now, but Ean had hoped they'd at least talk about it and try to come up with some sort of plan to keep seeing one another.

"It doesn't have to end, Lacey," he said, trying not to sound desperate. "I'll come back, or fly you up to Boston. Have you ever been there? It's beautiful! I can take you around to all the historic sites. You might even find some inspiration for decorating some of the homes."

She smiled and stroked his cheek. "Long-distance relationships rarely work, Ean." Lacey sighed and stood, "I never thought we'd get to a place where we'd be friends again. I spent a lot of years being mad at you and embarrassed at myself. Add the complication of our families being so close—they're bound to interfere."

"They wouldn't."

Laughing, she reached for his hand and pulled him to his feet. "That shows how little you know about our families. You've been away far too long. They would interfere and they'd start getting ideas and making plans and putting pressure on us, and soon it wouldn't be just you and me, it would be you, me, and everyone. I don't want that."

"I still think you're wrong about our families. They wouldn't be that bad."

"Oh please, Ean." She laughed. "As it is, Ava can never know about this because she's banking on this cottage as the be-all, end-all of fairy tales and she believes it's going to fix all of her and Mason's problems. If she finds out we stayed here, she'll find some way to blame us if their marriage fails. Never mind the reality that it's going to fail because clearly the two of them don't talk. We'll be the scapegoats!"

Ean stopped her tirade the only way he knew how. He kissed her. Deeply. Lovingly.

"I'm not ready to let you go," he said gruffly, his forehead against hers.

Lacey's heart ached just a little. "I'm not going anywhere yet."

———~~~———

When Lacey returned home the next day, her heart was in turmoil. Having been in love with Ean for most of her life, was she wrong to walk away now? When she'd finally left the Callahans' earlier that morning, Ean had told her again that they didn't have to end things. He said he wanted to continue to see her and find out where this relationship could go. Unfortunately, Lacey didn't see how it could go any other way than Ean returning to Boston, leaving her with her heart broken again. Not a road she wanted to go down.

With a flick of her wrist, she tossed her keys on the coffee table in her living room and collapsed on the couch. The time with Ean had been amazing— everything she'd ever dreamed it would be. It was the thought of all that went with making that kind of commitment that freaked Lacey out.

Kicking off her shoes, she sighed. It was the holidays and people were always more emotional during the holidays, plus Ava's wedding and her crazy Christmas Cottage story… It all had Lacey's head spinning. Maybe she was over-romanticizing her time with Ean because of where they were. And then all that talk about love and weddings…maybe neither of them were thinking very clearly. Perhaps all they had shared for those incredible forty-eight hours was nothing more than the influence of their environment.

That gave her some relief. Now she'd be able to get back to her real life without obsessing about what it all meant. Rising from the sofa, Lacey went and found the makings for a light dinner and decided to call Ava to discuss the cottage plans. It would be hard to omit any mention of Ean being there, but his refusal to tell his family of his whereabouts was between Ean and the Callahans.

Smiling, Lacey found herself eager, for once, to talk wedding plans with her best friend.

Chapter 7

LIFE WAS BUSY AND IT TOOK TWO DAYS FOR LACEY AND Ava to get together. They decided on takeout at Ava's; Lacey was bringing the Chinese food and Ava was providing the wine.

Arriving promptly at seven, Lacey had barely knocked when the door swung open and she was embraced by an overly excited Ava.

"Wow! That was some greeting! What's going on?" Placing the Chinese food on Ava's kitchen table, Lacey went about getting them set up to eat. Her day had been long and there hadn't been time for lunch, so traveling with the wonderful aroma of dinner in her car had kicked her appetite into overdrive.

"So? You saw it, right? Didn't you just love it? Did you bring the binder? You can see how all of my plans will fit perfectly, right?"

"Take a breath, Ava." Lacey laughed and handed her a plate. "I am not discussing anything until I have at least a couple of bites of food. I'm so hungry I could gnaw on my own arm!"

They each loaded up a plate and went to sit in the living room where, Lacey saw, Ava had laid out decorating and bridal magazines. She stifled a groan.

Ava was fairly vibrating with excitement. When she felt enough time had passed, she pounced. "So? C'mon, tell me, tell me, tell me!"

With great patience, Lacey put her plate down, got comfortable on the couch, and very diplomatically described what she thought would work in the cottage and what she felt would be overkill. Remarkably, Ava wasn't too disappointed with the results.

"So no cactus?" she asked.

"I think it's unnecessary. Between the Christmas tree, the wreaths, the roses... You want it to look romantic, not like the stockroom for an after-Christmas sale."

"Okay, I'll trust you on this, but everything else will work, right? You had no trouble with the other things, did you?"

Lacey thought about the flannel versus silk sheets discussion and figured now was as good a time as any to bring it up. "How attached are you to the idea of silk sheets?" she asked cautiously.

"It's my honeymoon, we have to have silk sheets!"

Rolling her eyes, Lacey made her pitch. "Yes, silk sheets can be very romantic, but you're also dealing with winter in the mountains. Even with the fireplace, you may not enjoy the feel of cool sheets. The cottage is your little winter wonderland, Ava. Think of how nice a good set of flannel sheets would feel." Lacey knew from personal experience how great those flannel sheets would feel, but she could never admit that to Ava.

"Well, I don't know..." Ava began.

"I'll tell you what, I'll stock the cottage with both of them and then you can decide."

"Lace, I'm not going to want to do laundry and change the sheets on my wedding night. Just stick with the silk, please?"

Reluctantly Lacey agreed, and they moved on from

talk of decor to food choices, and then finally the conversation turned to the traveling part of the honeymoon, which Lacey had no part in planning. Finally, she could sit back and enjoy herself.

"I wanted to go to Hawaii, you know, especially after having a winter wedding. I thought it would be nice to go someplace tropical to relax, to balance out the cool and hot."

"Wait, are you saying you're not going to Hawaii now?" Lacey was confused. Two weeks ago Ava had been modeling bikinis for her honeymoon.

"Mason felt it was more money than we needed to spend."

"So where are you going to go?"

"New York for four days," Ava said flatly.

"Why New York?"

"Well, Mason said we could spend time in Manhattan, see a Broadway show, go to Central Park and Rockefeller Center. It's beautiful this time of year."

Taking a sip of wine to fortify herself, Lacey waited a moment to respond. "Yes, I'm sure it's very beautiful, but it's also cold and crowded and not what you want. What did Mason say when you told him that wasn't where you wanted to go?"

"You know Mason, he made a good point. We don't want to start our marriage with a lot of debt, and he said he compromised on the wedding ceremony so I should compromise on the honeymoon."

This was all brand-new information. How much more was Ava keeping from her? They were supposed to be best friends! "How did he compromise on the wedding?"

"He wanted the big church ceremony, two hundred

people—you know, cousins you never knew you had—and then a big reception at one of those expensive hotels or catering halls. That's all fine and well for a lot of people, but we have a tradition in my family and I want to honor that. I never wanted a circus for a wedding, you know that," Ava said as if the whole thought of the wedding Mason described was repulsive. "I want a sweet, intimate ceremony, surrounded by people who mean the most to me, and that's what we're having."

Weighing her next words very carefully, Lacey was just about to ask Ava if she was sure she wanted to go ahead with the wedding when there was a knock on the door. She could only hope it wasn't Mason because that would certainly put a damper on talking about possibly breaking up with him.

Ava stood and went to the door while Lacey poured herself another glass of wine and settled back against the comfy cushions. She heard Ava squeal with glee. "Ean! You're here! You're really here! Lacey, look! Ean's home!"

A knot formed in Lacey's belly. What was Ean doing here? How was she supposed to act with him in front of Ava after their wild time together up at the cottage? She took Ean's lead and went with it after his rather formal hello.

"It's good to see you, Ean," she said softly, not making eye contact with him. "We didn't expect to see you until closer to the wedding."

Removing his coat and hanging it by the front door, Ean took a moment to drink in the sight of Lacey. He'd had no idea she'd be here tonight; he'd just had the urge to see Ava and figure out what was going on with her and Mason. Not that he had any reason to doubt Lacey, but he needed to hear it for himself so he could figure out how to help.

"I hadn't planned on coming home so early, but with Thanksgiving coming up next week I figured, hey, I'm the boss, I can take some extra time to come home and see how I can help my baby sister get ready for her wedding."

Ava beamed at his words and dragged him to sit next to her on the sofa opposite the one Lacey was on. She placed her head on Ean's shoulder as she smiled at Lacey. "Do I have the best brother or what?"

With a noncommittal sound, Lacey picked up her wine and took a long drink.

Sitting up, Ava turned to Ean. "I still cannot believe you're here! Did Mom and Dad know you were coming home?"

"No, I wanted to surprise everyone and you were my first stop. So tell me how the plans are going!" His tone was enthusiastic and it was all the encouragement Ava needed to plunge into the details of her grand fairy-tale wedding. The only things she seemed to omit were all of the disagreements she and Mason were having.

Ean looked at Lacey out of the corner of his eye and finally caught her attention. His eyes were saying *Do you believe this?* To which Lacey responded with a short shake of her head.

Having heard enough, Ean took one of Ava's hands and got her attention. "So you're telling me you and Mason are on the same page for everything? No disagreements?"

Ava pulled back and made a face at him. "What?

Why would you even ask that?" She looked between Ean and Lacey, looking very much like a caged animal.

"Relax, Ava," he consoled. "It's just that most engaged couples have a lot of disagreements where the wedding is concerned. I'm just wondering how it is that you and Mason managed to avoid all of the pre-wedding craziness."

"Well, maybe we're just more in love than most and..."

Lacey had had enough. "Ava? Can't you see that your brother is concerned for you? You need to tell him what is really going on. You won't seem to listen to me, but maybe Ean has something useful to say that will help you."

Standing, Ava lashed out. "Why can't you just leave this alone, Lacey? I told you I had everything under control! Why is it so hard to believe that? You know nothing about being in a serious relationship or planning a life together! I mean, honestly, when was the last time you even went on a date? Who are you to judge my relationship with Mason?" She stormed from the room and slammed her bedroom door. Lacey sat, mortified at her friend's outburst.

"Now that's the sister I remember living with," Ean said, trying to lighten the mood. Looking over at Lacey, he saw his remark fell short. "Hey, are you okay?"

"I just never expected that kind of rage from her."

"She's under a lot of pressure. From what you told me, it's got to be weighing heavily on her to keep up appearances when she's not happy."

Not knowing what else to do, Lacey went to the kitchen and cleaned up their dinner. She was placing takeout cartons in the refrigerator when Ean stepped up behind her. Wanting nothing more than to lean into him and feel his arms around her, she had to force herself to keep moving. This was not the time or the place to get into that with him again.

She could easily blame their passionate time at the cottage on proximity and perhaps getting one another out of their systems, but right now, she didn't want to look too closely at why she was still aching for his touch.

He pitched in silently, the two of them cleaning up Ava's kitchen as if they did this kind of thing every day. When everything was in its place and there was nothing left to do, Ean stood back and watched Lacey gather her things and prepare to leave.

"I'll give her a couple of days to calm down. I guess I shouldn't have pushed," she said quietly, needing to say the words out loud so she could convince herself it was the truth.

"Lace, she didn't mean any of that. You were just a handy target."

She smiled weakly at his attempt to make her feel better. "I think she meant it a little bit. What she doesn't realize is that you don't have to be married or planning a wedding to know that when two people disagree on so many things, it's not a good sign." When Ean tried to reach for her, she stepped aside, not trusting herself not to throw herself at him. "I better go."

"I'll walk you to your car," he said, reaching for his coat.

"No, it's okay. Go see how Ava's doing. She's the one who needs you right now." *So do I, but I can't let myself near you or I'll never want to let go!*

Merely nodding, Ean held the door for her and

watched from the porch as Lacey walked to her car. He waited until she pulled away and her taillights were out of sight before he closed the door and went to talk to his sister.

—∿∿—

"So I suppose she's been out here blabbing all about the problems Mason and I are having," Ava said as soon as she emerged from her bedroom at the sound of the front door closing.

With a patient smile, Ean walked over to her, took her by the hand, and led her back to the couch. "Care to tell me what that little temper tantrum was about?"

That was all it took. Ava burst into tears and told her brother about all the hurdles she was trying to overcome on her way to the altar.

"Has it occurred to you, Ava, that Mason might not be the man for you?"

"We do love each other, Ean. Opposites attract and all that."

If she had grown a second head, his expression couldn't have been more confused. "Ava, yes, it's true that opposites attract, but they usually have some common ground. It seems to me that you both like the idea of getting married—just maybe not to each other."

"What am I supposed to do? Everything is in motion! The wedding is a month away!"

He pondered that thought for a moment. "You need to sit down with Mason, maybe with an impartial third party, and talk about all of these problems. If you can't overcome them, then I'd have to say that this marriage is not a good idea. If you both agree to some compromises that don't leave you feeling devastated, you might have a chance. Marriage is hard work, Ava. Once the party and honeymoon end, you have to be able to live together. It doesn't sound like you're going to be able to do that."

"I want to. I really, really want to," she began.

"Do you? Or do you *really, really* want to experience this fairy-tale legend that our family has made up?"

"It's not made up, Ean! God, you sound just like Lacey!" And that's when it hit her. "Oh gosh, Lacey!" She looked around as if she thought her friend were still somewhere in the apartment. "Oh, Ean, I was horrible to her, wasn't I?"

He simply nodded and that brought on a fresh wave of tears from his sister. He wrapped his arms around her. "It's okay, Lacey will forgive you. You both just need a couple of days to cool down and then everything will be okay."

"I hope so, Ean. She's my best friend and I love her." He hugged her a little bit tighter and thought, *That makes two of us.*

The days leading up to Thanksgiving had been exhausting for Lacey. While no one was doing intensive interior design jobs, everyone seemed to want help decorating their homes for the holidays. She had averaged two homes a day, and as she pulled up in front of her parents' home on Thanksgiving Day, Lacey realized she'd missed out on all the traditional holiday preparations she normally did with her mother.

Sighing, she looked down at the store-bought pie in

her hand with disgust. They normally baked together every year, made a day of it. Unfortunately, Lacey's job required some unusual hours this time of year, and although she missed being a part of some of her favorite childhood memories, she knew it all went with growing up.

Several cars were parked in the driveway already, and Lacey had to wonder who was joining the Quinns this year. Her parents had a tradition of making an open invitation to everyone they knew and then being surprised by who RSVP'd. Some years they had over twenty people, while others it was just the immediate family. By the look of the cars, there had to be at least a dozen people here so far.

Sure enough, after she'd been greeted at the door by both of her parents and her two older sisters and their spouses, she heard other voices coming from the kitchen. It took less than a minute to recognize the Callahans' voices.

"Hey, Uncle Jack! Aunt Linda! How are you?" Lacey greeted them.

They each stood and hugged and kissed Lacey hello before turning her to face Ean.

"Surprise!" they said in unison. "Can you believe it? Ean came home early and is going to spend the month with us!"

Before Lacey could utter a word, Ean stepped forward and placed a gentle kiss on her cheek that made her go weak at the knees. "Good to see you again, Lacey," he said quietly. This time, she was unable to avoid eye contact with him, and for a brief moment it seemed as though it was only the two of them in the room.

"Oh, Lacey, thank goodness you're finally here!" Ava cried as she nudged her brother out of the way in order to get to her friend and hug her. When she finally released Lacey, Ava said a quick "excuse us" to everyone and led Lacey up to her old bedroom.

"So tell me the truth, do you hate me?" Ava asked dramatically, dropping herself onto Lacey's childhood bed.

"No, of course not. You're my best friend and I should have kept my mouth shut. After all, who am I to be doling out relationship advice, right?"

"I knew you were going to focus on that point!" She sighed loudly. "Look, I was angry because everything you were saying was right. I'm letting Mason call all the shots, and between you and Ean, I know I have to put my foot down and force him to listen to me so we can discuss these issues before the wedding."

"Why? What did Ean say?"

"It was a little spooky. It was like the two of you were completely in sync. He said everything you've been saying." She looked at Lacey through slitted eyes. "Did you call him and prompt him on what to say to me?"

Startled by the question, Lacey started to choke. "You think I just went and called your brother after not seeing or talking to him for like…ten years?" She went and stood by the window. "That's just crazy, Ava."

Ava considered Lacey's words. "I'm sorry, you're right. Gosh, I'm getting so paranoid! This wedding is making me crazier than usual. Please forgive me, Lace. I know I'm not myself, and I know you are genuinely concerned for me. What you've said hasn't fallen on deaf ears. I'm planning on talking to Mason this weekend and working it all out, and if that means giving up the cottage and the fairy tale"—she sighed again—"then it's for the best."

They walked back to the kitchen arm in arm, both with wide grins on their faces. "Everything okay?" Linda Callahan asked, concern marking her face.

"We're fine," Ava answered, and there seemed to be a collective sigh around the kitchen.

It was controlled chaos as everyone had a task to take care of in order to get the massive dinner on the table at the same time. It didn't take long to confirm that it was just going to be the Quinns and the Callahans this year, and while Lacey was happy to see everyone, she couldn't seem to keep herself from sneaking glances at Ean, and he at her. At this rate, someone was bound to question what was going on between the two of them, and that was something she just wasn't willing to deal with right now.

When it was finally time to sit down and eat, Lacey found herself sitting directly across from Ean. There was no way to avoid his gaze, and there was no way people weren't going to notice. They were seated at the center of the table, and Lacey was sure the lighting even seemed a little bit brighter over the two of them.

As plates were passed and conversation flowed, she began to relax. Everyone shared what was going on in their lives and what they were thankful for, and Lacey's heart was full with gratitude for all she had in her life: a wonderful family, dear friends, and—she thought with a sigh—the brief and romantic time with the man of her dreams.

If only things were less complicated and Ean lived closer. The possibilities of a future together would be easier to picture if there weren't so many miles between them. Even if they continued to see each other over the next month while he was home, their time together had an end date, and she wasn't sure her heart could handle it when it was time for Ean to leave.

She wanted to snap out of her melancholy thoughts. Sure, Ean had said he wasn't ready to let her go, but the reality was he *had* let her go. In the two weeks since she'd left the mountains, he'd made no attempt to get in contact with her. Seeing him at Ava's had been a fluke, much like today was. Maybe he had thought about it and realized what she had realized: A short-term affair was just not worth the effort.

While she understood, it certainly didn't make her feel any better. It would have been nice for him to try maybe a little bit to change her mind.

"So, Ava," Lacey's dad was saying. "How much longer till you graduate?"

All eyes turned to Ava, and Lacey felt a surge of panic for her friend. "Oh, um, well, if all goes as planned, I should be graduating next fall. I know I took a little bit longer to find my major, but by this time next year, I should have my degree in library sciences and be on my way."

"Actually," Mason cut in, "I think once we're married Ava won't need to go to school. After all, my practice is growing and I could use some help with organizing events to draw in new clients. Ava would be great with that."

You could have heard a pin drop for a full minute before the whole table exploded in conversation.

"She's been going to school for so long…"

"Ava? Is this true?"

"Your mother and I have spent a lot of money on your education, Ava…"

"A degree is never a waste of time. You may want that for your future…"

On and on it went. The only two who were silent at the table were Lacey and Ean, who looked at one another, shaking their heads. Lacey wanted to reach over and smack Mason upside the head for opening his mouth and bringing up such a sensitive subject over the holiday table, but clearly he was a man who only thought about one thing. Himself.

Lacey noticed Ava was crying.

"I think we should step outside to talk," Ava's father said sternly to Mason, and they stood and left the dining room. Everyone else started cleaning up the table in silence.

It was a nightmare. Lacey was about to stand and start helping with the cleanup when her mother whispered to her, "Make sure Ava's okay."

As they had earlier in the day, they found themselves back up in Lacey's old bedroom.

"Are you okay?" Lacey finally asked after handing Ava a box of tissues.

"I honestly don't know. I never would have thought Mason would bring up the topic so tactlessly. Gosh, Lacey, who is this man I'm marrying? How is it that I don't seem to know him at all?"

Unfortunately, Lacey had no words of comfort. "Maybe this will force some of the issues you've been avoiding, and you'll finally know once and for all if the two of you are meant to be."

With a teary sigh Ava nodded. "I know you're right, but I hate the fact that we've ruined Thanksgiving."

"It was pretty lively in there for a while." Lacey laughed. "Everyone had something to say!"

"Not you and Ean," Ava said, her expression perplexed. "Come to think of it, the two of you were particularly quiet during the whole melee. You've been pretty vocal up to now, why the silence all of a sudden?"

"It seemed like I didn't need to add any more fuel to the fire. Ean probably felt the same way."

"Maybe…" Ava said, still not sounding convinced. "Something's going on. I can feel it. Is there something going on with you and Ean?"

"What?"

"I can't quite put my finger on it, but the two of you are on the same page an awful lot lately. And then there are the long gazes I've been noticing all day." She stood and walked over until she was almost nose to nose with Lacey. "You *did* used to have a crush on him, and even though he's my brother, I have to admit he's mildly attractive. Admit it, Lace, you still have a crush on Ean."

Never, never, never! She gave a dismissive laugh and waved Ava away. Trying to put some space between them, Lacey walked over and sat down on her bed. "I mean, when I was younger, sure, I had a crush on Ean, but we're adults now. Seriously, Ava."

The lady doth protest too much, methinks…

"You can deny it all you want, but I'm telling you the vibes were flying down there earlier. I think it would be great if you and Ean hooked up. Then we'd *really* be sisters!"

"Okay, back up. For one thing, not everyone who

hooks up gets married, and for another, don't you think it would be weird if Ean and I did that?"

"What? Hook up? Oh please! He is totally into you! For all the secret gazes you were shooting at him, he was shooting them right back!"

The teenager inside of Lacey was doing a happy dance while her adult self did everything humanly possible to maintain her composure.

"Sure, whatever. Look, if thinking that helps you with the whole Mason thing, then let your mind go wild. Just do me a favor and keep it to yourself. No need to get everyone in an uproar over something you *think* you saw."

"Oh, I saw it, Lace, and you can be sure I wasn't the only one."

By the time they went back downstairs, dinner was completely cleared away and desserts were set out. Mason and Ava's father were deep in discussion, along with Lacey's dad, and from the looks of it, no one was happy. Ava turned to Lacey. "I guess I might as well face the music."

"Are you sure?" Lacey whispered. "Maybe now is not the time. Maybe you should let them talk before you throw in your two cents."

Ava hugged her. "I love that you are always looking out for me, but it's time for me to take responsibility for my part in all these disagreements." Lacey could only watch as Ava walked across the room. All three men stopped talking at her approach, and then made room for her to join them.

"Is she okay?" Lacey nearly jumped out of her skin at Ean's soft words in her ear.

"She will be. I think today was a real eye-opener for her, and the sooner they work this out, the sooner she'll know how to proceed."

In the large living room everyone was broken up into groups. In one corner was where Ava had joined what Lacey hoped was a productive conversation. Lacey's two brothers-in-law were watching the football game on the big-screen TV. Her mom and Ava's mom were talking animatedly with Lacey's sisters about Black Friday shopping, seemingly to keep themselves distracted, while Ean and Lacey stood and watched, unsure where they belonged.

In more ways than one.

While her heart was screaming at her to take Ean by the hand and sit on the sofa together, her head was telling her to play it safe and join the shopping conversation.

She hated when her head got its way.

Without conscious thought, Lacey gave a longing look over her shoulder at Ean before heading over to sit with the women. Once she was seated, she watched Ean sit to watch the football game across the room. If anyone noticed her staring, they chose to say nothing, and Lacey barely noticed the pause in conversation around her. With a brief sigh, she turned her attention to the women sitting around her and discussed their strategy for attacking all of the sales.

Every few minutes, Lacey found herself glancing across the room, first at Ean and then at Ava. She could only hope Ava and Mason's situation was getting worked out. Hers and Ean's? Well, that was another story completely. Did they even have a situation to work out? Sure, he seemed to be watching her as much as she was watching him, but they had already established that they were attracted to one another. Lacey just had to wonder if it was only attraction Ean felt, or something more.

Before she knew it, everyone was being herded back to the dining room table for dessert, and this time, thankfully, their time together was full of pleasant conversation and laughter rather than the loud arguments of earlier.

Looking around her, Lacey couldn't help but smile. There was so much love in this room, and she truly was thankful for each and every person there. Her eyes met Ean's, and she had to admit, exploring a relationship with him, even a short one, was not something she wanted to fight any longer. As soon as they were done with dessert, she decided she would seek him out privately and see if he was interested in spending time with her while he was home. She could only hope she wouldn't lose her nerve or make a fool out of herself.

When dessert was finished, her father called everyone back into the living room. As everyone filed in, Lacey found herself seated next to Ean and didn't even think of moving away.

"I am so thankful we had this day together," her father began. "It seems like we never have enough time to just come together and relax and enjoy one another's company. I know things were a little tense here earlier, and I just want to say to Ava and Mason that I hope the two of you realize the importance of communication. We had a good start here earlier, and I hope you'll go home and talk to one another about your future, and be honest."

Leaning over, Mr. Quinn reached for his wife's hand. "No relationship is easy, particularly in the beginning. But if you keep the lines of communication open and trust one another enough to say what's on your mind and what you're feeling, then you have a chance at having a successful marriage. Once you stop talking, or only let one of you talk, then you've lost everything."

Everyone nodded in agreement while settling into their respective seats to enjoy a Quinn family tradition and kick off the holiday season by watching *It's a Wonderful Life*. Lacey settled in a little bit closer to Ean and sighed contentedly as he reached over and put his arm around her, pulling her close as the opening credits began.

Chapter 8

TWO HOURS LATER, LACEY WAS FAST ASLEEP WITH HER head on Ean's shoulder. Everyone was getting up to leave and Ean hated to wake her. At first he nudged her gently to see if that would wake her. When it didn't, he quietly whispered her name until her lashes fluttered and her green eyes looked up at him.

"Ean," she sighed sleepily.

"Hey, look who's awake!" she heard her father say. It was like a bucket of ice water being thrown at her. "You missed most of the movie, sweetheart. Since when can't you stay awake past nine o'clock?" He laughed as he looked down at his youngest daughter.

"Since I ate my weight in turkey," she replied sweetly, lifting her head from Ean's shoulder and stretching. It took a moment, but she finally stood, although not too steadily, and was relieved to find Ean slipping an arm around her waist to catch her before she fell over.

At her father's speculative look, she quickly said, "Not to worry, I did not have anything to drink today and I'm fine to drive." It would have been a lot more believable if she hadn't followed it with a very loud and unladylike yawn. "Seriously, I'm fine." Another yawn.

"I don't think you should drive, Lacey. Why don't you just stay here tonight? You're going shopping with Mom in the morning so it wouldn't be a big deal."

Although the idea sounded tempting, Lacey was

anxious to go home, change out of her dress clothes, and sleep in her own bed. "Thanks, Dad, but I'll be fine." Ean released her as she stepped away from him, but Lacey began to wonder how smart it was to drive on her own. She was getting her coat from the closet when she heard her father and Ean talking.

"Ean, talk to her. Please."

"Don't worry, I'll drive her home."

Normally Lacey would have been annoyed to have them making arrangements for her like she wasn't even there, but in this particular situation, she knew it was the smartest thing to do. Plus, if she could get her sleepy brain in gear, she'd be able to talk to Ean about spending more time together before he went back to Boston.

After saying their good nights, Lacey locked up her car and followed Ean over to his. He held the door for her as she climbed in and she watched him as he walked around the front and got in beside her.

"You'll have to give me directions because the last address I have for you is right here," he said lightly.

Lacey could tell he was treading carefully, and it just made her heart beat that much faster for him. She typed her address into his GPS and they were on their way, silently at first, but then Ean spoke.

"So how did Ava seem when the two of you went upstairs after dinner?"

Lacey explained their conversation to him and how Ava took it as the eye-opener she'd needed. "Hopefully, between that and sitting and talking with our dads, she's got the confidence to stand up for herself."

"And the wedding? Is she disappointed?"

"Of course she will be if they decide to cancel it,

but she didn't seem ready to admit defeat yet. One of them is going to have to have a major change of heart and soon in order for everyone to be comfortable going forward with it."

"So no more talk of the cottage being the answer to it all?" he asked as he turned and grinned at Lacey.

She couldn't help but giggle. "No, no more talk of the magic of the cottage and how that's all she needs to survive it all." Then she stopped and gave some serious thought to what they were saying. "I think Mason's outburst came as a surprise to her. It forced her to see the situation for what it is rather than through rose-colored glasses. I felt bad for her."

Ean reached for her hand and held it as they drove silently to Lacey's home. It wasn't a long drive, and when they pulled up in front of her town house, she could sense Ean's uncertainty. "Would you like to come in?" she asked shyly and was relieved when he agreed.

Standing by her side as she unlocked the door and reached in to turn on the lights, Ean enjoyed having the opportunity to prolong their night.

"I'd offer you some coffee, but just the thought of any more food is enough to make me feel a little bit green, how about you?"

"Agreed." He laughed, looking around Lacey's home. Everything was warm and inviting, just like Lacey. He walked into the living room and admired the built-in bookcases that surrounded the stone fireplace. Her eclectic collection of books was mixed with shelves of family photographs. It was a home. He thought of his own place back in Boston and realized it was lacking the kind of warmth he felt here. Maybe there were some simple adjustments he could make on his own that would make his place a little more appealing.

"Your home is beautiful, Lacey." *Just like you.*

She blushed at his compliment. "Thanks. I get a lot of inspiration from my work and I think this place is going to be a work in progress forever. I just wish I had more space."

"More room to play with?"

"Exactly! One of the things I loved about this place was that it was brand new, so the walls were blank, the floors were bare, and I only let the builders do the bare minimum before I moved in. My folks thought I was crazy, but I had a blast spending my spare time choosing paint colors and carpets." She sighed. "Most people don't want to take their work home with them, but I don't mind."

"That's what happens when you love what you do. Plus, your work is something you can bring home and use. For me, I'm on a computer all day and when I bring my work home, it's all still on the computer. Not a whole lot of fun, if you know what I mean."

By now they were seated on one of her sofas and Lacey had lit the gas fireplace to warm the place up a little. There weren't too many lights on, and overall the setting was nice and romantic.

"So how long have you been here, then?"

"About two years."

"How many times have you re-finished a room?"

Lacey smiled sheepishly. "This is the third color I've tried on this wall."

"That's not too bad," he said, looking around the room appreciatively.

"And my fourth area rug…" she added.

"O-kay…"

"And the second set of living room furniture." It sounded crazy when she admitted it out loud. "You have to understand," she began, laughing as she spoke.

"No, no, you don't owe me an explanation," Ean said, laughing along with her. "I'm sure in your line of work, it's completely normal to keep changing your surroundings."

She didn't believe him for a minute. "Can you imagine what would happen if I had more rooms?" she asked.

"Well, it would probably mean your rooms would stay with one color scheme for a bit longer because you'd have more rooms to play around with."

"That does make sense," she said, and then they both fell silent. With the fire roaring beside them and at a loss for anything else to say, Lacey leaned in a little closer, her eyes never leaving Ean's.

"I thought we weren't going to do this," he said, inching closer himself.

"We weren't," she whispered, her tongue darting out to delicately lick her lips.

Ean's smile started slow and then spread as he saw the twinkle in Lacey's eyes. "It feels like we're doing this," he said, his lips a breath away from Lacey's.

"Then I guess we are," she said, finally closing the gap and resting her lips against Ean's. It felt better than she remembered, more exciting than she thought possible. In an instant everything changed; what had started sweet and gentle was now frantic and urgent. What was tentative and teasing was now suddenly very serious.

"I want you to be sure, Lace," Ean said breathlessly,

his mouth traveling around her jaw, her throat. "I did what you asked and stayed away, but it damn near killed me."

"I'm very sure, Ean," Lacey assured him.

Closer they moved, until it was impossible to tell where one ended and the other began. Their lips never leaving one another, Lacey sighed with contentment. This was where she wanted to be. It didn't matter that Ean would be gone in a month; it didn't matter if their family wanted to meddle. All that mattered was that she was here right now with this man in this moment.

She pulled back briefly and smiled. "I just recently did some work in the bedroom."

Ean looked puzzled for a moment and then caught on. "Is that right?" He kissed her throat, the delicate spot below Lacey's ear. "That sounds very exciting."

"Oh, it is," she said breathlessly. "I only just learned about the wonder of flannel sheets, so I invested in a set." She felt him chuckle against her skin. "Would you be interested in checking them out? Only to make sure I bought quality flannel, of course."

She was teasing him, and Ean realized it was one of the things he loved most about her. With Lacey, there would always be joy and laughter surrounding him, something that was missing in his life currently. "That would require some close inspection," he said thoughtfully. "Good quality flannel can be hard to come by."

With a smile that blinded him, his beautiful angel pulled Ean to his feet and he let her lead the way, thankful for second chances.

— ᨓᨓ —

It was still dark out and Lacey was asleep in Ean's arms when she heard a knock at her front door. Sitting up, she glanced at her bedside clock and saw that it was 4:32 a.m. Who would be…?

"Oh no!" she cried.

"Lace?" Ean whispered. "You okay?" The knock on the door came again and Ean sat up. "Is someone at your door?"

"Yes!" Lacey cried, crawling from the bed to find her robe. "Your sister! We're supposed to meet up with our moms at five to go Black Friday shopping! I completely forgot!" *Crap, crap, crap!* Her cell phone rang next and Lacey ran to the living room to grab it.

"Hello?"

"Lace, come on, open the door. It's cold out here!" Ava said, annoyance the obvious mood of the day.

"Just give me a minute…"

"*Now!* I see Ean's car here so don't bother trying to hide him."

Oh, this was so not good. Lacey hung up and nearly cried out when Ean appeared beside her. "I have to go let her in," she said and when he went to go back to the bedroom, she stopped him. "No need to hide, she already saw your car."

Lacey walked to the door, opened it, and was nearly plowed over by Ava. "I *knew* something was going on!" she yelled. "You covered it up, Lacey! How could you?"

"Well, in my defense you were already dealing with enough with Mason, so I didn't want to bother you with my personal…you know, stuff."

Lame, Lacey, very lame.

"And you!" Ava turned and focused on her brother.

"You're sleeping with my best friend? When did this happen?"

Lacey tried to get a signal to him to please say that it just happened tonight, that this was the first time they were together, but for some reason this was the one time their brains weren't in sync.

"I ran into Lacey when she was up at the cottage. We got snowed in together and it just…happened. We didn't plan on it and we didn't plan on it happening again, but we're trying to figure out where we go from here."

Standing between the two of them, Ava's mind raged. She looked from one to the other, not sure who to scream at first. "So you went up to *my* cottage and spent the night there with my brother?" Though her tone started out controlled, she was nearly screeching on the last word.

"Ava, listen," Lacey began.

"This is all your fault! All the problems Mason and I were having just escalated in the last two weeks and do you know why?"

Lacey had a feeling she wouldn't have to wait long to find out.

"It's because you *stole* my magic from me." At the ridiculous words, Lacey looked at Ean with an expression that clearly said *I told you so.* "Mason and I could've worked out our problems, gotten married, had our night in the cottage, but you had to swoop in there, with Ean of all people, and steal it away from me!"

"You're talking crazy, Ava," Lacey tried again.

"No! This is the absolute worst thing you could have possibly done. I will never forgive you!"

Ean finally stepped in. "Ava, this had nothing to do

with the cottage or stealing any of your so-called magic. What happened between Lacey and me just happened. We weren't doing it to hurt you, or anyone for that matter."

"Don't you see, Ean? Don't you think it's odd that you two hadn't seen each other for over a dozen years and you get snowed in together at the cottage and now all of a sudden you're in love?"

"Hey, wait, nobody said we're in love," Lacey interrupted but was promptly ignored.

"That had nothing to do with the damn cottage! Lacey and I have a history together, and now that we are both adults we decided to act on some feelings we had for one another. The cottage didn't make that happen!"

"No, the cottage just takes what you have and makes it wonderful! And that was supposed to be mine, Ean! Mine! That feeling, that wonderfulness, that was for me and Mason and you took it away!"

"*Ava!* Do you hear yourself? Has someone hit you on the head? There is no *wonderfulness* that an inanimate object can give you! There is no magic! There is no fairy tale! Grow up!" Ean's words sounded harsh to Lacey and she wanted to cry at him to stop, but Ava was getting out of control.

Ava turned to leave and Lacey tried to reach out to her one more time. "Ava, I am so sorry, but like Ean said, this wasn't about you. It wasn't about the cottage. I had no idea he'd be up there, he had no idea I was going to be there, and when we got done talking and going over all the plans for *your* wedding night, the snow had really piled up. Believe me, neither of us wanted to be there! It was all just a series of circumstances. You have to believe we never wanted to hurt you!"

"Well, whether you wanted to or not, you did." She looked at the two people before her and felt an overwhelming sense of sadness and loss. "You took away more than my fairy tale," she said quietly. "You took away my hope." A lone tear escaped down her cheek. "And for that I cannot forgive either of you."

She ran out the door, and when Lacey tried to run after her, Ean stopped her. "Don't, Lace. You'll only make it worse."

Turning in his arms, she felt her eyes fill with tears. "What am I supposed to do, Ean? How on earth am I supposed to make her see that we weren't trying to hurt her?"

"Damned if I know, sweetheart." He held Lacey close to him and led her over to the couch, where they sat while she cried.

A few minutes later, her cell phone rang again; this time it was her mother. Lacey answered and gave her mother a very short version of what had happened, mortified to have to admit she'd spent the night with Ean. Not that she was ashamed of being with him, but she couldn't believe she had to share that fact with her mother this way. She apologized for missing their shopping spree, but under the current circumstances, Lacey thought it best if she stayed home. She greatly doubted that Ava would be out shopping, but just in case, Lacey decided to stay out of her way.

After hanging up, she sat back in the comfort of Ean's arms.

"What can I do, Lacey? Tell me what I can do to make this right."

She sighed wearily. "I knew this would happen. I was

afraid she would react badly, and now the whole family is involved and it's going to just get messy and complicated."

Ean stroked her long auburn hair, loving the feel of it, wanting to comfort her. "It's none of their business what we're doing. This was something that took us both by surprise. Neither of us showed up at the cottage with the thought of seeing one another, right?"

Lacey nodded.

"We had unfinished business between us, but even that didn't prepare me for the feelings I found that I have for you, Lacey." He gently cupped her face and tilted her chin so that she was looking up at him. "You took my breath away and it wasn't because of the cottage or any family fairy tale, it's because of you and who you are. Do you believe me?"

She wanted to just say yes, but something niggled in the back of her mind. All the years of Ava recounting that silly story of the cottage kept coming through. "What if it's not just a story? What if it's true?"

Ean released her face and stood up. "Please don't tell me you suddenly believe in that story now, too, because of what Ava said?"

"Well, the timing is a little suspicious…"

"Lacey, listen to me," he said sternly. "I saw you in the damn grocery store before you got to the cottage. I saw you, two lanes over, before I knew it was you, and all I could think was 'I have to meet that woman.' I feel the way I do about you because it's real and it's true. You have always been on my mind. You've quite possibly always owned a part of my heart! Don't let the rantings of my sister ruin this for us."

"I can't help it, Ean. She was so sure of what she was

saying! Every time she told that story, she told it with such conviction that it's hard for it not to play a part in what I'm thinking right now!"

"How can I convince you that what I feel is not about the cottage? How can I make you believe that the feelings I have for you are because of who you are, and what we can have together?"

"What we can have together?" she cried. "Ean, we have a month together and then you're going back to Boston. That's where your life is. Mine is here. That's not going to change."

"So what are you saying? That all of this tonight was, what? Killing time?"

"No!" she cried, needing Ean to understand. "Look, I have no idea what's going to happen after Christmas when you go back to Boston. All I do know is I'm not ready to let you go yet either. There was no plan, and believe me, for someone like me who always has a plan, this was a little out of my comfort zone." She stepped closer to him. "This is all new territory for me. I wasn't expecting this to happen. Not with you."

Ean inhaled sharply. He knew exactly what she meant. Never in his wildest dreams had he thought he'd have the opportunity to be with Lacey, to make love with her, to fall in love with her.

Fall in love? Yes, looking into her upturned face right now, worry lines etched from the events of the morning, Ean knew he was falling in love with her. He reached up and gently stroked the side of her face, loving the softness of her skin, and the sound of her soft sigh gave him hope. "I wasn't expecting you either, Lace, but here we are." He kissed her softly. "The thought of not being with you was tearing me apart, and I hate that you doubt what we have all because Ava was having a temper tantrum."

"It's not just that, Ean…"

"Shh." He placed a finger over her lips. "Let me finish." She nodded. "Twelve years ago we started something, or rather you started something. It just took me a long while to catch up." He smiled sheepishly and was rewarded with a small smile from Lacey. "This isn't about anything else except me and you. There is no cottage, there is no magic story. It's about us. Do you believe me?"

When Lacey looked into his eyes, she did believe him. She could hardly believe the man she had always wanted stood right here in front of her, telling her he cared for her, but the look in Ean's eyes said it all.

"Have a little faith in us, Lacey."

Oh gosh! Could it be this easy? Her heart said yes while her head was saying no, but for once, she let her heart win. "I do believe you, Ean," she whispered. "And I do have faith in us."

Wrapping her in his arms, Ean kissed her, slow, wet, and deep. While what he wanted most was to take her back to bed, he knew there'd be plenty of time for that later. Right now he just wanted to sit in front of the fire holding the woman he loved, and luxuriate in the perfect moment where everything was possible. He kissed her temple and felt her relax into him as they both stared into the fire, a sigh of contentment escaping his lips.

Chapter 9

THE NEXT THREE WEEKS FLEW BY. WORK KEPT LACEY busy, and she was thankful for it because she needed the distraction. Things with Ean were perfect. They spent nearly every night together either going to dinner, the movies, or just staying in, but there was an underlying tension within the families where Ava was concerned.

According to Lacey's mom, the wedding was still on. Ean was able to confirm it, but apparently his sister was being tight-lipped with everyone, not just with him and Lacey. No one was sure how it was all going to come together considering the bride wasn't speaking to the maid of honor or best man, but to keep some sense of peace, they all let Ava be.

Coming home late Friday night, Lacey was walking toward her front door when she noticed someone standing in the shadows. Clutching her cell phone in her hand, she was just about to call Ean when she recognized who it was.

"Ava? This is a surprise!" That was the understatement of the year. Lacey unlocked the door and heard Ava following behind her. "Are you okay?" Turning, she saw great distress written all over Ava's face.

"No, I'm not okay." Her tone was very defensive. When Lacey just stared at her, Ava finally spoke. "Look, I'm not proud of my behavior from the morning after Thanksgiving. To say I've been out of sorts over this wedding would be an understatement."

Lacey merely nodded.

"I'm sorry," Ava continued. "I know you and Ean aren't trying to sabotage me or my wedding." She sighed and looked at Lacey desperately. "Everything is falling apart and I don't know what to do!"

Lacey grabbed her friend and hugged her. "It's all going to be okay, Ava. I know you're under a lot of pressure. But you need to relax a little." She released Ava and looked at her, noticing the dark circles under her eyes. "How are things going with Mason?"

"Oh, if anything, they've gotten worse."

"Worse? How is that possible?"

"Remember his former best man, Brian?" Lacey nodded. "Well, I asked him again why they weren't talking. You know, sort of commiscrating on how we had that in common." She had the grace at least to look sheepish. "Anyway, he got all defensive and said it was none of my business and I was to stay away from Brian. I don't even know Brian all that well. We hung out together a couple of times, but Mason made it all sound like an accusation, like somehow his not talking to Brian was my fault! I'm telling you, Lace, this whole situation is getting worse and worse the closer we get to the wedding."

So many thoughts were swirling through Laccy's brain, but she was not going to voice anything that could possibly set Ava off again. "Why do you think he's so crazy about Brian? And what could it possibly have to do with you?"

"I don't know. We don't really socialize a whole lot with Mason's friends; it's mostly business associates and colleagues and whatnot. I guess there have been a lot of warning signs I was blind to, huh?"

"You're in love. You didn't have a reason to think anything was amiss."

They were silent for a moment. "Are you in love with Ean?" she asked, her eyes locked on Lacey's.

"That's not something I'm going to discuss with you. That's between me and Ean."

"For real? We're best friends and we tell each other everything and you won't share this with me?"

"Have you given me a reason to want to share anything with you lately? You've turned this whole wedding into a movie-of-the-week drama! I'm afraid to say anything to you that might upset you, and basically everything falls into that category lately!"

"Fair enough," she said. "But if I had to guess I would say you are definitely in love with him and have been for a long time."

"Ava…"

"It's all right. I think Ean feels the same way."

"How do you know?"

Ava smirked. "I don't think it would be fair to discuss that theory with you. That's between me and Ean." They broke into a fit of giggles and embraced. "Gosh, I missed you."

"Same here," Lacey admitted. "C'mon, I'll call in an order for takeout and let's get caught up with what's going on with each other."

"Isn't Ean supposed to come over?"

"One step ahead of you." She sent Ean a quick text telling him what was happening and that she'd see him tomorrow.

Text sent, food order placed, and two friends sitting together talking about their future. Maybe it was all going to be okay.

By the time the food arrived, it was like the past three weeks had never happened. They were laughing and joking, and it wasn't until they were sitting down to eat that the conversation turned serious.

"So seriously, what are you going to do about Mason?" Lacey asked hesitantly. As much as she hated to ask, she could no longer sit back and say nothing.

"We've done a lot of talking and he's agreed to my finishing school."

"Well, that's a start!" It was small, but at least he was giving in to something. "And the honeymoon?"

"We're going down to Key West," Ava responded and smiled. "I can compromise, too."

"Okay, so you guys are making progress. This is a good thing."

"Oh, yeah…sure."

Lacey pushed her plate aside. "Ava, I've said this a thousand times. I love you, you are my best friend, but I am tired of playing this game with you. Can we please skip all of the nonsense and get to the bottom of this? Do you even want to marry Mason?"

"I thought I did," Ava began, "but the more we talk, the more I think I've made a mistake."

Finally! "You don't have to marry him. Call off the wedding. Your parents will be fine with it, everyone will be fine with it. I've got to imagine that if you've come to this conclusion, Mason may be feeling the same way."

"I said almost those exact same words to him last night, and you know what he said?" Lacey shook her head. "He said we make a good team. That marriage is a partnership, and that we work well together and we could eventually make a great power couple."

"Yikes. For real?"

"Those were his exact words. I kid you not." They broke into another fit of laughter.

"I have to ask, what first attracted you to him?" Lacey asked. "I never quite understood that."

"Mason is smart and confident, and when we talked, he really seemed to listen to me." Ava's expression turned sad. "And then one day, he stopped."

"I'm so sorry, Ava. Are you disappointed about canceling the wedding?"

Ava considered her words for a moment. "I'm not quite ready to throw in the towel."

Lacey was stumped. "But…you just…you said…it's only two weeks away!"

"I know, I know, but I have to make sure I try everything before I just give up. You know me, I don't give up easily when I want something."

"Yes, but what is it that you're fighting for? Mason or the wedding?"

They sat in silence, picking at the last of the food. Shaking her head to clear it, Ava brought up the subject that had been on her mind. "So, you and my brother? How's that going?"

At first Lacey thought it would be awkward to have this conversation with Ean's sister, or any family member, but as it turned out, it wasn't that bad.

"I never thought Ean would be attracted to me," she began. "I chalked it all up to a childhood crush. When I first saw him at the cottage, he was flat on his back in the snow. I think there were little cartoon birds flying around his head!" She relayed the story of that first night and how awkwardness turned to a renewed friendship, and how that turned to something more.

"When I left the ranch, I thought I would be okay with just having that brief moment in time with him, but the more I fought it, the worse I felt. Seeing him at your place and then leaving? It was harder than leaving the ranch. And then Thanksgiving?"

"Oh, the sparks were flying on Thanksgiving!" Ava joked. "We all noticed it."

"You did not! Well, you did, but no one else did."

"Are you sure?" Ava teased.

"Seriously? We were that obvious?"

"It wasn't until the two of you snuggled up together to watch the movie and you fell asleep on Ean. He was just watching you like he was mesmerized. He was touching your hair, your cheek… It was actually kind of sweet."

"Well, if you thought it was sweet, why did you freak out on us the next morning?" Lacey was prepared for the impending fight.

"I thought you guys were just flirting with one another. I didn't realize something had already been going on, and I was a little bit pissed that you kept news like that from me!"

"It's weird! He's your brother!"

"And you're my best friend!"

"I'm sorry. I was afraid to talk about it because at the end of the month, Ean's going back to Boston and I'm staying here. End of story."

"End of story? Why?"

"Um, he'll be in Boston and I'll be in Raleigh?

Hundreds of miles between us? Long-distance relation-ships are rarely successful, and I'd rather us end it while we're still friends than resent one another when the dis-tance becomes a real issue."

"Wow, insecure much?" Ava asked.

"What is that supposed to mean? I'm not insecure."

"Oh please! You are the queen of Insecureville! You're willing to end a relationship that seems to be making both of you nauseatingly happy because of a little geography!"

"It's not a little, Ava, it's over seven hundred miles! That's not a hop-in-the-car-for-the-weekend relation-ship, it's a second mortgage in airfare! It's not seeing one another for weeks on end and coordinating work schedules to get time away. Ean's the boss, so he can pick up and go almost whenever he wants, but it's not like that for me and I wouldn't expect him to be the one to do all of the traveling."

"So you work something out! You've been preaching to me about communication and not letting things go without a fight, and it seems to me you're not willing to fight for this relationship with Ean. Maybe you don't love him."

"Of course I do! I always have, but…"

"Aha! I knew it!" She did a little victory dance around the table. "I knew I'd get you to admit it!"

Lacey couldn't help but laugh. She had certainly fallen for that one. "Yes, I love Ean. The thought of ending this relationship is killing me, but I don't see a solution. He's not prepared to move back here, and I'm not prepared to move up to Boston."

"So you've talked to him about this." It wasn't a question.

"Not exactly," Lacey responded, not daring to meet Ava's knowing eyes.

"Lace, you've essentially put an expiration date on this relationship without letting Ean know about it. Maybe he is willing to compromise. Maybe he would be open to moving back if you asked him."

"That's just it, Ava. I wouldn't want to ask him to do that. I would hate for him to make such a huge sacrifice for me. What if things don't work out down the road?"

"And what if this is the best thing that's ever happened to him? What if his business grows and he gets to marry the love of his life? Have you thought of that?" When Lacey didn't answer, Ava took the last drink of wine and placed the glass down on the table before forcing Lacey to look at her. "I didn't think so."

⁃⁃⁃

The next night, Lacey and Ean were lying in bed, limbs tangled together. She had told him about the night before and the Ava and Mason part of the discussions. "I just wish I knew what she was going to do," Lacey said.

"If I know my sister, she's going to wait until the last minute to decide, just for the dramatic effect."

Lacey groaned. "Gosh, I hope not. I hate the thought of your parents going through so much for the wedding and then have it not happen."

"Well, to them, it's just Christmas with an extra celebration thrown in," he said lightly. "They'll be a little disappointed, I'm sure, but in the end it will just mean more food and cake to enjoy all the way through to New Year's." He kissed Lacey's head.

"They still have so much to work through. I don't know how they'll do it."

"When you love someone, you do what it takes to make them happy."

Leaning away from Ean slightly, Lacey looked into his face. "But it can't be all one-sided. You make it sound like one person has to give up everything so the other person can be happy."

Ean sat up and faced her. "That's not what I meant. In the case of Mason and Ava, they've come to some great compromises. She'll finish school like she wants, and then she'll help him with the firm like he wants. He didn't want to spend a fortune on a tropical vacation but knew that Ava wanted to go someplace warm, so they compromised and are going to Florida. See? They are each giving something in order to make the other happy."

Lacey eyed him suspiciously. "Okay, I see where you're going with that, but do you hear the one word that keeps coming up? Compromising. They aren't in agreement on anything. Every decision has required a compromise. Shouldn't they have enough in common that there wouldn't have to be so many compromises?"

Now that she kept saying the word "compromise" he realized she had a point.

When Ean didn't agree or comment, Lacey continued. "Take the two of us, for example. When we were up in the mountains, and even since Thanksgiving, we haven't had to negotiate everything. We enjoy the same restaurants, we have similar taste in movies. No one is keeping a scorecard on who is getting their way more. At least, I'm not. Are you?"

"Hell no," he answered sternly. "But you have to

remember that we're still in the early stages of our relationship. Who's to say that it won't change in time?"

Lacey wanted to argue that they probably weren't going to get to a point where they could change, but decided to keep that can of worms closed for now. "If you start out with common interests and mutual passions, that won't change," she argued lightly. "It's not like I'm going to wake up one morning and tell you I don't ever want to eat Thai food again." Since Thai was one of her favorite cuisines, it was a safe bet she was speaking the truth.

"What if you got a bad case of food poisoning? That might put you off Thai food." It was a flimsy argument at best.

"You know what I'm saying, Ean," she chided. "I'm not trying to make light of it, but…"

"I know, I know. I do understand what you're saying, but ultimately, it's up to them to decide what they can and can't live with. What is perfectly acceptable for them may not be for you, and that's okay. Whatever they decide, we have to be supportive."

Lacey wasn't so sure she would be able to do it, and the look on her face must have conveyed that thought to Ean. "Lacey, you've voiced your opinion to Ava until you were blue in the face. You've been friends with my sister long enough to know she never does anything she doesn't want to. If she decides to marry Mason, there's a reason for it, and we have to hope she'll be happy."

"And when it falls apart?"

"Boy, I never knew you were such a pessimist," he teased, leaning over and kissing her on the nose. "Have a little faith, Lacey. Ava's happily ever after may not be conventional, but if the version she gets makes her happy, then we should be happy for her."

She supposed Ean's words made sense. If nothing else, the real-life drama of having to deal with their disagreements had finally moved Ava off the Christmas Cottage story. A quiet chuckle escaped her lips at the thought of it, and Ean reached for her and rolled her on top of him. "Something funny?"

Kissing him soundly before raising her head, she replied, "I'm just thankful she's finally given up on the cottage story. There's a little less pressure on us to make everything so precise now that she's calmed down a bit."

Ean wasn't excited about the fact that they still had to make time to go and decorate the darn place. Still, it was a reason to have some alone time with Lacey in the place where it all began. Maybe someday they could look back and admit that, perhaps, there was a little magic in the place.

"What has you smiling?" she asked, leaning forward again and placing tiny kisses along his jaw.

Not ready to share it all with her, he merely said, "Just enjoying the view, sweetheart."

Chapter 10

THE WEDDING WAS TWO DAYS AWAY. LACEY WAS PUTTING finishing touches on the Christmas tree in the cottage while Ean hung the large wreath over the fireplace. Normally, setting up Christmas decorations brought Lacey joy, but in this particular case, she was having trouble finding any.

"Okay, what's the matter?" Ean asked, stepping down off the ladder.

"What? Why do you ask?"

"Because that's, like, the tenth time you've sighed like that. What's going on?"

Even though they'd had this discussion multiple times over the last several weeks, Lacey was still having a hard time coming to grips with the fact that Ava and Mason were getting married. Mason was barely involved in any of the preparations, and although Ava was being more than agreeable, something just wasn't sitting right with Lacey.

"I'm sorry. I guess I still can't believe they're going through with this."

"Lace, we've been over this. You have to let it go. Everyone is going to be arriving tomorrow. We only have tonight to ourselves, and I don't want to spend it discussing my sister and Mason. Please."

He was right. The cottage looked beautiful, and they had brought the makings for a wonderful dinner they were going to share later that night right here in the cottage. Lacey didn't consider it bad luck to be staying there; after all, if the legend was true, it only applied to those who spent their wedding night there. That certainly did not describe her and Ean.

"Okay, no more talking about Ava and Mason," she said. "Or the huge mistake they're making," she added quietly, but Ean shot her a look.

"I heard that."

Packing up the last of the decorations, Ean put the boxes back in the closet and then started a fire for them. While he was doing that, Lacey started their dinner. They worked so well together. Ean's comment about still being in a new relationship came to mind, but Lacey didn't think it applied to them. After all, they'd known each other practically their entire lives. They were so comfortable around each other because they were already friends.

"Ean?"

"Hmm…?"

She voiced her theory to him and he seemed to agree.

"Although there is a big difference between being friends and being lovers," Ean added. "As your friend, I would want you to be happy, but I wouldn't feel the overwhelming need to make sure you're happy."

Lacey smiled and walked over to him, wrapping her arms around his waist. "You have an overwhelming need to make me happy?"

Ean chuckled and kissed her. Then, leading her to the bed, he showed her just how important her happiness was to him.

∽∽

Looking around the cottage, Lacey thought everything looked perfect. The table was set with candlelight, there was a fire roaring in the fireplace, the Christmas tree lights twinkled, and she was here with the man she loved. *So this is what a fairy tale could look like*, she thought.

When they were seated, Ean reached across the table and took her hand and looked intently at her. His gaze scanned her face as a slow smile crept across his own. "I need to go back to Boston for a few days next week between Christmas and New Year's," he said slowly. "It will be a quick trip and I'll be back for New Year's Eve." He waited to see how she responded to the news.

"Oh." Her heart actually ached. It was starting already. In her mind, they had another full week before they had to deal with the reality of being apart. She wasn't ready for it to happen so soon. She cleared her throat as she carefully pulled her hand from his, taking great care in rearranging her place setting before speaking. "What day will you be leaving?"

Ean wasn't a fool. He knew she was upset and could tell she was insecure about what this all meant. "I was thinking of leaving the day after Christmas and driving back, but…"

"That's right, you drove down. You have your car here and all that. So it takes, what, two days to drive back? Then you'll have your meetings or whatever, and then you'll have to turn around and drive for another two days to be here for New Year's, only to turn around again and drive home? That seems a little silly, Ean. You don't have to worry about being here for New Year's. I mean, I know we had some tentative plans, but you don't have to…"

He cut her off before she ran out of breath. "Lacey,

listen to me. First of all, I had thought about driving back, but then I realized how time-consuming it would be, so I was considering flying there and back to save on time. I want to be with you for New Year's, but I wanted to run something else by you."

No, it was all too much. Lacey cursed herself for having gotten caught up in the romanticism of the whole thing—the cottage, the man, and, dammit, the fairy tale. She knew there wasn't going to be a happily ever after for them, but having to sit here and listen to Ean spell it out, the ending of their relationship, was too much to bear.

"Ean, seriously, you're getting all worked up over nothing. We both knew you had a life up in Boston to get back to. It just so happens that you have to get back to it sooner than we thought. It's okay. I'm okay. You don't have to inconvenience yourself on my account."

"What are you saying, Lace? That you don't want me to come back?"

Most men would be thankful to have an out, but of course she had to be involved with the one man who needed to drag it out. "I'm saying I don't *expect* you to make such a big production out of coming back only to have to leave again."

Ean sat quietly for a moment. "What if I didn't leave again?"

Lacey's eyes shot to his. "Excuse me?"

"What if, when I came back from Boston next week, I wasn't leaving again? What if I came back here to stay?"

She did not want to misunderstand him; it was important that she not read more into this than there was. "Why? Why would you do that? What about your business?"

"I want to be with you, Lacey. I want to move back here to be with you."

"I can't ask you to do that, Ean," she said, panic lacing her voice.

"You're not asking me, it's my decision."

"Yes, but you're making it based on me."

He chuckled and grabbed her elusive hand again. "As much as I'd like to say that was true, I can't. Two months ago, if anyone had asked me, I would have said my life was fine. But the truth is, I wasn't very happy. One of the reasons I came down here to the ranch before going to Raleigh was because I was reevaluating my life. I was ready for a change, for a new challenge, and as much as I've always said I enjoy being away from my family, I've missed them."

"You can't just uproot your entire office, though. Can you? I mean, what are you going to do?"

"I'm not uprooting anyone, at least not yet. I'm going back to finally promote one of my VPs to take over operations in the Boston office. I'm going to delegate more. I'll work from here or from Raleigh and get an office set up, and during the transition I may have to travel a little bit, but in the long run I'll be here permanently." He looked at her expectantly. "Do you think you can live with that? Having me around permanently?"

Tears started to well in her eyes. "Ean, there is nothing I'd like more than having you around permanently, but I would feel so guilty if you were compromising…"

"I never want to hear that word again, Lacey Quinn! I am not compromising anything. This was something

I'd thought about doing, and seeing you, being with you, falling in love with you? That just solidified it for me. This is where I want to be!"

Falling in love with you? Had he really just blurted that out?

"You're in love with me?" she whispered, so afraid she'd heard him wrong.

Ean couldn't help himself—he let out a laugh that was part joy and part relief; he'd wanted to say it out loud for so long. "Yes," he said, softly, sincerely. "I know it seems crazy. We've known each other our whole lives, and then it's been so long since we've seen each other. But one look at you, Lacey, was all it took. I love you."

Emotion overcame her and the tears ran freely. Ean reached over and cupped her face, wiping her tears away with the pads of his thumbs. "Don't cry, Lace. I never want to make you cry."

"It's just that I'm so happy, Ean. I never thought we'd be here, in this place, together. Not just the cottage, but together like this, in love. It's more than I ever dared dream of."

"I want to be the one who makes your dreams come true," he whispered, emotion clogging his throat.

"I do love you, so much." Then she laughed out loud. "I never thought I'd get to say those words to you. I never thought you'd say them to me first!"

"Well, get used to it, because I'm going to be saying them a lot from now on." Standing, he came around the table and took Lacey in his arms and kissed her. He lifted his head and stared down into her beautiful green eyes. "Every day, possibly several times a day. You think you can handle it?"

"Most definitely," she sighed, happiness filling her. They stood like that, locked in each other's arms for several minutes, before sitting back down to their meal.

"So you're going to fly back to Boston?"

"Well, I was thinking maybe we can both fly back to Boston. You mentioned that you don't have to work next week, so I thought maybe we could get away for a few days."

"But you'll be working. I wouldn't want to be in the way…"

"You couldn't possibly be in the way. I want to show you my company and where I've been living. Then, when we get back, I'll show you where I'm looking to set up my offices and the houses I'm looking at."

"You're already looking at houses?" she asked, stunned that he had so much in motion already that she wasn't even aware of.

"Sweetheart, once you came back into my life, I knew I had my answer about what direction I wanted to go. Now if only I knew a decorator who could help me make the transition happen quickly…" He smirked. "You wouldn't happen to know anyone, would you?"

"You just try to find somebody else!"

"There is nobody else I want handling it for me, Lace. Honestly, I figured if you saw what I'm living and working in now, you'd get a feel for what I'm looking for down here." They talked decorating and Ean's plans for his new spaces as they finished the meal, and when everything was done and put away, they moved the conversation to the love seat in front of the Christmas tree, next to the fire.

"This is turning out to be a pretty fabulous Christmas." Lacey sighed, reclining in Ean's arms.

"There's still the wedding to get through."

She elbowed him in the ribs.

"Don't ruin the mood!" She laughed. "No matter what happens, it's going to be a fabulous Christmas."

Ean smiled to himself. It most certainly would be if he had anything to say about it.

Chapter 11

CHRISTMAS EVE MORNING ARRIVED AND LACEY WOKE up in a luxurious hotel room not far from the Callahan ranch, alone. While she missed waking up with Ean beside her, it had been necessary as part of the bachelorette ritual the night before. She and Ava had spent the previous day being pampered at a local spa—getting manicures, pedicures, facials, and massages—before doing some last-minute honeymoon shopping for the soon-to-be newlyweds.

As much as it pained her, Lacey kept quiet on her concerns about the upcoming nuptials, and decided that if Ava was happy, then she would be happy for her. During their ultimate girls' day out, they laughed and talked about the future, and Laccy told Ava all about her and Ean telling each other that they loved each other.

"Told you so," Ava had said, tongue-in-cheek. "I'm glad the two of you have finally gotten together. If I had to spend one more holiday with the two of you pretending you weren't interested in each other, I would have had to kill myself!"

Lacey knew it was said in jest, but a little part of her wanted to remind her friend that it wasn't any picnic watching her and Mason during the last couple of months either. Staying quiet seemed the better option.

Now, lying in the king-sized bed alone, she allowed herself a good long stretch before beginning what was sure to be a very busy day. She and Ava were supposed to meet in the hotel restaurant for breakfast before going to get their hair done. After that, they had planned to get a light lunch before heading to the Callahans' to begin getting the bride ready.

A glance at the clock told Lacey that her time of peaceful reflection was over and it was time to hit the shower and get downstairs in time for breakfast. In record time, she was waiting at the elevator, mentally congratulating herself on her ability not only to get ready quickly but also look good.

Stepping off the elevator and into the restaurant, all good feelings seemed to come to an end. Ava wasn't there. Lacey checked her watch again and frowned. Where was she? It was her wedding day; wouldn't she be anxious, particularly more anxious than Lacey, to get things moving?

Lacey followed the hostess to a table with a view of the gardens, and as soon as she was seated, she called Ava. "Where are you?" she demanded when Ava finally answered on the sixth ring.

"Oh, Lacey, hi," Ava said a bit breathlessly. "What's up?"

"What's up? I'm sitting here in the hotel restaurant waiting for you. Where are you?"

There was a moment of silence. "Something came up. Listen, why don't I meet you at the salon. Will that work?"

"Ava, are you okay? What's come up?" Lacey was starting to get a bad feeling.

"It's nothing. No worries. I just needed to get some last-minute stuff done and lost track of the time. We'll meet up and get our hair done and do lunch and be back on track, okay?" Before Lacey could answer, Ava added quickly, "I'll see you in a bit. Bye!" and hung up.

Lacey stared at her phone for a full minute before she realized what she was doing. Her mind raced. *Last-minute stuff?* Considering the events of the last two months, Lacey knew without a doubt that every detail of the wedding had been handled: the dresses, the tuxes, the food, the flowers…everything was ready and waiting. Just yesterday, she had helped Ava pack for her honeymoon.

As she continued to tally all the details, she thought of the cottage. The cottage was like a scene out of a decorating magazine. Lacey had taken pictures of it to show clients because it looked that picturesque and perfect.

What the heck is Ava up to?

The waitress came to take her order, and rather than leave and seem rude, Lacey ordered a fruit platter and some coffee. Her appetite was gone, but she supposed it would be better to have a little something in her stomach just in case anything else crazy happened to come up on the way to the wedding. While she waited for her food, calling Ean seemed the natural thing to do.

"What do you mean 'last-minute stuff'?" Ean asked after Lacey explained her cryptic conversation with Ava.

"I was hoping you'd know. Did something happen over at the house that I'm not aware of?"

"All we need here is a bride and groom, everything else is in place. Do you think she's all right? Do I need to go look for her?"

"I'm hoping everything is fine and that I'll have an explanation when we meet up to get our hair done."

"Call me when you're leaving the salon so I know everything's okay," he said, concern lacing his voice. "Unless she doesn't show. Definitely call me if she doesn't show." Lacey promised she would and hung up when her food arrived.

"Please don't make me have to call your brother to tell him you didn't show, Ava," Lacey said under her breath as she stuck a fork into a piece of melon.

—⁓—

Ava was fifteen minutes late.

Lacey paced the waiting area of the salon and dialed Ava for the tenth time. When her voice mail came up again, she left yet another message. "Ava? You are starting to freak me out now. I'm here at the salon and you're not. I don't know what I'm supposed to do. I need to know where you are and that you're okay. I called Ean earlier and he wanted me to call him if you didn't show and I'd rather not do that and put the whole family into a state of panic, but you *need to call me!*"

The bad thing about smartphones was that you couldn't slam them down in a fit of anger when you were hanging up on someone who'd just ticked you off. With no other choice, she pulled up Ean's number, not sure what she was going to say that wasn't going to sound dramatic. Clearly Ava was missing and didn't want to be found, but why? Of all days, why did she have to choose today to pull a stunt like this?

Her finger poised on the Send button, Lacey very nearly dropped the phone when it rang and Ava's picture showed up. "You'd better have a damned good explanation for this," she said as her greeting.

"I know, I know, I'm late," Ava said, her voice as cheery as ever. "I decided to do my own hair. My mom does a beautiful French braid and I think that's what I'm going to do. Plus, it will give us a little mommy-and-me time before the wedding."

"Well, that sounds like a very sweet thing to do, but it doesn't change the fact that I've been getting the runaround all morning," Lacey grumbled.

"I'm sorry, Lace. My nerves are a little more than I expected this morning and I just needed some time alone. I'm better now and I'm heading to my parents' house."

"So what am I supposed to do?"

"Get your hair done, grab your dress, and meet me here as planned."

"We'd planned to have lunch," Lacey reminded her.

Ava sighed wearily. "Can you cut me some slack today, Lace?"

Lacey halfheartedly agreed, but made a mental note to be more considerate of her friends and family when it was her turn to get married.

"Fine. I'll see you at the house around two o'clock, okay?"

"That's the plan," Ava said and then hung up.

So Lacey sat and got pampered a little more. Her hair was left long, but with her curls more defined. With the extra time on her hands she decided to indulge and let one of the girls glam her up a little and do her makeup. By the time she was ready to leave, she barely recognized herself. Looking in the mirror, all Lacey could think was *I should totally do this more often.*

When she returned to the hotel to grab her dress and other necessities, all she could do was pick up a yogurt parfait from the restaurant. Where had the day gone? One minute she had all the time in the world, the next she was practically running late! And after all of the grief she'd given Ava today about being where she was supposed to be, it would not look good if she, herself, was late!

A lot of cars were already in the driveway. Lacey recognized her parents' car and Ean's in the bunch. Carefully she emerged from her car and carried her dress and bags to the house. When she opened the door, she was greeted by a dozen pairs of eyes and complete silence.

Stopping short, she took in the scene in front of her. "What's going on?"

Ava stood. "Good, you're finally here." Walking toward her, Ava took Lacey's dress and hung it on the coat rack and then took the bags Lacey had in her hands and placed them on the floor beside it. Without a word, she took Lacey by the hand and led her into the living room, where everyone else was seated quietly.

Taking a seat next to Ean, Lacey was beyond confused. Ava and Mason stood in front of the large stone fireplace, hand in hand, and faced their audience. *Isn't it bad luck for the bride and groom to see each other before the wedding?* was all Lacey could think until Ava finally spoke.

"Mason and I wanted you all to know how happy we are that you care so much about us that you were willing to spend your Christmas with us instead of as you normally would with your families." She turned and smiled at Mason and then turned her attention back to the group at large. "As most of you know, things have been a little tense since Thanksgiving, and we took some time to get counseling and did a lot of soul-searching to make sure we were ready for our future together."

"It was the best thing we could have done," Mason said seriously. "We learned a lot about each other, and I want to thank everyone who encouraged us to do it."

"The thing is," Ava said tentatively, "after all the counseling and soul-searching and discussions, we realized we aren't ready. We each have an idea of what we want for our futures, and unfortunately, they aren't the same thing. So we've decided not to get married."

The entire room erupted in conversation. Lacey felt an odd sense of déjà vu.

"You waited until today…?"

"What about all of the planning…?"

"Do you have any idea the amount of time we put into this?"

"How could you be so selfish, Ava?"

The only two people in the room not speaking again were Lacey and Ean. Relief washed over Lacey at the thought of her friend not going through with the wedding. Deep down, she knew it was the right decision.

Ean sat back, holding Lacey's hand, watching the chaos around him. After a few minutes, he leaned forward and whispered in Lacey's ear, "Should I say anything?"

"Like what?" she whispered back.

"I feel like someone needs to come to Ava's defense."

Not sure it was going to make any difference, Lacey agreed and watched as Ean stood and got everyone's attention.

"Look, I think we can all agree that the timing of this announcement could have been better. After all, as you yourself said, a lot of people gave up their

Christmas plans to come and celebrate with you."
Everyone nodded in agreement. "However, we are all
here together and there's no reason why we can't still
have a festive Christmas Eve together. There's plenty
of food and everything is set up already."

"Ean," his mother chimed in, despair in her voice,
"we were set up for a wedding! There's a wedding
cake in the dining room! That's hardly part of the
Christmas menu."

He walked over and kissed his mother on the
cheek. "Well, it will make for a funny story for future
Christmases. We'll all remember the Christmas where we
had wedding cake and no wedding." Everyone laughed,
and some of the tension in the room disappeared.

Turning back to Ava, he continued. "I think we can
also all agree that we'd rather be here right now hearing
that you've made the decision together to call off your
wedding with no hard feelings rather than sitting here
years from now hearing you cry about a bitter divorce. I
think what you're doing is very brave, and I for one am
proud of you."

A single tear escaped down Ava's cheek as she said
thank you to her brother not only for his kind words, but
for bringing peace back to the room. "I really am sorry
there won't be a wedding today," she said. "It wasn't my
intention to do it this way. Mason and I kept thinking
our feelings would change, but in the end, they didn't."

Lacey went to stand beside Ean as conversation died
down and plans were made on how the rest of the day
would play out now that there wasn't going to be a wedding. The sound of the doorbell ringing brought everyone's heads around.

"Oh dear," Mrs. Callahan said, walking toward the door. "That will be Pastor Steve! Now we'll have to explain all of this mess to him."

"Such a shame…" seemed to be the phrase of the moment because Lacey heard it from more than one person around the room. She sought out Ava and pulled her into a hug.

"Well, I can't be too disappointed," Lacey admitted. "After all, if it wasn't for you and your wedding, Ean and I probably would have never found each other again. We'd have kept up our own version of 'keep away' and never realized what we could have together." She turned and saw Ean across the room and smiled. "I would never have known the love of the man of my dreams. And who knows," she added, turning back to Ava, "maybe someday we'll be the ones getting married right here and you can wear my maid of honor dress!" It was meant as a joke, but Ava's face was suddenly very serious.

"That's it!" she said, looking around as if it was obvious to everyone what she was thinking.

"What? What's it?" Lacey asked, confused.

"You and Ean! There can still be a wedding here today!" Ava's voice got louder with each word and Lacey pinched her on the arm to quiet her down.

"Are you crazy? What is the matter with you? How could you even suggest such a thing?"

"Oh, I don't know, maybe because the two of you are crazy in love with one another? Maybe because we have all the makings of a wedding right here, right now? And finally, because that cottage on the hill is ready and waiting for a couple of newlyweds tonight and should not be disappointed!"

"For the last time, Ava! It's a house! It's not waiting for anything!"

Just then, Ean walked over. "What's going on?"

Before Lacey could stop her, Ava told him her plan. "Don't you see, it's all right here, ready and waiting! You can avoid all the arguments and tears of planning a wedding because it's already done. What do you say?"

The silence was awkward. If Ean asked her to marry him today, would she be able to say yes? It would be so unlike her. Lacey was a planner; she made lists! She certainly didn't do spontaneous things like get married at a moment's notice! Although, if there was one man she'd do that for, it would be Ean Callahan. Why wouldn't he say anything? He wasn't even looking at her! Not wanting to seem obvious, she snuck a quick glance at him and saw him staring at Ava, a small smile on his face. Ava arched a brow at him, and Lacey had to wonder at the brother/sister connection. It was like they were having a conversation without saying a word.

"Can I have everyone's attention?" Ean called out as he took Lacey's hand and turned to face the roomful of guests once again. "I have something else to say."

All eyes were on them and Lacey had no idea what he was doing. If he was going to ask her to marry him here today, shouldn't he have asked her first? Alone? Her heart was hammering in her chest and she looked at him just as expectantly as every other person in the room.

"As we've already established, Mason and Ava will not be getting married today. I know we're all disappointed that it came to this, but I for one cannot be sorry. You see, two months ago I came up here to get away from life for a little while. I needed some time away from work and family and pretty much everything to figure out what I wanted for my future. What I didn't know was that my future was waiting for me, right here."

He turned and faced Lacey. "I saw you first in the grocery store, and then again while I was flat on my back in the snow with stars in my eyes—and they weren't only from banging my head." He chuckled and reached out to caress her cheek. "Just the mere sight of you brings me to my knees. I look at you and my heart races. You challenge me, you make me laugh, and you made me realize I was missing so much. You brought joy and laughter into my life, and most of all, you filled my days with love."

There was no way to stop the tears from flowing and very nearly ruining her expensive makeup job. Ava swooped in with a tissue and then stood nearby with the entire box. Ean wiped her tears away the same way he'd done days before. "I know you like to plan things, and I know this isn't something we had discussed but, Lacey Quinn, I love you. I knew from that first night that I wanted to spend the rest of my life with you. There is no one else in this world for me but you." He got down on one knee. "And it would be an honor if you would agree to be my wife."

Oh my gosh! This is really happening! Ean is proposing! I'm getting married! Wait, have I answered him yet?

"I had it all worked out to do this tomorrow," he said with a sheepish grin. "I'm a planner too." He winked. "Hopefully you won't mind me giving this to you a day early."

Looking down, she saw the ring in his hand and realized she had not yet given him an answer. Taking a deep breath, she smiled. "Ean Callahan, I have waited since I was fourteen to be your wife." She laughed through the tears. "I don't want to wait any longer. Yes, I will marry you!" In a flash, the ring was on her finger and Ean was kissing her. All around her people were clapping and cheering.

"You'll have time for that later," Ava said as she dragged Lacey away from Ean. "It's time to get the bride ready!"

With a last glance over her shoulder, she said to Ean, "I guess I'll see you soon." His grin was the biggest she'd ever seen. "I'll be the one in white."

He laughed. "I'll be the one waiting."

Hopefully not long was all Lacey thought as she was swept away into the Callahans' master bedroom, surrounded by her mother and Ean's, plus her sisters and Ava.

"You can totally wear my dress," Ava said, taking her dress down from its hook on the door. "I know it may not be what you would have picked out, but you're going to look gorgeous."

"Ava," Lacey began, looking around at all of the activity going on around her, "we're not the same size… Maybe I should just…"

"Never fear," Linda Callahan called out. "I've got my sewing kit, and I think with a few nips, tucks, and creative accessorizing, we can pull this off!"

People were fussing all around her, and at some point Lacey realized it was a good thing, because she was sure if she were given a moment to herself, she'd probably have a panic attack over what they were about to do.

"Am I crazy?" she asked her mom when they had a moment to themselves.

Denise Quinn looked at her youngest daughter and smiled. "Lacey, I know you've been wild about Ean most of your life. Seeing the two of you together these last couple of months was always like watching a private moment. The love the two of you share is so obvious to everyone." Lacey blushed at her mother's words. "You are a very levelheaded woman, you always have been, and I don't think you're crazy for deciding to marry the man you love. Neither of you are the type to take such a thing lightly, and I trust Ean to make you happy."

"Thank you, Mom." She did not want to start crying again, so Lacey forced herself to take a couple of deep breaths. "I know this isn't how you probably imagined your youngest daughter getting married…"

"Are you kidding me?" She laughed. "After what your sisters put me through with their weddings, this is an absolute gift! We got off easy! I'm just sorry we didn't have more time to prepare and do something special for you."

"Mom, I don't need anything else. Like you said, I'm marrying the man I love. He's all I've ever wanted."

For the next thirty minutes, Lacey felt like a human Barbie doll. She stood still while her gown was quickly altered.

"Ava's a bit curvier than you," Linda said. "I think we'll take the red sash from your maid of honor dress, Lace, and use it to hide some of the tucks we did. It will make for a festive accessory to the gown."

"Okay…I love it," Lacey said with a nervous laugh, still trying to wrap her brain around the fact that this was her wedding day.

"I've got the top secured as best I can, but being

that the gown is strapless, I wouldn't make any sudden moves."

"Wait!" Ava called out. "You have a white stole, don't you, Mom? We can use that to sort of hide any gaps, right?"

"That's a wonderful idea! It's in the back of my closet. Someone go and grab it!"

Taking a step back and looking at her daughter, Denise took off the pearl choker she had been wearing and carefully placed it around Lacey's neck. "These were your grandmother's," she said softly. "I think she would have been thrilled for you to wear them on your wedding day."

"Oh, Mom…" Lacey sighed as she reached up and touched the necklace, staring at her reflection in the mirror. Turning to her mother, she said, "This is really happening."

Denise nodded. "It certainly is."

Lacey swallowed hard. "I still can't believe… I just hope…"

"Okay, everyone, it's time!" Ava yelled from the bedroom doorway. "You ready?" she asked, looking at Lacey and grinning.

Taking a steadying breath, Lacey smiled. "More than."

"You know, I really should hate you," Ava said when they were alone and waiting for Lacey's dad to come for her.

"Hate me? Why?"

"Well, for starters that dress looks better on you than it did on me!"

Lacey turned and looked at her reflection for what was probably the twentieth time and smiled wickedly. It did look great on her. The form-fitting, strapless style wasn't what she would have picked for herself, but she couldn't be sorry for it. Ean was going to love it.

"You have good taste," Lacey said simply. "But I have a great body." They laughed and hugged. "Thank you for being willing to share all of this with me. I cannot tell you how much it means to me."

"Good, because I'm not done telling you why I should hate you," Ava said, wiping tears from her own eyes. "I have got to stop doing that today!"

"So you still hate me, why?"

"Oh, right. First, there's the dress."

"We've covered that."

"Right. Then there's the cottage."

"We're not having this conversation again…"

"Yes, we are. You proved the fairy tale right, Lace. You'll be telling stories to future generations about how you met up with Ean again and fell in love and lived happily ever after thanks to the Christmas Cottage. That was going to be my story!"

Lacey wanted to argue with her but just didn't have it in her. Ava was right. As much as Lacey wanted to dispute the tale, the truth was, had it not been for the Christmas Cottage, there would be no wedding today. Still, they had to get to the ceremony in order to get to the honeymoon so that her future could begin.

Her dad popped his head in to the room. "Ready, sweetheart?"

And she was: for the ceremony, for Ean, and for her happily ever after.

Epilogue

MUCH LATER THAT NIGHT, LACEY AND EAN WERE relaxing in what was quickly becoming known to them as "their" cottage, and talking about their wild day.

"Who knew I could actually be spontaneous?" she said, clearly amused with herself.

"You pulled it off quite well," he said, kissing her head. "You definitely have a future being a rebel."

"Let's not get carried away." She laughed. "This was an exception. No one else but you could possibly make me do something this far out of my comfort zone."

They lay together staring into the fire, both realizing how fortunate they were. "Was Ava terribly upset?" he finally asked. "It couldn't have been easy watching you have the wedding that she'd planned."

"She was amazing. It seemed like it was almost a relief for her." Lacey shared with him Ava's list of grievances against her but how, in the end, it was all said in good fun. "I just wish she could have made it work with Mason."

"He wasn't the one for her. End of story. Not everyone is fortunate enough to know someone for twenty-something years and then realize they're in love, like we are," he joked and felt her elbow to his ribs. "What? Am I lying?"

"No, but when you say it, it sounds ridiculous."

"Ava will find someone, and in no time, we'll be back

up here having to decorate this cottage again." And then he paused. "You do realize we decorated this cottage for ourselves, right?"

She agreed. "Thank goodness we scaled it down a little bit or we'd be choking on the overwhelming Christmas theme."

"I feel a little bit gypped. When Ava gets married, she's decorating the damn cottage herself." Lacey laughed. "And we'll make her do it to our specifications. How does that sound?"

"Like a plan." Lacey looked up into Ean's face and pulled him forward for a kiss. "I love you, Ean Callahan."

"Thank God." He sighed and sank back into kissing his wife, sending up another prayer of thanks for the wonderful Christmas present he had received.

EVER AFTER

Prologue

It was hard to stand there feeling sorry for yourself when everyone around you was so damn happy.

On what was supposed to have been *her* wedding day, Ava Callahan willingly relegated herself to the role of maid of honor due to a last-minute substitution of the bride and groom in the form of Ava's brother and her best friend, Lacey. While she could admit there was some lingering sadness at the breakup of her engagement to Mason Brooks, her primary emotion was relief. She hadn't really loved Mason; she'd loved the idea of getting married and having her fairy-tale wedding.

A wedding that was now being celebrated by another bride and groom. Looking across the room at the happy couple, Ava couldn't help but smile. Dang it! She'd always known Lacey had been in love with Ean, and seeing them dancing together now, Ava did envy them just a little. Not in a green-eyed-monster kind of way, but in a wistful, can't-help-but-sigh kind of way.

They hadn't seen each other in a dozen years, and yet in less than two months Lacey and Ean were so in love that it was obvious to anyone who was in the room with them. How did one find that kind of love? How do you find your soul mate? Was there even such a thing?

Ava took a long sip of her champagne and looked around the room. Everyone was happy, everyone was smiling. Occasionally she'd catch someone looking at

her with a little sadness, a little pity; she could understand why and didn't hold it against them.

Earlier in the day, when she and Mason had decided
not to go through with the wedding, it had all been very
civil, very dignified. She guessed that's how it went when
neither party felt overly emotional about the other.

How had she missed all the signs? When had she and
Mason gone from being in love to being just two people
planning a wedding? When had they fallen out of love?
Ava wracked her brain, trying valiantly to remember
the last time she had actually *felt* anything resembling
love for the man she almost married, and was shocked
to realize that she couldn't.

That wasn't a good sign.

In the last couple of months, she'd immersed herself
in wedding planning and ignored the now obvious signs
that something was wrong with their relationship. The
chance at having her fairy-tale wedding, including her
night in the famous Callahan Christmas Cottage—a
place that promised love everlasting to any couple who
stayed there—was too strong of a draw to slow her down
enough to see reality.

She didn't love Mason and he didn't love her. End
of story.

They both had an agenda: Ava's was to get married,
Mason's was to have a wife to help cement his image
in his law firm. In the end, Ava realized that the kind
of wife Mason wanted was never something she was
capable of.

Thank goodness they had come to their senses before
walking down the aisle!

As the wedding had drawn closer, people tried to

warn her, especially the now happily married Lacey and Ean. Unfortunately, Ava's stubborn streak refused to let them be right. When she and Mason had finally come to an agreement earlier in the day, it turned out he'd had people warning him as well.

Particularly vocal on that end was Mason's friend and former best man, Brian McCabe.

A shiver ran down Ava's spine at the thought of Brian, and she could feel a blush creep up her cheeks. She turned to look out the window just in case anyone had noticed. Looking out at the wintry landscape, she vowed that no one, not Mason or Lacey or anyone, would ever know Brian had come to see her last night or his reasons why he was so opposed to her marrying his best friend.

"I'd like to make a toast," someone yelled from across the room, and Ava turned, a genuine smile on her face, her glass raised. "To Lacey and Ean! May you have a lifetime of love and happiness and may your fairy tale never end!"

Everyone raised their glasses and cheered as the happy couple sipped their drinks and then kissed. Ava sipped her own champagne before turning to look out the window again, wondering *When will my fairy tale begin?*

Chapter 1

"You're doing it again."

"Doing what?"

"You're looking."

"Looking at what?"

"The bump."

Ava rolled her eyes. "You are almost eight months pregnant, Lacey! Stop calling it the bump!"

Smiling, Lacey ran a hand over her rounded belly. "Doesn't change the fact that you were staring at it. What's up with that?"

"Why can't you just call it a baby?"

Now it was Lacey's chance to roll her eyes. "Because your brother is making me crazy! When I refer to it as a she, he reminds me that we could very well be having a boy. Then he gets suspicious that I've had some secret ultrasound he wasn't invited to and that I actually know the sex of the baby! I don't know who's going to be more of a handful when I give birth, the baby or your brother!"

"So because you can't say anything gender specific, you've decided it's better to call it 'the bump'?" Ava asked. "That's just weird."

"No, what's weird is watching an intelligent, grown man trying to wrap me and everything around me in bubble wrap so I don't get hurt."

Ava had to agree on that score. "He loves you and he wants to make sure you're okay. I think it's sweet."

"Oh, it is, and believe me, I love him more every day because of it. I just wish he'd relax a little bit."

"Ean doesn't know how to relax. You've known him your whole life and you married him. Clearly this can't be news to you?"

"It's not," Lacey sighed, "but it's exhausting, too."

Ava would have been worried, but Lacey's tone held nothing but affection. As much as she might be griping, there were no two people more in love than the expectant parents. It was enough to make a person sick.

"So, you invite a pregnant woman who cannot have caffeine to a coffee shop," Lacey began as she inhaled deeply. "This must be important."

"He's getting married."

"Who?"

"Mason."

Lacey was glad she wasn't drinking anything because she surely would have spit it out. "How did you find out?"

"I ran into him."

"Where?"

"Here."

Knowing Mason wasn't here at the moment, Lacey still couldn't stifle the urge to look around. "Is this the first time you've seen him?"

"Since the wedding?"

Lacey nodded.

"Yes, it is," Ava replied, finally taking a sip from her own now-cool latte. "It's weird because we used to come here all the time, and to not run into Mason once in eight months seemed unusual."

"Was he alone or was he with…her?" Lacey asked cautiously.

"Geez, you don't have to be so dramatic, Lace. I was in line and Mason walked in, alone, and it was a little bit awkward but we got our drinks and sat down and that's when he told me."

Lacey waited to see if there was going to be more to the story, and then got tired of waiting. "And?"

"And what?"

"Talking to you is painful sometimes, Ava, you know that?"

"Her name is Melissa. She's a paralegal at his firm. They met three months ago." Funny, but it didn't even bother her to say those words out loud.

"Wow, how very *When Harry Met Sally* of him."

Ava's brows furrowed. "What?"

"Oh, come on! Remember the movie? When her ex announced he was getting married to the paralegal?"

"Seriously? You think *now* is the time to go quoting romantic comedies to me?"

Immediately Lacey felt remorseful. "Sorry, I was just trying to lighten the mood. Are you okay?"

"The thing is, I'm fine. I really am. I thought I would be more upset. It's just that—"

"Are you still upset that you didn't marry Mason?"

"Oh, gosh no! No, I realize that would have been a huge mistake. It's just that—"

"Are you upset he found someone so quick?"

Ava almost growled in frustration. "No, I'm not upset that Mason found someone else. I want him to be happy. It's just that—"

"Was he unkind? Did he gloat?"

"For the love of it, Lacey, if you would just shut it for one minute I could tell you exactly what *it* is!"

Ava's tone was a bit loud and several heads turned to stare at them.

"Sorry," Lacey mumbled and sat back in her seat.

"It's just that I thought I'd be married by now. What's wrong with me that I'm not on my way to being married? Am I that horrible?"

Lacey reached across the table and grabbed her friend's hand. "Oh, sweetie, that's not it at all! You aren't a horrible person. You've taken the time to pursue your education and you're getting your degree in less than a week! Don't focus on what you don't have, Ava, think about all that you do!"

"Well, a library sciences degree is not helping me get down the aisle or start a family."

"Dramatic much?" Lacey asked, her light sarcasm bringing a smile to Ava's face.

"I'm twenty seven. I'm just beginning to doubt that it will ever happen for me, Lace. I was so wrapped up in reaching the goal of getting married that I almost married the wrong man!"

"But you didn't! You came to your senses, and although your timing was a bit off, you knew Mason wasn't the one for you."

"I guess."

"Look, falling in love is not something you can arrange or mark on your calendar. It just happens. It's going to happen for you," she said and then paused. "You do realize that would mean you'd have to actually start dating again."

Ava frowned. "I was afraid you'd mention that."

"It's been eight months. Enough time has gone, by and it's time for you to go out and meet some people."

"I meet people all the time, Lacey."

"Right. Other students, in the bookstore where you work. All very safe. How's that working for you?"

"Gosh, you're annoying when you're right," Ava mumbled. "I hate the dating scene! That's what was great about Mason, he struck up a conversation with me in a coffee shop."

"I think you need therapy. You spend way too much time in coffee shops…"

"So what am I supposed to do, huh? Online dating? Place an ad in the personals? You're right, there's no one at work I'm remotely interested in. I'm telling you, Lacey, dating is hard work. The hair, the makeup, the fake giggle… It's not me!"

"Who says it has to be? Why can't you just strike up a conversation with a man you find attractive—even if it is here in a coffee shop?"

Ava looked around and frowned. "There's no one here, Lace. And in case you haven't noticed, no one is tripping over themselves to come talk to me, either." She sat back in her chair and her look dared Lacey to argue with her. "You see? It's just…"

"Hello, Ava," a masculine voice said from directly behind her.

Oh gosh! Oh no! Ava squeezed her eyes shut and prayed that her subconscious was playing tricks on her. There was no way this was happening right here, right now. Slowly opening her eyes, she looked at Lacey, who was staring back at her, her eyebrows raised expectantly.

Swallowing the lump that had lodged itself in her throat, Ava slowly turned around. "Oh, hi, Brian." She took in the sight of him: all six-foot-plus of solid muscle that shouldn't look as good as it did in a pair of faded jeans and plain T-shirt.

"May I join you?"

"Of course!" Lacey said before Ava could stop her.

Brian grabbed a vacant chair and pulled it up to the table. "So, Ava, how've you been?"

"Fine, thank you," Ava replied nervously. God, how she hated small talk. It was tedious and annoying, and what was worse was having an audience to her misery. "Brian, this is my friend Lacey."

Lacey leaned forward to shake Brian's hand. "Nice to meet you," she said, smiling.

"You too," he responded and then nodded toward her belly. "Congratulations. When are you due?"

"Another five weeks and believe me, I cannot wait!"

"Honeymoon baby?" he asked and both Lacey and Ava's eyebrows shot up. Brian cleared his throat before speaking. "Oh, um, Mason mentioned that you and Ava's brother took their places back at Christmas."

Ava was shocked but before she could say anything, Lacey was speaking. "As a matter of fact, it was! Ean and I couldn't be happier. After waiting so long to be together, it didn't seem necessary to wait to have a baby."

"Well, pregnancy certainly agrees with you," he said with a wide grin. "You are positively glowing."

Lacey blushed. "Thank you, Brian." She was about to say more but noticed the scowl on Ava's face and quickly silenced herself.

Brian continued to smile as he turned his attention to Ava. He took a slow sip of his coffee and had to stifle a sigh. He'd waited; he'd kept his distance. Now that

Mason was engaged again and Ava was ready to gradu-ate, Brian felt the time was perfect to seek her out.

A million questions were racing through Lacey's head as she watched what could only be described as the most awkward encounter between two people ever. With a quick glance at her watch, Lacey got to her feet.

"Listen, Ava, I'll call you later. I'm supposed to meet Ean in a little while to do some final touches on the office remodel." She pushed her chair in and noticed the slight look of despair on her friend's face. She threw out the life-line. "You're more than welcome to come with me. We'll be grabbing dinner afterward and you could join us."

Ava considered Lacey's words. "No, um, thank you. You go on, and tell Ean I said hello. I'll see you this weekend."

A smile beamed across Lacey's face. "You'll be the one in the cap and gown, right?"

Ava smiled in return. "And you'll be the one with the bump." They both laughed and said their good-byes.

Brian looked at them both curiously. He waited until Lacey was out the door before returning his attention solely to Ava. "The bump?"

"Sorry, private joke." The silence stretched on between them and Ava nearly jumped when Brian spoke again.

"So, did you hear about Mason?"

She nodded. "I'm happy for him. I want him to be happy, and if this Melissa girl can do that, then I'm happy for them both."

"That's a lot of happy," he said.

"Well, what would you have me say, Brian? That I'm angry, sad, hurt?"

"Are you?"

"Am I what?"

"C'mon, Ava. Are you angry, sad, or hurt?"

She smiled weakly. "No, I'm really not, and that in itself makes me a little sad."

"Mason wasn't the right man for you, Ava. You and I both know that." His voice was fiercer than he intended, and when her gaze snapped up to meet his, he realized it. "Sorry, that was…"

"Completely arrogant of you? That seems to be your MO, Brian."

Unable to disagree, Brian had no choice but to let that particular subject drop. "So you're graduating this weekend. That was fast."

A halfhearted laugh escaped her lips before she could stop it. "Fast? If anything, I'm about five years behind."

"Nonsense, you just took your time in choosing what you wanted. I meant, compared to where you were this time last year, I thought you had at least another semester left."

"I doubled up after Christmas so I could graduate sooner."

"That had to be rough."

She shrugged. "I needed to keep busy." The admission was brutally honest and for the first time, Ava wasn't so proud of the accomplishment. "What I mean is…"

"It doesn't matter, Ava. You worked hard and you're graduating. Good for you. So what comes next for Ava Callahan? Your own business? World domination?"

This time the laugh was genuine. "World domination? I don't think I'm ready for that. I thought I'd want to open my own little bookstore, but I don't think there's a market for that sort of thing anymore. With all of the big online retailers and the few mega bookstores, the days of the mom-and-pop shop are long gone."

"So what will you do? Your degree is in library sciences, right?"

She nodded. "It is, and while I thought my choice limited me, it turns out it's opened a lot of doors."

Brian leaned forward, sincerely interested in what she was saying, and was rewarded with a smile. "I can keep working for the university, and not just in the bookstore; I can put in to work in the library there, which is the traditional route. But if I wanted to challenge myself a little bit, think out of the box if you will, I can use my degree to become an archivist, or find a corporation that needs someone to establish or maintain a library for their organization."

"I don't follow," he said. It wasn't a field he knew much about.

"Well, places like hospitals, med schools, law schools, museums…lots of places you wouldn't think of right away have a library."

"That sounds like a very challenging job," he said, taking another sip of his coffee.

"It could be, but I enjoy a good challenge, and I love all kinds of books, so researching and getting the opportunity to stock a library would be amazing!"

Her enthusiasm was contagious and Brian knew that Ava certainly could handle any task—even world domination. "Have you started submitting résumés to any place in particular?"

Ava took a sip of her long-cold latte and made a face. Pushing the cup aside, she looked back at Brian. "I've sent out a few to some local companies and I've talked to human resources at the university, but I'm not sure I want to stay in Raleigh."

That bit of information stopped him cold. "What? Why? Where would you go?"

"I don't know," she admitted. "I just think I'm ready for a change. I've lived here my whole life and nothing's happening for me."

"What do you want to happen?"

"I want to travel a little. I want to meet new people!" she said heatedly. "I'm tired of living in everyone else's shadow and having people look at me with pity because—" She caught herself, unable to believe she had just said that out loud, and especially to Brian.

"Because you and Mason called off your wedding?" he asked cautiously.

"Exactly. It's been eight months and people still look at me with that 'oh, poor Ava' look. I'm tired of it. I need to get away and prove I'm more than someone who got left at the altar."

"Well, you didn't *really* get left at the altar, did you?" he began. "It was a mutual decision not to go through with the wedding. Big difference."

"Yes! But it didn't seem like that to the people who were there," she grumbled. "It took months before people let me be around sharp objects, they were so afraid I was going to hurt myself in my despair."

"Were you? In despair?"

"No," she said sadly. "I wasn't. But everyone just thought I was putting on a brave face. It wasn't brave, it was just my face," she said, trying to lighten the mood.

Brian looked at the face that had haunted his dreams for more than a year. Her blond hair was a little shorter than it'd been the last time he'd seen her, but her sea-blue eyes still twinkled and captivated him. In that moment, he wanted nothing more than to reach out and touch the smooth skin of her cheeks, to kiss those glossy pink lips and know that he had the right to do so. But he didn't.

Not yet.

Silence returned. Ava glanced at her watch and realized it was getting late and she had the evening shift at the college bookstore. "I've got to go," she said and almost cringed at the regret she heard in her voice.

"Already?" he asked, not ready to let her go.

"I've got work in a little while and I have some things I have to do before I go in." She stood and grabbed her cup. "It was good to see you, Brian. Take care of yourself."

Brian stood and reached for Ava's arm before she turned away. "I know you've got graduation this weekend, but I'd like to see you again, Ava. Can I take you to dinner next week?"

She hesitated for a few seconds before responding. "I don't think that would be a good idea, Brian. It would be awkward."

"Because of Mason?" he asked, angry that Mason would still be part of the equation.

Ava nodded. "I just don't think it would be appropriate. Please understand."

He didn't want to understand. He'd played by everyone else's rules and he'd be damned if he didn't at least try to get Ava to give him a chance. "Mason's getting married, Ava. He's moved on. Isn't it time for you to do the same?"

Regret immediately came when he saw the hurt on her face. Brian had to give her credit, she quickly recovered before turning to him and saying, "Thanks. You have no idea what I've been doing or what I've moved on to, Brian. All things considered, I just don't think we should see each other again." She pulled free of his grasp and took a step back, scanning his face before finally saying, "Have a good life, Brian."

And then she was gone.

———

It took most of the ten-minute drive from the Starbucks to the campus for Ava's heart to stop thundering in her chest. As she shut off the car, she banged her head on the steering wheel. "Seriously?" she grumbled to herself. "I have to run into Brian the day after hearing about Mason getting married? What are the odds?"

Leaning back in the driver's seat, Ava realized she was twenty minutes early for work and had nothing to do. She'd only told Brian what she did because she needed to get away from him. He evoked too many emotions in her, too many memories. She'd relived that night in her mind countless times and yet seeing him today made it seem like it was only yesterday…

Closing the door to her hotel room, Ava sighed. She'd had a wonderful day of pampering and shopping with Lacey, and tomorrow was her wedding day. She and Mason had overcome many obstacles, but she felt certain they were doing the right thing in getting married. Any other issues they could work on after their honeymoon. Neither of them was over-romanticizing their relationship, but Ava had finally reached a point where she was okay with her future.

A knock on the door took her momentarily by surprise, but she assumed it was Lacey wanting to hang out a little bit more; she had joked earlier about them having one last sleepover like they used to when they were kids. Besides, if Lacey were waiting with her pillow and some chocolate chip ice cream, she'd be more than happy to have the company.

When she opened the door it wasn't Lacey staring back at her, but Brian McCabe. To say she was shocked was an understatement. He and Mason hadn't spoken in months, and it was because of their disagreement that Ava's brother was now standing in as best man at their wedding. Truth be known, she'd kind of missed his company. Now here he was, standing larger than life in her doorway.

"Brian! What are you doing here?" she asked.

"May I come in?"

Ava thought on that one for a second. Brian had been a long-time friend of Mason's—she always enjoying going out with him and Mason, sometimes more than going out with Mason alone, if she were being totally honest—and she really did want to know what had happened between them. She stepped aside and motioned for him to come in. "So, how are you?" she asked shyly.

Apparently trying to collect his thoughts, Brian glanced around the room and went to sit in the lone chair in the corner. Taking a deep breath, he said, "I needed to see you, Ava. I couldn't keep what I have to say to myself any longer."

She stood rooted to the spot some ten feet away from him. "I don't understand, Brian. What is this all about?"

"Marrying Mason is a mistake. He's not right for you."

"What gives you the right to say that?" she demanded.

"I've known Mason for a long time. He's like a brother to me. And I'm telling you this marriage is a mistake. He won't make you happy."

She wanted to cry. They had been under attack about their relationship for months, but Brian's words hurt the most. "You don't even know me! That's an unfair assumption to make!"

Now he stood and walked slowly toward her. "But I do know you, Ava," he said. "You love to read and you're excited about your education and your career. You love to sing and dance to music from the '80s. You hate documentaries, love a good chick flick, and cry at commercials."

"How—how do you know this?" she whispered, mesmerized at the fact that Brian was quite possibly the first man to really see her.

"I listen to you when we talk, and I love spending time with you. I watch you as you interact with people. You're social and genuine, and Mason doesn't appreciate that. I'm sorry I never told you, but how could I say that to my friend's girlfriend? But then you got engaged... Mason is looking for a partner, but you're looking for someone who's as passionate about life as you are. He'll smother you. He's already doing it, Ava." Brian stopped directly in front of her and reached out and touched her cheek. *"He'll stifle your creativity and he'll kill the passion you have inside of you."* His words turned to a mere whisper as he leaned forward. *"Don't let him do that to you."* His lips were a breath away from hers. *"You've got too much passion to give."*

Ava couldn't answer so she moved beyond him and farther into the room. She walked to the wall of windows and hugged herself.

"Why are you doing this, Brian?" she cried. "Why now? Why couldn't you just let us be?"

She saw his approach in the reflection before her and then his hands were on her shoulders, turning her around.

Ava wasn't prepared for such tenderness. Both hands reached up and cupped her face, his eyes softening as they scanned her features as if memorizing them. "You deserve someone who loves you for who you are, Ava. Someone who shares your passion and delights in all the things that make you who you are, not someone who is trying to mold you into someone else."

"That person may not exist," she said weakly, mesmerized by his intent gaze.

"But he does," he whispered. "And he's going to kiss you right now."

And then his lips claimed hers.

Ava knew she should push Brian away, but everything he said was true and the feel of his mouth on hers was so perfect. It had been a long time since Mason had kissed her with such tenderness, such emotion! She was helpless; she had no choice but to respond.

The instant Ava went from being cautious to participating in the kiss, Brian seemed to take full advantage and wrapped her in his arms. She went willingly, pressing closer to him until nothing else mattered. He deepened the kiss and it went on and on. Ava's fingers ran through his hair as his hands roamed her back. It was mindless and passionate and…wrong. That thought hit her hard, and she forced herself to step back.

"I'm sorry. You have no idea how long I've waited to do that." Brian looked down at Ava's flushed face *and smiled sadly. "You can't marry him, Ava," he said. "Don't marry him."*

A knock on the car window startled Ava out of her daydream. She turned to see her coworker Julianne standing there waving. Grabbing her purse and keys, Ava climbed out of the car, feeling a little more aroused than she should be. "What's up, Jules?"

"I wasn't sure if you were awake in there," she said with a smile. "Sorry if I scared you!"

"Just relaxing before heading inside," was all Ava could say as they headed into the bookstore discussing their nightly to-do list.

Chapter 2

BRIAN MCCABE WAS A PATIENT MAN. SOMETIMES THAT worked to his advantage, while other times—like now—he wasn't so sure.

He'd waited eight long months to call Ava. Sure, he'd known there would be a period of time during which it wouldn't have been appropriate for him to call her. After all, she had ended her engagement on the day of the wedding! To some people it might have seemed inappropriate for him to pick up the phone and call his best friend's ex-fiancée.

But the possibility of never seeing Ava again wasn't an option. Brian was exceptional at judging people, and he believed Ava had been just as attracted to him as he was to her. After this accidental meeting at Starbucks, he felt like the universe was giving him the go-ahead.

He wasn't quite sure how it was all going to play out. All he was sure of was that he was in love with Ava Callahan and now was the time to prove it to her.

Finishing his own coffee, Brian eventually left the shop and realized he had nowhere in particular to go. The sun was still shining bright in the late August sky, and he felt momentarily at a loss what to do. There was always the possibility of going to the campus bookstore and trying to talk to Ava again, but he had a feeling that would only serve to hamper his campaign to win her over. No, he needed to let her have a day or two to think about how she felt about seeing him again.

He thought about his friendship with Mason and how his actions were going to affect them, and then stopped himself. When Mason had called him yesterday to tell him he'd seen Ava and told her of his engagement, Brian had been shocked. Not by Mason's call—they had resumed their friendship not long after the canceled Christmas wedding—but by the fact that Mason had seen Ava and was actually telling Brian about it. They had known each other too long to stay mad, and Mason had admitted that Brian's disapproval of his wedding was a real eye-opener to him.

It wasn't until well after the smoke had cleared that Mason figured out Brian had feelings for Ava. He never said whether he approved or disapproved, but it was by silent agreement that she was never brought up in conversation.

Until yesterday.

Was his friend trying to tell him it was okay for him to see Ava? Date her? Brian shook his head, unsure of whether any answer he came up with would be legit or a figment of his own inner desires. Eventually they would have to talk about it because Brian's ultimate goal was to have Ava fall in love with him and marry him. He didn't want his friendship with Mason to end, but if he had to choose, he was choosing Ava.

As Brian walked along the city street, his mind strayed back to the night he'd shown up at Ava's hotel the night before her wedding. It was never far from his mind, but seeing her today, having her so close and not being able to do anything about it, had his subconscious in overdrive. That first kiss only solidified what he already knew: Ava was the one for him. He thought they'd been on the same page, until she'd stopped him.

The windows were fogged, as if from the steam of their kiss. If Brian had his way, he'd never stop kissing her. He felt Ava pulling away but wanted to keep her close, scared of what she was going to say.

"Brian, we have to stop," she said as he continued to kiss her cheek, her throat. Carefully, she pulled out of his embrace and he could see her trembling. "I'm getting married tomorrow," she said weakly.

"Don't do it, Ava," he pleaded. Hadn't she heard anything he said? "I love you."

"You don't love me, Brian, you barely know me!" She turned away from him and now it was her turn to pace the room. "We hung out a couple of times and now you're saying you're in love with me? It's not possible!"

"You may not want to believe me, Ava, but it's true! I knew the first time we met that you and I were perfect for one another."

Ava stared at him incredulously. "Isn't Mason supposed to be your best friend? How can you stand here and talk to me like that? What kind of friend are you?"

"I'm the kind of friend who speaks the truth. I'm not saying anything to you that I haven't already said to him. It may not be pretty, but at least it's the truth."

"I can't understand what you hope to accomplish by doing this. Is it so important for you to be right that you would destroy peoples' happiness? Is your ego that big?"

"This has nothing to do with my ego. I hate seeing the people I care about mess up their lives, and that

is exactly what the two of you are doing. You both deserve to be happy; it's just not going to happen if you stay together."

"Brian, do you have any idea how long and hard I've worked on this? The amount of time, money, and effort that went into this wedding? And because of your own selfish desire, you swoop in and ruin it!"

Tears welled up in her beautiful blue eyes, and Brian cursed himself for putting them there. As one lone tear escaped he reached out and wiped it away with the pad of his thumb, lingering for just a moment to caress her cheek. Ava didn't pull away and he took that as a good sign. He leaned in and kissed her one last time.

Reluctantly, he raised his head, wiped away one last tear, and walked out the door just as she'd asked.

Thanks to his need to speak his mind and voice his disapproval over Mason marrying Ava, not only had Brian been replaced as the best man, he was told not to show up at the wedding at all. It wasn't until a week later that he'd found out the wedding had been called off. He'd been at a New Year's Eve party when he'd seen Mason walk in alone. Brian had frantically looked around for Ava, but it was soon blazingly obvious she wasn't there. That fact was confirmed when Mason approached him, beer in hand, and greeted him with, "Any eligible ladies here tonight?" And just like that, it was as if the previous months had never happened.

That again only stood to confirm his belief that Mason and Ava had been wrong for one another. Now Brian had to figure out how to convince her how right they could be.

—∿∿—

Saturday morning dawned bright and beautiful, and Brian was a man with a plan. Ava was graduating today; he'd heard her and Lacey mention that. He was going to surprise her at her graduation and present her with a beautiful bouquet of her favorite flowers. It was the perfect plan and nothing could go wrong.

Except it did.

The campus seemed unusually deserted considering there was a graduation today. After driving around in circles for what seemed like hours, he located a campus police officer and stopped to question him. "Excuse me, but where is the graduation ceremony being held?" he asked.

The officer looked at him with confusion written on his face. "There's no ceremony today. The university holds graduation ceremonies in May and December. Students graduate in August but there's no official ceremony." He looked at Brian with compassion. "Sorry."

Brian thanked him and drove off, frustrated at this turn of events. Driving around the campus wasn't going to get him anywhere so he drove to the first place he could think of as a good place to regroup—Starbucks.

He climbed out of the car, and when he stepped inside Starbucks and removed his sunglasses, his smile returned. There, in line, was Ava. *Thank you, universe*. She looked crisp and cool and beautiful. Her blond hair was playfully curled and loose, her floral dress hugged her to perfection with tiny little straps and a row of dainty pearl buttons down the back.

"Can I buy the graduate a latte?" he asked, getting in line behind her.

Ava turned to see Brian smiling down at her. "Brian?" she said, returning his warm smile involuntarily. "What are you doing here?"

"Same as you, I'd imagine. Getting some coffee." He simply smiled and looked at her. "You look beautiful today, Ava."

"Oh, um, thank you. Today's my graduation, but there is no real ceremony. I'm meeting my family in a little while to get some pictures with me in my cap and gown and then we're going to lunch."

"If there's no ceremony, why the cup and gown?"

"I have the option of participating in the December ceremony so I just ordered them now. I'm not sure where I'll be in December so they wanted some pictures of me in it just in case I'm not here to be a part of it."

"Makes sense," he said, nudging her forward to place her order. "It would be a shame not to take part in the ceremony after working so hard toward the degree, though, wouldn't it?"

"Not really. I accomplished what I wanted to, and it's just a ceremony. I still have my diploma and that's all I need." She waited while he placed his order and once they both had their drinks, Brian led them to a corner table. Once they were seated Ava took a sip and then looked at Brian expectantly. "So what are you up to today?"

He stalled by taking a sip of his own beverage before answering. "Well, I was hoping to surprise you at your graduation ceremony."

"Seriously?"

He nodded. "Oh, absolutely. I've never had the opportunity to be an observer at a college graduation. Only ever been to my own, and I was curious to see what it was like from a spectator point of view." He kept his tone playful and light, and he could see Ava's mouth twitching with the need to smile.

"Well, sorry to disappoint you, but there's no spectator seating or ceremony today. Just a couple of pictures in the park with the Callahans. Nothing exciting."

"That depends on your definition of exciting." Ava arched an eyebrow at his words, but Brian continued. "You see, for a guy with no family in the area, observing another family, particularly one celebrating such a momentous occasion, would be very exciting."

Ava leveled him with a glare. "So basically you're telling me you want to come and watch me get my picture taken with my family. Do I have that right?"

"When you put it like that, it sounds ridiculous," he teased. "Look at it this way, it could be very beneficial to have me there."

"Oh really?" she said, humor and disbelief mingled in her tone. "And why is that?"

"For starters, who is going to take the group shot?"

Ava merely stared. "I think Dad has a tripod and a timer on his camera."

Brian waved that idea off. "Sure, that can work, but then someone is always having to run and set up the shot and then has to hope they don't look like they've just jumped into the picture. Wouldn't it be easier to have an impartial third party there to help take the pictures so everyone can relax?"

"Are you into photography or something?"

"Not particularly."

"So then this all just falls in the 'for fun' category?"

Brian nodded, his grin widening when he realized she was actually considering inviting him along. "So what do you say, Ava? Wouldn't it be nice to let everyone relax and have fun on your big day?"

Truthfully, she didn't need to contemplate it for long. She'd always enjoyed Brian's company, and even though she thought it *should* feel awkward, it didn't. Not wanting to seem too anxious, she paused for a moment, admiring his strong features and the hopeful look on his face. "Oh, all right."

"Why don't we head over now and scope out some good locations?"

If there was one thing Ava loved, it was being prepared and having a plan. Arriving at the park early had already been part of her plan, but the fact that Brian was on the same page and wanted them to be ready and have a location selected before anyone arrived made her smile.

Brian knew the instant Ava realized he was a planner just like she was, and her smile pleased him. Common interests, common ground; the sooner she began to see how much they truly did have in common, the sooner he could see her agreeing to go out with him.

—◦◦◦—

"It's going to clash with my dress."

"It's going to look beautiful."

"I am going to blend into the background!"

"You could never just blend, Ava. You're too beautiful; you'll stand out no matter where we take the picture."

His kind words took a little of the heat out of their current disagreement. So far they'd looked at a half dozen locations in the park for the family picture and Ava had a problem with each of them. One spot was too green, another too "woodsy," the third had too many people milling about. Ava didn't mean to be so disagreeable, but she wanted the pictures to be perfect and stated that point again to Brian.

"Sometimes things can't be perfect, Ava. Sometimes the best things in life are a little less than perfect and it still makes them wonderful."

She had to wonder if they were still talking about the location for the picture. Brian was staring at her so intently that she had a hard time looking away. He drew her in like a magnet and she was just about to take a step toward him when she heard her name being called from somewhere behind her.

"Ava!" She turned and saw her parents heading her way, with Lacey and Ean not far behind. "We thought you'd be waiting by the car," her mother said, stopping to fuss with Ava's hair. "You could have called and mentioned you were walking around. Poor Lacey shouldn't have to be traipsing aimlessly in this heat."

Lacey gave her an apologetic look and then stepped in between mother and daughter to hug her friend. "No worries, the doctor said a little exercise is good for me!" She kept her tone overly cheery in hopes of defusing any arguments. It was bad enough that Ean was overprotective; it was worse when her in-laws chimed in.

Ean stepped in and hugged Ava right before her father did. "So, where are we thinking for these pictures?" her dad inquired.

"Ava and I were just discussing that," Brian said, suddenly taken aback when all eyes turned to him as if just now realizing he was part of their group.

Lacey looked at Ava quizzically before greeting Brian and then introducing him to everyone. "Ava didn't mention that you'd be with her today," she said casually, fishing for a little info since Ava had clearly left her out of the loop.

"It just sort of happened," Brian responded as he glanced at Ava. "We ran into one another at Starbucks and when she told me what you had planned, I offered my assistance."

"Well, isn't that sweet?" Linda Callahan gushed. "Honestly, Ava, don't you think that was sweet of him?"

It didn't take a rocket scientist to see the wheels turning in her mother's head.

"So where are we thinking?" Lacey asked, turning to take in the landscape. "That area over there is beautiful with all of the flowers."

"Ava believes it will be too much with her dress," Brian said, his tone playfully disapproving. "However, I think if she puts on her cap and gown, we can get some great shots over there and then move someplace else for some poses without the graduation finery. What do you say?"

It was hard to protest when the man made such a convincing argument. Dang it!

"I just have to get my stuff from the car," Ava said and turned to go. Brian's hand on her arm stopped her.

"Give me your keys," he said simply. "You're in high heels and it's very warm out. Let me run to the car and you find a shady spot with your family to wait and I'll be right back."

She hated that he was saying all of the right things and making such a good impression. At this rate her parents would start planning the wedding and asking when they'd be grandparents again. Dang it, dang it, dang it!

"That's very nice of you to offer, Brian, but I don't mind."

"Oh, nonsense, Ava," her mother chimed in. "I'm sure Brian will be back in a jiffy, and in the meantime we can discuss poses and stay cool. It is oppressive out here today." Ava was no fool; her mother wanted Brian out of earshot so she could grill Ava about him. There was no way around it without getting into an argument, so she quietly handed Brian the keys and sent him on his way.

"So, the flowers? Everyone okay with the possibility of bee stings?" Ava asked, hoping her sarcasm wasn't too obvious.

"Knock it off, brat," Ean said. "What's the deal with this guy? Isn't he Mason's best friend?"

"He is." Ava nodded in agreement.

"So why is he with you? What's up with that?"

It was the implication that bothered her and raised her defenses. "What's up with that? Well, let's see, he's a nice guy who happened to want to help out some unappreciative people, apparently."

"That's not what I meant and you know it," Ean snapped back. "I'm just wondering why he would even want to help out. You broke up with his best friend. Does this guy know anything about loyalty?"

"Please, Ean, stop being such a chick." Ava sighed. "First of all, it's not like I broke Mason's heart. Our breakup was mutual. Second, Mason's already engaged again, so clearly he's doing okay. And finally, I never did anything to Brian. He's just a good guy who wanted to help us out. Do you have a problem with that?"

Four pairs of eyes stared at her in disbelief and then everyone started talking at once.

"Mason's getting married?"

"Did you know?"

"Do you think he was cheating on you with her?"

"Are you okay?"

"How did you find out?"

"I never trusted that guy…"

The funny thing was, none of them seemed to wait for an answer before asking another question! She listened halfheartedly to the conversation and was relieved to see Brian heading back her way. A smile tugged at her lips as she took in his appearance. He was dressed semi-casually in dress pants and a polo shirt, his sandy brown hair in disarray from the heat and running back and forth from the car. His brown eyes twinkled when he caught her smiling at him, and when he winked at her and broke into a smile of his own, his dimples made an appearance.

All in all, he was quite a fine example of the male species, and for the first time in a long time, Ava found herself appreciating the male form.

When he got back to her side he noticed all of the chatter going on around her. "What's going on?"

"Oh, I just told them that Mason's getting married."

Brian stopped and listened. "Interesting. Do they ever come up for air, or will this continue for a while?"

"If you say something to them, you'll break the spell and we can get this photo shoot back on track."

"Why me?"

"Because you're new and shiny and a distraction. Trust me on this one."

"Shiny, huh? Do I only distract them, or do I distract you too?" he asked softly so only she could hear.

Before she could answer, however, the Callahans noticed his return. "That was fast, Brian," Jack Callahan said. "I've got the camera and a tripod. Tell us where you want us to pose and we'll get you set up."

"Thank you, sir," he responded and then turned back to Ava. "Here's your cap and gown," he said as he handed her the garment bag, "and here's a little something extra," he said as he handed her a beautiful bouquet of tulips.

Tears welled in her eyes. "These are my favorite," she said reverently. "How did you know?" How was it possible that this man knew her so well?

"I told you a long time ago, Ava, I pay attention." His voice was soft yet firm, and it sent thrilling little chills down her spine. With that, he turned and walked toward her family and helped them get set up for their perfect shot.

~~~

Two hours later Ava's head was spinning. She liked to know exactly what was going on, and right now, seated next to Brian in her favorite restaurant, she had no idea how she had gotten here.

He had dazzled and won her family over. They had taken dozens of pictures all over the park, and he managed to find something to talk about with each family member to keep them all engaged and entertained. And all the while he somehow managed to make her feel as though it was only the two of them. Something was going on, and she was going to get to the bottom of it.

She glanced around, looking for clues indicating how Brian McCabe had managed to charm the people who were originally skeptical of him. Not that it was too hard to imagine—he really had been nothing but charming and helpful all day. She focused on some of the conversations going on around her.

"Wait a minute, wait a minute," she said out loud, her voice one of disbelief with a hint of hysteria. "Did you just invite Brian to play golf?"

"Well, yes," her father responded, suddenly cautious at his daughter's tone.

"In the year that Mason and I dated, you never once invited him to play golf," she accused. "And you!" She turned to Ean. "A couple of hours ago you were wondering why Brian would want to do anything nice for us and questioning his loyalty to his friend, and now here you are inviting him over to your house!"

Everyone was staring at her, except for Brian. He was smiling into his water glass.

"Well, of course we invited him to our home, Ava," Ean explained. "We want to do some renovations on the house and he can't bid on the job if he doesn't come to the house."

"Bid on the job?" She looked around, confused. "Renovations?" she asked, turning her attention back to Brian. "Um…what do you do for a living?"

Brian cleared his throat and took a sip of water before facing Ava. "I'm a contractor. I have my own firm and while we primarily do commercial work, I enjoy taking on residential jobs, too. I'm more than happy to take a look at what your brother wants to have done, and hopefully we can work together."

"Oh yeah, I think I remember Mason mentioning that," Ava mumbled. She reached for her water, embarrassed by her outburst. Conversation resumed around her, and she excused herself to the ladies' room. Lacey followed.

"Are you okay?" Lacey asked when they were alone.

"Am I a good person?" Ava asked.

"Of course you are. Why would you even ask such a thing?"

"Really? Because I can remember a time not that long ago when I was so wrapped up in myself I couldn't even see you were struggling with your feelings for Ean."

"You were planning a wedding, Ava. You were under a lot of pressure."

"Was I? Because it was a home wedding. There was no big venue, no church, nothing big or important that needed the constant attention I gave it. I made you and everyone around me crazy with tiny details and didn't seem to take note of the fact that I was acting that way!"

Lacey took a deep breath and looked at Ava. Something was going on and she had a fairly good idea it had to do with Brian. "Ava, we all understood why you were so consumed and we all love you and got over it. Now come on, what's this all about?"

"Did you hear me out there?"

"When?"

Ava rolled her eyes. "When I snapped at everyone for being nice to Brian?"

Lacey didn't bother arguing the point with her. "What about it?"

"Did you notice the bouquet of tulips he gave me earlier?"

"Of course I did! They were beautiful!"

"Yes, yes, they were beautiful, but do you know why he got them for me?"

"Because he's a nice guy?" Lacey suggested.

"No. I mean yes. I mean… He got them for me because he remembered that *one* time I mentioned tulips were my favorite. Mason never remembered that tulips were my favorite. He got me roses all the time, and no matter how many times I commented on my love of tulips, he never once got them for me."

"And this makes you mad at Brian why?"

Ava sighed impatiently. "Geez, Lace, I think the bump is sucking too many brain cells from you! You used to understand me!"

"Well, in my defense, you are being extremely difficult to understand right now. It has nothing to do with the bump. Now will you please tell me what has you all upset?"

"Brian remembered that tiny detail about me and I couldn't even remember what the man did for a living! A person's favorite flower is a minute detail, but what someone does for a living? That's huge! That's like in the top ten things you cover with someone when you first meet them, and then again every time you see them, you ask about their job." She tried and failed to stifle a sob. "And I never once did that," she cried. "Why? Because I was too damn focused on myself! I'm a horrible person!" And then she burst into tears.

"Oh gosh, oh, Ava, honey, no, you're not. Come on now, no crying. My hormones are a mess and if you keep crying, I'm going to cry, and if I go out there and Ean sees I've been crying, he's going to freak out and think something's wrong with the baby." She grabbed a fistful of tissues and shoved them in Ava's hands. "So if you care anything about me and your unborn niece or nephew, you'll stop this crying right now!"

Amazingly enough, Ava stopped crying. "Lacey Callahan, that was low, using your unborn child to bribe me!"

"Worked, didn't it?" They laughed and then they hugged. Ava took a minute to fix her makeup before they turned to head back to the table. "Are you going to be okay?" Lacey asked as she checked her reflection for any signs of tears.

"I don't know, Lace. Brian…asked me out, and I don't know how I feel about it."

Lacey punched her on the arm.

"Ow! What was that for?"

"A handsome man asked you out and you didn't tell me? How could you?"

"Well, you slept with my brother and didn't tell me. Now we're even."

"Gosh, you can be such a child," Lacey mumbled. "So he asked you out. Are you going to go?"

"I don't know."

"What? Why?"

Ava sighed. She had sworn she would never let anyone know about the night before her wedding, but suddenly it seemed like the natural thing to do. She gave Lacey the *Reader's Digest* version and then stood back and waited for her reaction.

And waited.

And waited.

Finally, when she couldn't take it any longer, Ava rolled her eyes and said, "Don't you have anything to say? I wanted to tell you, Lacey. But I just couldn't handle that on top of everything else at the time."

Lacey looked at her sympathetically. "Ava, honey, after all the planning you did, you gave up your wedding and graciously gave it to me and Ean. In the midst of all that, you weren't just dealing with ending your relationship with Mason; you had to deal with the fact that Brian had feelings for you. That's way more than any girl should have to handle on her own."

"So you forgive me?"

"Of course I forgive you! I'm sorry you felt you had to keep it to yourself," Lacey said sincerely. "We've been friends our whole lives and in the last year we've kept some pretty big secrets from one another. I don't want that to become a habit."

Ava sighed with relief. "It's not, I swear it's not. From this point forward, no more secrets."

Lacey nodded with approval and smiled. "That brings me back to my original question—are you going to go out with him?"

"I don't think it would be a good idea."

"Because of Mason?" Lacey asked.

"For one thing, yes!" A guilty flush stole across Ava's face. "Liking my ex-fiancé's best friend is just a teensy bit awkward, but I can't get him out of my mind."

"Is he a nice guy?"

"Well, yes, but…"

"And do you enjoy having him around?"

"He is…persistent."

"So whose feelings are you trying to spare by denying your feelings for Brian? Mason's?"

Ava had nothing to say to that.

"You listen to me, Ava," Lacey continued, her voice firm. "Sometimes it's okay for you to lead with your heart even when your head is saying it isn't a good idea. If I had listened to my head, I never would have given my relationship with Ean a chance. So speaking from experience, I can tell you that you need to give this a shot. Besides," Lacey said with a naughty grin, "Brian's really attractive, wouldn't you say?"

The blush on her cheeks answered Lacey's question.

"It isn't all about being attracted to him," Ava said hesitantly and then broke into a huge grin, "but the man kisses like nobody's business!" They broke into a fit of giggles and stopped short when Linda Callahan opened the ladies' room door.

"Is everything okay in here? Ean was getting worried!"

"Of course he was," Lacey mumbled. She checked her reflection one last time before smiling at her mother-in-law. "We were just on our way out."

"Oh good." Linda looked at her daughter and quirked an eyebrow at her. "Are you okay?"

"I'm fine, Mom," Ava replied, and for the first time in days, she believed it. "Did I thank you and Dad for taking me to lunch today?" Leaning over, she gave her mom a kiss on the cheek and linked their arms together as they followed Lacey back to their table.

Conversation continued to flow, and Ava allowed herself to relax. Brian wasn't doing anything wrong; if anything, his presence took some of the pressure off her to give her family an answer about what she was going to do now that she had graduated. She was sure she would eventually figure out exactly where she wanted to be and what she wanted to do, but right now Ava just couldn't put her finger on it.

She wanted to move, but to where? She wanted a job, but doing what? She wanted to be in a relationship, but with whom? Her eyes immediately strayed to Brian, and she blushed when he caught her staring. It wouldn't be the worst thing in the world to have dinner with him sometime. What were the odds that one little dinner would lead to anything more? Maybe once he spent some time with her, Brian would realize she wasn't as close to perfection as he'd built her up to be.

Just the thought of that made Ava frown. No, going out with Brian would be safe; it would be like having dinner with an old friend while at the same time taking that leap back out into the dating world. They'd go out once, settle her curiosity, and then she'd be able to move on.

What could go wrong?

Chapter 3

"So he hasn't asked you out?"

"He hasn't asked me out."

"You're sure?"

Ava glared at her friend. "I think I would remember if, sometime before he *raced* away from the restaurant, Brian had asked me out!"

"Well, I'm stumped," Lacey said as she leaned back on her comfy sofa. "Maybe you misunderstood the original invite?"

"How could I misunderstand 'Can I take you to dinner next week?'" Ava growled. It had been almost two weeks since Brian had asked her out at Starbucks. She had been certain when they had all walked out of the restaurant after her graduation lunch and said their good-byes that Brian would repeat the invitation.

But he hadn't. Standing in the parking lot, he'd merely thanked her for letting him join the festivities, congratulated her on her graduation, and walked away. The thought of it still made her mad!

"Maybe he's just giving you a little space since you didn't necessarily respond as he'd hoped the first time."

Ava slouched down next to Lacey and felt miserable. "Or maybe he's just doing exactly what I asked."

"What's that supposed to mean?"

Sighing wearily, Ava turned to Lacey. "When he asked me to dinner, I kind of told him I thought it would be awkward and that we should both move on with our lives."

"You didn't say no more asking you out," Lacey supplied.

"It was implied, don't you think?"

Unfortunately, Lacey couldn't disagree. "Well, it is what you wanted, right?"

"I don't even know what I want anymore," Ava admitted. "I like having a plan of action, and right now I have no idea what action or direction I want to take." She noticed Lacey wince slightly. "I know, what a conundrum, right?"

When Lacey didn't answer right away, Ava sat up a little straighter. "What's going on? Are you okay? Do I need to call Ean?"

Closing her eyes, Lacey took a deep breath and then counted to ten. "No, I'm fine. I've had some Braxton Hicks contractions, but the doctor says they're normal. I just don't like them."

Ava wasn't completely convinced that all was well but kept that opinion to herself. Maybe some distraction would be helpful. "Anyway, I've got an interview next week out in Charlotte for a position with a new charter school. They're looking for a librarian to create the library and then maintain it."

Lacey let out another breath. "Are you excited about it?"

"I'm not sure 'excited' is the right word, but it's worth looking into."

"Charlotte's not that far away," Lacey considered, her hand running over her rounded belly. "We'd still get to see you on weekends, right?"

"Of course. You're going to get tired of seeing me

once this baby comes. I am going to be the absolute best aunt in the world!"

"I know you will be." Lacey began to stand and then doubled over.

"Oh my gosh!" Ava cried, standing up next to her. "I knew something was up! What do I need to do? Call Ean? The doctor? The hospital?" She began frantically looking around the room as if the answer were going to magically appear.

"First," Lacey said calmly, "you need to relax. If anyone here gets to freak out, it's me. Next, let's not panic yet. It was just a bad contraction. It doesn't mean anything until my water breaks."

"Water breaks? That can't be good!"

Lacey rolled her eyes. "Ava, please, you're not an idiot. You know what water breaking means. Now let's just both take a deep breath and calm down. The baby isn't due for almost another three weeks. I'm sure everything is fine." There was a knock at the front door. "Could you answer that? I think I need to sit back down."

Ava looked at her nervously. "I don't want to leave you alone."

"The door is twenty feet away! Believe me, if anything happens, you'll know."

"Fine. But I just want it noted that I did not want to leave you."

"It's noted, Ava." Another series of knocks sounded from the door. "Now, could you please answer that?"

Ava headed to the door and opened it, her jaw nearly dropping to the floor. "Brian? What are you doing here?" That seemed to be her standard greeting for him and she grimaced at the realization.

"Hey, Ava," he said and smiled. "I'm meeting Ean here to go over the plans for the extension."

"Oh, Ean's not home yet. And Lacey didn't mention you were coming over." Ava wanted to smack herself in the head for being so blind. Lacey never invited her over at midday just to hang out. This was probably Lacey's way of getting Ava and Brian together. Part of her wanted to yell at her friend while the other part wanted to hug and thank her. "Come on in. If you had an appointment, I'm sure Ean will be home shortly." Stepping aside, she held the door open as Brian entered, and then they stood in the foyer simply looking at one another.

"So," he began, taking off his sunglasses and looking around the entryway, "how've you been?"

"Good, good. Can't complain." Even though that was exactly what she wanted to do. But she felt justified in complaining—it wasn't right to tell someone you love them and then never do anything about it! She was just about to say something to that effect when she heard Lacey cry out from the living room.

"Uh-oh…"

"What's going on?" Brian asked, quickly following Ava to where Lacey was.

"Lace?" Ava cried. "What's up? Another contraction?"

"My water broke."

"Her water broke?" Brian croaked. "That's not good, right?"

"No, it's not good!" Ava cried. "She's in labor! Tell me what to do, Lacey! Where's Ean? Where's your doctor's phone number?"

"Do we need to call an ambulance? Do I need to boil water or something?" Brian chimed in.

Lacey looked at the two of them and wanted to laugh, but the contractions were pretty strong. "If I could interrupt the two of you for a moment, you need to both be quiet and I'll tell you exactly what to do." They instantly silenced. "Ava, call Ean and tell him to call Dr. Williams and meet us at the hospital." She turned to Brian. "As you can probably guess, we'll need to reschedule." He nodded mutely. "I have a bag by the stairs, Ava. If you can grab that, Brian can help me out to your car and we'll be on our way."

The three of them moved as quickly as possible, but once outside Ava saw that Brian's truck was blocking her car in. They so didn't have time for this! Fortunately, Brian was on the same page.

"Let's help her into the truck and I'll drive to the hospital while you get Ean on the phone and help keep Lacey calm."

"Thank you, Brian. Even though I would have had it under control if you weren't blocking me in…"

"In case either of you haven't noticed, I'm about to have a baby and I would prefer that to happen in a hospital and not in my driveway."

Quickly and quietly, they got Lacey settled into Brian's truck and were on their way. Ava reached Ean and told him what was going on, and then had to take turns between calming him down and letting Lacey squeeze her hand during the contractions. Brian only spoke to ask very simple questions: which hospital, which route, and if Lacey was feeling all right.

Luckily the hospital was only twenty minutes away, and in no time Ava could see Ean pacing outside the emergency room entrance. The truck had barely come to a stop when he yanked the door open and nearly threw Ava to the ground in his haste to get to his wife.

"Oh, Ean, for the love of it, look what you've done to your sister." Lacey sighed as she climbed out of the truck. Ean barely spared his sister a glance and mumbled a very halfhearted apology as he helped Lacey sit in the wheelchair that Brian had secured.

The next several hours seemed to drag. Brian stayed and waited with Ava and her parents and the Quinns, anxious for any news on Lacey and the baby. He brought coffee and sandwiches to them all in the waiting area, and as the night wore on, he urged Ava to relax and try to sleep a little while as they waited for Ean to come out with an update.

A quick glance at his watch showed it was going on ten o'clock. Somehow, while he had been engrossed in an evening news show, Ava had fallen asleep on his shoulder. With a little maneuvering, he had her reclined on the sofa, using his legs as a pillow. She looked so peaceful and beautiful, and it was nice to have the opportunity to observe her without her noticing. Returning his attention to the TV, he absently stroked her hair away from her face, sometimes taking a moment to gently caress her cheek. The expectant grandparents were all seated across the room and had long since given up trying to stay awake.

Sometime near eleven, Ean came out. Brian noticed him first and gently shook Ava awake. She sat up immediately and then called out to her parents and the Quinns. They all stood and looked at Ean expectantly. "Well?" Ava finally said.

"It's a girl! I have a beautiful, healthy daughter." He

beamed. "She's tiny—five pounds, three ounces—but she's perfect."

"How's Lacey?" Ava asked, her voice laced with concern.

"She was a trooper. As fast as the labor came on, it stalled for a while and the baby was in distress. The doctors were just about to prep her for a C-section but then everything seemed to kick into gear."

"So she's okay now?"

"She's exhausted but thrilled," he replied, looking exhausted himself. He sat down on the sofa that Ava and Brian had vacated, leaned back, and closed his eyes, his grin never fading. "A daughter. I have a daughter."

"Does this daughter have a name?" Jack Callahan asked.

Ean opened his eyes and sat up. "Olivia Harper Callahan." He smiled at the collective sighs of his family around him.

"Such a beautiful name," his mother said. "Now when do we get to see her?"

Ean led them down to the nursery, explaining that because it was so late they'd only be able to see her through the glass. They'd have to come back when visiting hours began in the morning. He shared their disappointment because he wanted to show his daughter off, but knew everyone needed their sleep; plus he was anxious to get back and check on Lacey.

Ean waved good night to them all and watched as they headed toward the elevator. The doors had barely closed when he ran to return to his wife's side.

"She's perfect, absolutely perfect," Linda Callahan kept saying in the elevator.

"You're just biased, Mom," Ava teased.

"No, I'm not, you saw those other babies in the nursery. Olivia was, hands down, the most beautiful."

As much as Ava would have loved to poke fun at her mom a little bit more, the truth was she was exhausted. It was after midnight and she still had to get her car from Ean and Lacey's and head home. "Do you need a ride to your car?" her father asked.

"Oh, yeah," Ava said, stifling a huge yawn.

"I can take Ava back to her car," Brian offered.

"Thanks for offering. Are you sure?" Jack said, looking at Ava. She shrugged and smiled sheepishly, trying to hide her blush and the flutter in her stomach.

"Absolutely. It's late and I'm sure you both want to get some sleep."

"Can't argue with that," Jack said, shaking Brian's hand. "Thank you, Brian. We're grateful you and Ava were there to get Lacey to the hospital."

Ava looked around for his truck. "So I guess you're stuck driving me to my car," she said.

"I don't mind," Brian replied mildly, turning her to lead her in the right direction. "Are you sure you don't just want me to take you home? It's late, and you look pretty tired. Are you sure you're okay to drive?"

"I'll be fine in a little while. It was all that sitting around and waiting that put me to sleep. Once I saw Olivia, I was wide awake."

Brian thought she looked adorably sleepy, but he didn't argue. They got to his truck and drove in companionable silence back to her brother's house. Once there, he sat and waited for Ava to speak.

"So, um, thanks for the ride," she said shyly, not

looking directly at him. When Brian remained silent, she finally turned to face him. What she saw made her want to gasp; the look of desire on his face was so strong it left her feeling a little breathless. Time seemed to stand still. They sat facing one another, and Ava was sure her expression now mirrored his. Her breath quickened and she silently prayed that he was going to lean over and kiss her.

But he didn't. She wanted to be bold; she wanted to make the first move and show him she had been wrong. She wanted to have the confidence it took to do it.

"So…you're okay to drive?" he finally asked, breaking the spell.

Ava shook her head to be sure she heard him correctly. *Okay to drive?* Here she was thinking about kissing him senseless and he was worried about her driving skills. When she didn't immediately answer, he asked her again.

"Oh, um…I'll be fine. Thanks." Feeling foolish for her wayward thoughts, Ava scrambled from the truck and ran over to her car.

Once inside she took several deep breaths to calm her nerves. "Well, this is what you said you wanted," she reminded herself out loud. "You told him no more and that's exactly what you got."

Sometimes getting what you wanted wasn't all it was cracked up to be.

Brian pulled out of the driveway and waited for Ava to do the same. He knew she was tired and he probably should have just driven her straight home, but he wasn't sure he would be able to handle the temptation. Oddly enough, he'd enjoyed himself today. Even though he'd been sitting around in a hospital waiting room, spending time with Ava and her family had been a pleasant experience.

Ava had been quite chatty when she let her guard down. It didn't happen often, but over the course of the day they had engaged in several long conversations about everything and nothing at the same time. He loved talking with her, hearing her laugh, and getting her input on current events. Her parents were friendly and talkative, and several times Brian found himself just as excited as the rest of them waiting for the arrival of the newest Callahan.

As Ava's car disappeared down the road, Brian smiled sadly. He'd seen the way she'd looked at him moments ago. He knew if he had pushed even a little, they'd both still be in his truck and he'd be kissing her as he'd longed to do all day. But she had told him to back off, and as much as he was trying to respect her request, it wasn't easy. If Ava wanted him, she was going to have to make the first move. He wanted her to be sure; he wanted her to want him as much as he wanted her.

When her car turned right at the end of the block, Brian finally put his own vehicle in gear and smiled. The clock read 1:00 a.m. Hell, her father would surely kill him if he didn't make sure she got home safely. So with a renewed sense of purpose, Brian set off to follow Ava home, telling himself it was only as a favor to her parents.

That would sound believable if she caught him, wouldn't it?

Chapter 4

AVA FELT A MOMENT OF PANIC WHEN SOMEONE PULLED into her driveway behind her. It wasn't until their head-lights turned off that she realized it was Brian. What was he doing here? Why had he followed her? Her heart leaped. Had he followed her because he felt what she did back in his truck? Knowing her luck, he had merely followed her home like a good boy scout to make sure she didn't fall asleep at the wheel.

Great, now she had a problem with responsible men who were concerned for her well-being. Clearly she needed therapy.

Getting out of her car, she turned as Brian was get-ting out of his. She was just about to ask what he was doing here and then stopped herself, remembering that had become her opening line every time she saw him. Playing it safe, she merely stood next to her car and waited for him to come to her. Ava looked at him expectantly when he stopped in front of her.

"I wanted to make sure you made it home safe," he said softly. The look on her face told him he'd said something wrong. "It's late and you were tired and…"

"It's fine," she mumbled. "I appreciate your con-cern." Her voice lacked any form of sincerity, and she wished him a good night and turned and started to walk toward her condo.

"Ava, did I say something wrong?"

Why wouldn't he just leave? She took another couple of steps and then stopped when he called her name again. Before she knew it, Brian was standing before her. "It's nothing, Brian. Like you said, it's late and I'm tired."

Placing a finger under her chin, Brian tilted her head so that Ava was forced to look at him. "I don't think so. What did I say? Clearly I've upset you and I don't have a clue as to why!"

She moved his hand away, took a step back, and sighed wearily. "I don't know why I'm upset, okay?" She was mortified when tears started to well in her eyes. "You've been nothing but helpful all day and it's like… you just keep showing up everywhere and I don't know what to do with that!"

One lone tear escaped and it nearly brought Brian to his knees. "Ava, it was never my intention to make you cry. I'm sorry," he said in a near whisper. "I didn't realize I was making you miserable. I should have respected what you asked of me and stayed away." He hated saying the words but he hated seeing Ava cry more. Clearing his throat, Brian took a moment to find a way to say good-bye. "I only wanted to be near you, to get to know you. I thought maybe if you spent some time with me, you'd want to get to know me, too. I never wanted to cause you any pain. I'll keep my distance. I just want you to be happy, Ava. I won't bother you again."

He'd almost made it all the way back to his truck before Ava called out to him. "You don't tell someone you love them and then walk away!" she cried.

Brian turned, stunned at her words. Ava angrily walked toward him. "Was it all a lie? Was that your way of making sure I didn't marry Mason, by telling me you loved me?"

"What? No! I wouldn't lie about something like that, Ava, I swear!"

"Loving someone means staying with them, standing by them," she stated. "Yet every time you even hint about caring about me, you leave."

"Well, it didn't seem as if you wanted me to stay."

"Well, then maybe you don't know me as well as you think," she said, folding her arms across her chest.

"So what you're saying is that all those times you told me to leave, I should have stayed. Do I have that right?" He quirked an eyebrow at her and was rewarded with a small smile from Ava.

"I don't know. Maybe."

"How about now, Ava?" Brian leaned in close, his mouth a breath away from hers. "Do you want me to leave right now?" he whispered.

Ava felt his warm breath against her cheek and couldn't help but lean into him. She could no longer deny the attraction they shared, and if she was honest with herself, she could admit she'd been waiting for this moment for far too long.

"I don't want you to go anywhere," she admitted softly and was rewarded when he slowly touched his lips to hers. It was a gentle kiss, one of reacquaintance. When Ava sighed and relaxed into him, Brian deepened the kiss and Ava found herself winding her arms around his neck and combing her fingers through his hair.

Far too soon, Brian pulled back, his breathing labored. "As much as I hate to stop, I certainly don't want us to be entertainment for the neighbors." The night air was cool but his skin was on fire. All he wanted was for them to be alone and someplace private, but he was afraid to admit that out loud. After finally finding themselves on the same page, he hated the thought of scaring her off.

"I have to agree," Ava admitted and then looked from Brian's truck to her condo, indecision written all over her face. "It is getting late," she said after a moment and Brian's heart sank. He was going to have to leave, and while he was sure it was going to be okay, the selfish part of him was reluctant to let the night end. He'd waited so long, and now to be so close to finally being alone with Ava and having to leave was torture.

He simply nodded in agreement and was about to suggest they go out for dinner tomorrow when she surprised him and grabbed his hand.

"We certainly don't want to waste what's left of it," she said saucily, and led him inside with a seductive smile on her face.

———

Ava woke up early to a long-forgotten sensation: a man sleeping beside her. She took a moment to take in Brian's features relaxed in sleep. He was so handsome. His hair was in sexy disarray, and she had a hard time deciding if she should reach out and run her fingers through it or focus her attention on his strong jaw, shadowed with stubble.

Although now that she let her eyes wander, she saw there was so much more to admire in the light of day. Broad shoulders, tanned skin, strong arms… Her hand skimmed lightly along the hard lines of his chest and abs before she let out a sigh of appreciation.

Memories of their night together made her smile. Carefully, she rose from the bed and tiptoed to the bathroom, and gasped at her own reflection. Not wanting to make too much noise, she quickly ran a comb through her hair and brushed her teeth. She was just about to creep back into the bedroom when she made a quick grab for her deodorant and put some of that on for good measure. Feeling slightly more human, she was about to turn out the bathroom light when her lip gloss caught her eye. What harm could that do?

When she finally was back under the blankets, Brian rolled toward her and then took her into his arms. He kissed her forehead and said a sleepy good morning to her before even opening his eyes.

Praying she had fixed herself to the point of not scaring him, Ava held her breath as he opened his eyes and scanned her face. "You're even beautiful first thing in the morning," he said with a smile and leaned in for a deeper kiss.

Ava smiled to herself, luxuriating in the feel of him wrapped around her. Hopefully her attempts at freshening up weren't overly obvious. She ran her fingers along his roughened jaw and purred. A girl could get used to waking up like this.

"Do you have plans for today?" he asked, hesitantly raising his head from hers.

"I was planning on doing a little baby shopping before going to see Lacey and Olivia. Why? Did you have something in mind?"

"I just figured you were getting ready to go somewhere, with all the hair brushing and lip gloss," he teased, and flinched when she pinched him.

"A gentleman wouldn't have mentioned that!"

"Darlin', I never claimed to be a gentleman," he replied and then rolled her on top of him. "Now, this baby shopping, that would entail going to a mall or something like that, right?"

Ava nodded. "Are you offering to go with me?"

In the blink of an eye he reversed their positions and had her pinned beneath him and was rewarded with a genuine laugh from her. "It wouldn't be my first choice for how we might spend the day, but for you, I wouldn't mind a little shopping."

Her eyes softened as she looked at him. "That's very sweet of you," she said, "but I think you would be terribly bored. When I shop, I'm a woman on a mission." Reaching up, she kissed him softly on the cheek. "But thank you for offering."

"My pleasure," he said with a smile. "So, were you planning on shopping early or later on or…"

Ava shook her head. "I hadn't planned it out that far." Then she chuckled. "And that's saying something. I almost always have a plan."

"Sometimes it's good to go with the flow and not have a plan—you know, just to wait and see what happens."

"Hmm… I guess it might not be such a bad thing. What about you? What are you doing today?"

"I was too busy enjoying the moment to give it much thought. But going to the mall is probably *not* what I'd choose to do."

A broad grin spread across Ava's face. She wound her fingers in his hair. "Well then, what *would* you choose to do?"

Brian didn't miss a beat. "I guess I must have done

something wrong last night if you've forgotten already." And with that, he showed her how his time could be better spent.

———ᨆᨆᨆ———

Much later that day, after Ava had exhausted herself first with Brian and then with shopping, she arrived at the hospital with both arms loaded with packages. When she entered Lacey's room, Ean grabbed what he could and laughed. "We're going home tomorrow, Ava. How much stuff did you think we'd need?"

"Oh, be quiet. As Olivia's aunt, it is my duty to make sure she is spoiled rotten and extremely well-dressed." She raised her arms and shook the shopping bags dangling from them. "Nothing is too good for my little princess."

Lacey sat up in the bed and clapped her hands with excitement while Ean rolled his eyes. "I am seriously outnumbered," he grumbled.

"And you'd better get used to it," Ava responded smartly and went to hug Lacey. "How's the new mom today?" she chirped.

"A bit sore but so, so happy." She glanced over at Ean. "Um, I would love a snack from the cafeteria, sweetheart. Do you mind?"

Ava nearly laughed out loud as Ean jumped to his wife's assistance and went in search of food for her. "Nice," she said blandly. "Does he roll over when you ask, too?"

"Very funny. But there was no way for us to talk with him hovering." She studied Ava for a moment. "You slept with Brian, didn't you?"

"What? How…?" Ava sputtered. "Okay, I don't even have it in me to deny it. How did you guess?"

"Other than the glowing complexion and the sappy smile on your face? Please. I've known you your whole life. Nothing gets by me."

"Especially now, since the bump isn't sucking your brain waves," Ava deadpanned.

"Olivia better be a genius for all she took from me." Lacey smiled. "So, tell me all about it."

While Ava knew Lacey wasn't asking for graphic details, she managed to give her the highlights without blushing too terribly. "Honestly, Lace, it was wonderful. He's wonderful! I'm so happy!"

"I'm so glad, sweetie. You deserve to be happy."

"I wasn't sure I was capable of it. I don't remember feeling like this before. I feel like I'm walking on air and I can't stop smiling!"

"Smiling's a good thing and you have a gorgeous smile."

"This is completely different from what I had with Mason." Ava knew she was gushing and she didn't care. What were friends for? "Brian knows me better than Mason ever did. I think that, in time, this could be something completely amazing. Lace, this could be my happily ever after."

Lacey would be happy never to hear of fairy tales or happily ever after coming from Ava's mouth ever again. But it was good to see her friend happy, so she kept any creeping doubts to herself and listened as Ava waxed poetic about all the things she wanted to do with Brian and all the places she wanted to go.

"What about the job interview next week? You're still going on that, right?"

"Hmm… I had forgotten about that. Of course I'll go, but it would have to be a spectacular job offer to make me consider moving away now! Between you and Olivia and now Brian, I don't want to leave!"

"Oh, Ava, no!"

"What? What did I say?"

Although Lacey had not one minute ago vowed to keep all negative comments to herself, she couldn't help but let one last one slide. "Ava, it's starting already!"

"What? What is?"

"You haven't even gone on the interview and already you don't want to go because of other people! You have to live your life for you, not for anyone else! Don't let me or Olivia or Brian keep you from living your dream!"

"I'm not!" Ava cried. "Geez, since when did it become a crime to not want to move away from your family?"

"It's not a crime, Ava. It's just that less than forty-eight hours ago you were open to the idea of moving away, and now after one night with Brian you're reconsidering."

It was hard to argue with the truth. Again. "Look, I'm not committing one way or the other. I'm simply keeping my options open."

Lacey's disbelief was written all over her face. "I certainly don't want to be the reason for you to start doubting yourself…"

"You mean again?" Ava interjected, referring to Lacey's attempts the year before to convince her to cancel her wedding. It had all worked out for the best, but sometimes having a friend who didn't have a problem voicing her opinions hurt.

"I just had a baby and I am emotional, and for that reason alone I get a free pass to say what's on my mind."

That made Ava smile. "Okay, but you only get to use that excuse once."

"Deal," Lacey agreed and relaxed. "All I'm saying is I want you to take it slow and don't give up the things you want. If Brian cares about you, he's going to take your feelings into consideration. Right?"

"When you're right, you're right," Ava said, and then turned when her brother entered the room carrying enough snacks and beverages to feed at least a dozen people. She turned back to look at Lacey as they both broke into a fit of giggles.

Ean sighed. "I am just completely outnumbered..." he mumbled.

Chapter 5

THE NEXT SEVERAL WEEKS FLEW BY. BETWEEN HER job at the bookstore, her search for a career, spending time with Lacey and Olivia, and settling into her relationship with Brian, Ava's life was beyond full. Each day she woke with a smile on her face and a sexy man by her side. They went on dates to the movies, museums, and dinner. They talked for hours about their jobs and careers, and mostly, Brian encouraged Ava to share her dreams.

In all of their conversations, Brian was careful neither to fully encourage nor discourage Ava when a job opportunity presented itself that would have her moving away from Raleigh. Should she decide to take a job that meant relocating—well, he'd deal with it when the time came. He wasn't foolish enough to believe that would be easy, but Brian was walking a fine line. He remembered well enough what had happened a year ago when Mason had tried to control Ava's future, and that was not something he ever wanted to be accused of doing.

Ava was an intelligent woman. He could only hope the things that drew him to her also didn't take her away from him.

As Brian was trying to find the proper balance where Ava's career search was concerned, Ava had a dilemma of her own: wondering why Brian wasn't weighing in more. If he truly felt for her the way he said he did, wouldn't he be trying to persuade her not to even look at jobs that would take her out of the area? Granted, there hadn't been that many, but when they came up, he wished her luck on her interviews and was waiting for her when she came back, anxious for a report on how it went. He never mentioned moving his business, and Ava knew it was time for those questions to come to the surface.

They were sitting on the sofa in Ava's condo watching a movie one October evening when she finally decided to broach the subject. "I was thinking more about the job with the med school up in Richmond," she said casually, reaching for the bowl of popcorn on the coffee table in front of them. She said it without making eye contact, just something she seemingly threw out there, and waited for his response.

"Richmond, huh? I didn't think you were all that crazy about that one. The starting salary was a little low, wasn't it?"

Ah, so he had paid attention to her ramblings about the pros and cons of the job; that was promising.

"It was a little low, but the area was really nice and I've been looking at houses online. I think I can find something a little newer and a little bigger than what I've got here for around the same price. It might be nice to upgrade in the process," she said, still looking as if she was actually interested in what was on the TV.

"So this is about a house?" he asked, confusion lacing his voice. Grabbing the remote, he muted the television. "You'd take a job you weren't crazy about because of a house?"

Ava finished chewing her snack before turning to face him. "Of course it's not just about a house, Brian.

I'm trying to look at the total picture. I mean, the job has potential. I may be starting out with a lower salary than I want, but the possibility of advancement and growth within the company is promising. If I'm going to find the perfect job, then I want to have the perfect house to go with it. You know me, Brian, I want the total package."

He stifled a groan. Her and her damn *perfect*. "I think your quest for all things perfect is admirable, Ava, but sometimes you have to take a good look around you and realize that what you have is satisfying and good and be happy with it."

"So I should settle?" she said a little too defensively.

"No, not settle, just have more...gratitude." There, that sounded good, didn't it?

"Brian, that night you came to my hotel room, do you remember what you said to me?"

"Of course I do."

"You told me I was a passionate person and Mason was stifling me. Well, what I learned is that you're right, I am passionate, especially about the things I want. I don't think my expectations are too much. I want a job with potential and a home I love. What's wrong with that?"

"Nothing's wrong with it per se, it's just that you keep tacking on the word 'perfect' and there is no such thing."

"Brian, you worry me," she said wearily.

"Why?"

"Because it sounds as if you are the one who is settling. That you'll never be truly happy because you'll just take what's in front of you and never dream of more."

He stood, his frustration rising. How could he make her understand? She had no idea how hard he'd worked to get where he was or how long he'd dreamed of having the woman he loved just simply sitting beside him on the couch! It may not seem grand or extravagant, but that was his vision of perfect. He was about to say as much when Ava stood beside him, her hand on his arm.

"I don't want to argue with you, Brian. I just don't want to see you settle when there's so much out there in the world to see and do!"

"Has it ever occurred to you that I sincerely like my life the way it is? I have a great job, great friends, and a very supportive family. I built my dream home and it's *my* dream home. It may not be perfect to somebody else, but that doesn't make me love it any less!"

"Your house *is* perfect!" she cried. "I didn't mean to imply otherwise, it's just that…"

"And on top of all that," he interrupted, "I finally have the woman I love beside me and *she,*" he stopped and placed a gentle kiss on her lips, "is damn near perfect."

Ava couldn't help but smile. "I'm glad you think so." She shrieked as Brian scooped her up in his arms and headed toward her bedroom, where he showed her all through the night just how perfect she was.

⌘

It didn't take long for some of Brian's words to start making Ava think. Was she being realistic? Was she searching for something that didn't exist? Was there really no such thing as fairy tales and happily ever afters? She wasn't sure, but she wasn't willing to stop searching yet. Her job at the campus bookstore was a dead end, and while she had sent her résumé to over a dozen companies, nothing thrilled her yet.

Well, at least not in the job department. Her time with Brian? Now that was thrilling. She loved it when Brian challenged her. Mason had often *yes*'d her to death on the little things merely to appease her, but Brian wasn't afraid to say no to things he didn't want to do or to let her know when he thought she was making a mistake.

That one took a little getting used to.

After a lifetime of no one telling her no or disagreeing with her, having someone point out her mistakes and imperfections, but not in a mean or bad way, was a brand-new experience. The first lesson learned came after their very first night together: Ava never made the mistake of getting out of bed to freshen up in hopes of fooling Brian again! He still teased her about it, and looking back, she realized how silly it was. Brian wasn't with her because she woke up with lip gloss on and her hair perfect; he was with her because he loved the person she was inside.

That took a little getting used to, as well. Ava wasn't vain, but she knew she was attractive and most men gave her what she wanted because of how she looked. Not Brian. She could walk around without any makeup and her hair in a ponytail and he'd still want to take her out. Not that she tested that theory too often, but he never made a big deal about her appearance.

That thought made her frown a little, and her pesky insecurities started to bubble up. Clearly he found her attractive, but was it normal to not even acknowledge when she went from one extreme to another? Mason had often made her feel bad when she would be at home in her sweats on a Saturday, just wanting to hang out. He'd ask if she was going to do her hair or put on some makeup, but Brian never said anything like that. He accepted her no matter what.

It left her feeling a little unbalanced. How did she go about pleasing him when he didn't seem inclined to share with her what she did that pleased him? Well, she *knew* the things she did that pleased him, but that was in the bedroom; she was curious how to keep Brian satisfied out of the bedroom, because eventually that part of the relationship died down too, didn't it?

To be honest, that part of their relationship just kept getting better and better, but how long would that last? Shouldn't they be cooling down by now? Settling into things? Talking about the future? It had been about six weeks, and although she could still hear Lacey reminding her to take it slow, Ava felt that at age twenty-seven, there was only a certain level of slow she was willing to go! The bottom line still remained: she wanted to find a job first and foremost, but her ultimate goal was to get married and have a baby before she was thirty.

That wasn't too much to ask, was it? Was Brian going to be the man to make that dream come true? She wracked her brain trying to remember if in any of their lengthy conversations he'd mentioned his plans for a family, but somehow that never seemed to come up. Why was that? Was Brian not interested in having a family, or was he not interested in leading Ava to believe he wanted a family with her?

She frowned for a moment. The more she thought about it, the more she realized that, in all the time she and Brian had been together, he hadn't said he loved her again—not like he had that night in her hotel room before her wedding. She could feel it in the things he did for her, but he never said the words, never looked deeply into her eyes and professed his love for her, not like the first time.

Then again, she hadn't said those three little words to him either. Was Brian waiting for that? Waiting for her to profess her love for him before he was okay with saying it to her? Did she love him? Was she seriously ready for that?

"Ugh," she grumbled. "Why don't relationships come with manuals?"

———~~~———

That weekend they took in a local music festival. As they wandered the streets holding hands, Ava thought that life didn't get much better than this: a beautiful day, good music, good food, and spending time with Brian. She wanted to tell him she thought it was the perfect day, but decided to omit that one little word from her vocabulary for a while so as not to upset Brian.

"Ooo…cotton candy," she commented as they stopped to listen to a three-piece bluegrass band.

"Where?"

"Across the parking lot. Want some?" she asked, already fishing through her purse for her wallet.

Brian smiled—that purse looked innocent but actually contained enough to keep a person alive in the forest for days. "Thanks, but I'm still full from the corn dog earlier."

Ava raised her head and looked at him as if he were speaking a foreign language. "But it's cotton candy," she stated.

"And?"

"And there's always room for cotton candy. Weren't you ever a kid?" He laughed, and the sound was the sweetest music at the whole festival. "Seriously, how can you pass it up?"

"Okay, okay, if it means that much to you…"

"No, it's fine, more for me then," she said and sauntered across the parking lot to get in line for her treat. Once she had it in hand she fairly skipped back to Brian. "Mmm…there is nothing better than some cotton candy on a day like today."

Brian watched her enjoying her snack and felt his throat go dry. It shouldn't have been sexy; he most certainly should not have been aroused by the sight of Ava enjoying a sticky, messy treat. Yet right now all he could think of was kissing her, tasting her, and getting them out of this crowd of possibly a thousand people to get her home.

Without conscious thought, he grabbed her hand and started dragging her toward where they were parked.

"Is that it?" she asked. "Did we see all the bands already?" Looking over her shoulder and around at all of the festivities, she was confused. They hadn't been there that long; where were they going? "Brian? Are you okay?"

Suddenly he stopped. He let go of her hand and cupped her face and brought his mouth down on hers. It wasn't gentle, it wasn't sweet. The kiss was all pent-up tension and arousal and Ava found herself right on board with it. "You taste so sweet," he said huskily before diving in again.

Ava pulled away slightly and sighed. "That's not me, it's the candy."

"No," he said firmly, "it's you, it's always you. God, what you do to me, Ava." He stared down into her face and just felt himself falling deeper. Her blue eyes were fathomless and he wanted to dive right in and never leave. "You're so damn beautiful, do you know that?"

She shook her head, confused as to where all this emotion had come from. The question was on the tip of her tongue, but for the life of her she didn't want to do or say anything to ruin the moment. Brian's eyes scanned her face for another heartbeat before he kissed her again; this time it was a little less consuming but still just as powerful.

"I want to take you home," he finally said.

"But the bands? You said you wanted…"

"All I want is you, Ava." It was a simple statement, but the raw emotion in his tone made it more powerful than any words he'd ever spoken. In that moment, nothing else mattered.

Ava simply took Brian's hand in hers and took the lead. "Then let's go home."

It was hours later, when passion had been spent, their skin had cooled, and heartbeats returned to normal, when Ava finally had her answer: She was in love with Brian McCabe.

Chapter 6

AVA'S HEART WAS BACK TO BEATING WILDLY THE next day when she sat down on Lacey's couch. "Okay, so I did something crazy," she said, unable to meet her friend's worried gaze.

"Crazy? How unlike you," Lacey said, trying to lighten the mood. When Ava didn't respond, she knew something was seriously wrong. "Ava? C'mon, that was funny. What's going on?"

"I fell in love with him," she said quietly.

Lacey sat back, her infant daughter cradled in her arms. "And this is bad why?"

"You told me not to rush into anything! You told me to take my time and it's been what? Two months and I'm already in love with Brian!"

"Oh for goodness sake, Ava, is that all?"

"All? Isn't this the part where you lecture me on not making the same mistakes I made with Mason?"

Sighing, Lacey made herself more comfortable and faced Ava. "I am so sorry you think that is going to be my first reaction to anything going on in your life. That was never my intention. I just want you to be happy, and I have to tell you, it's been a long time since I've seen you this happy."

"Really?" Ava asked, uncertainty in her tone.

"Yes, really," Lacey assured her. "I know this relationship you have with Brian is completely different

from the one you had with Mason. You seem more like
the Ava I grew up with. You were more solemn and
moody—and yes, bitchy—when you were with Mason.
Now you're all cheery and sassy and full of smiles
again. I love that the old Ava is back!"

"It feels good to be back. It has been so long since I
felt this way that I wasn't sure at first what I was feeling." She sat back and sighed. "He makes me happy,
Lace. We don't have to be doing anything or going anywhere and I'm just happy."

"So did you tell him?"

"Tell him what? That I'm happy?"

"No, that you love him!"

"Oh, no," Ava said a little too quickly.

"Why not?"

"Well, I don't want to scare him off, for starters."

"Starters? Wasn't he the one who told you he loved
you almost a year ago when you two barely knew
one another?"

"Well, yes, but…"

"So then what are you waiting for?"

Ava grimaced at Lacey. "You know you can be
irritating sometimes, right?" Lacey merely smiled in
response and waited for Ava to speak again. "I guess
I'm a little gun-shy. I mean, what if I tell Brian I love
him and then he says he loves me and then I go and get
all crazy again?"

"Crazy how?"

"What if I start obsessing about getting married?
What if I end up ruining another relationship because
I'm a wedding-crazy lunatic?"

"Okay, for the record, your being a…what did you

call it? A wedding-crazy lunatic? That was not the reason for your breakup. You and Mason weren't meant to be, and I think you obsessed about that wedding because you subconsciously didn't want to admit to other problems in the relationship."

Unfortunately, Lacey was right. Again. "Well, for the record," Ava said tartly, "I'm getting a little tired of you playing amateur psychologist."

"Stop pouting, it gives you wrinkles," Lacey said sweetly. "Look, this is a new relationship with a new future ahead of you. You have to stop comparing the two, and I can promise I'm done doing that, too."

"I don't know, it seems risky…"

"Sometimes the best things in life require the biggest risks. Believe me, I didn't think I could take the risk with Ean, but I am so glad I did! Look at how wonderful everything's been!"

"Well, the two of you are just disgustingly adorable and none of us like it," Ava said, but her words were full of love. "You got the fairy tale, Lacey. You spent the night in the cottage and…"

"Ava! We swore to never bring up the cottage myth ever again!"

"I know, I know, and I'm sorry, it's just that I have to wonder if…"

"No! No wondering, Ava," Lacey cut in. "No more talk about the cottage or fairy tales or ever afters. Are we clear?"

"Why do you hate it? I want you to think about that and give me an honest answer," Ava said after a moment of contemplation.

Lacey sighed. "Okay, I don't hate it, all right? It's

just…you took a sweet story and sort of wore it out. And while you were wearing it out, you put too much importance on it. I love the cottage. It holds nothing but wonderful memories for me and Ean. And someday, I hope it holds wonderful memories for you. But I want you to be able to be okay with your life without basing it on a story." She looked at Ava and smiled sadly. "Can you understand that?"

Ava nodded but she wasn't so sure she could let it go so easily. What if she waited and took Brian up to Asheville to spend the night in the cottage? She'd feel comfortable telling him she loved him there, wouldn't she? After all, if the Callahan legend were true, if they spent the night there in the cottage, they'd be guaranteed love everlasting. That's what happened to Lacey and Ean. Was it so wrong to want that for herself? Wasn't she entitled to her share of magic? Good luck? Love everlasting?

She looked over at Lacey, who was stroking her daughter's cheek with a look of pure bliss. That's what Ava wanted. The desire for it was so strong that she knew what she had to do. For now, she'd let the subject drop with Lacey; no need to perpetuate the argument. But once she got home, Ava was going to put a plan into action that would help her overcome her fear of telling Brian she loved him and get her on the path to her own happily ever after.

—∾∾—

Several nights later Ava found the perfect opportunity to get her plan in motion. Handing Brian a glass of wine before dinner at her condo, she motioned for him to join her on the sofa. She waited for Brian to take his first sip before she spoke.

"So, I got a request for an interview with a college up near Asheville," she began, searching for any reaction from Brian.

"Is that right?" he asked. "What's the position?"

Ava described it to him, adding a little more excitement to her tone than she actually felt for the job. In all honesty, the job didn't interest her much, but it was a means to get Brian up to Asheville for a weekend at the cottage.

"Seems to me they're not offering anything more than any of the other local positions you've looked at," he said neutrally.

"Well, I still want to go and meet with them. You know, this way I can make an informed decision." Brian nodded at her words, but his face remained expressionless. She hated when he did that. "Anyway, I'm scheduled to meet with them a week from Friday and I was hoping you could take the day off and go with me and then we can spend the weekend up in the mountains. What do you think?"

Brian seemed to consider her words. "That sounds good. There's a great resort up there and I think we should see if we can make reservations…"

"No!" she cried a little too enthusiastically. "Um… what I mean is, that won't be necessary. My folks have a place up there where we can stay."

Eyes narrowing, he looked at her. "Your parents' place? I'm offering you a weekend in a five-star resort with spas and room service and you want to stay with your folks?"

232 SAMANTHA CHASE

Ava rolled her eyes. "Not with my folks, they won't even be there. The place stays empty for most of the year, but I love going up there and don't make the time to do it very often. I just thought we could stay there. You know, two birds, one stone, and all that."

She was rambling, and Brian could tell there was more to this than Ava was letting on. He wasn't sure where she was going with all of this, but she was a little too jittery and excitable for this to simply be about going to Asheville for an interview.

"So you want to go on this interview for a job that isn't very interesting just so you have an excuse to stay at your family's place? Why not skip the interview and we can just go up there?" Again, his tone gave nothing away; as far as Ava could tell, he wouldn't mind if she went on the interview or not.

"It would be rude to not go on the interview after I've already scheduled it. Besides, what if I misjudged them based on the phone interview? What if I fall in love with the campus and find out there's some great opportunities for me in the future?"

Brian sighed and took another sip of his wine. "Whatever you want to do is fine with me, Ava. We'll go and make a weekend out of it."

"Yeah!" She squealed and launched herself into his lap, nearly knocking his glass from his hand. "Oh, I'm so excited! Our first weekend away together! It's going to be great!" She kissed him soundly before rising to skip into the kitchen to finish making their meal, talking the entire time.

"My appointment isn't until four in the afternoon but if we leave in the morning we can get up there and get settled in. The property is beautiful. It's particularly spectacular in the winter when it snows. Lacey and Ean got snowed in up there last year and that's how they ended up reconnecting with one another. We got some beautiful pictures from their wedding…"

That elusive something that had been nagging at the back of his mind finally clicked into place. Her parents' home. The cottage. Her wedding to Mason.

He was completely blindsided. Why on earth would she want to take him to the place where she'd almost married his best friend? What could she possibly gain from that? What kind of game was she playing? Looking over at her, he couldn't comprehend how it was that he could love Ava and completely not understand her.

"So what do you think?" she asked anxiously, placing their dinner plates on the table.

Shaking his head to clear it, he asked, "I'm sorry, what do I think about what?"

She looked crushed. "Haven't you been listening? I was telling you we can go hiking and set up a fire outside in the fire pit that my grandfather built and go exploring the town, or we can maybe just spend a cozy weekend in the cottage…" Her voice trailed off a bit at the end of the statement, and that was the final piece of the puzzle for Brian.

"I'm not spending the night in the cottage, Ava," he said bluntly.

"What? Why? I don't understand."

"Seriously?" he asked. "You don't understand why I wouldn't want to spend the night in the place where you were going to honeymoon with Mason? Don't you think that's a bit of an odd request to ask of me?"

She looked truly puzzled. "I don't see why. It's not like we actually *did* spend the night in the cottage. Mason didn't even see the cottage, let alone sleep there! I just thought it would be a nice little getaway for us and a little less boring than spending the night at my parents' house."

"Under any other circumstances, Ava, it would be, but to me it feels a little weird. I want us to make our own memories, not tack on to somebody else's."

"We're not, honestly, we're not. I just thought it might be nice, that's all. Eventually you are going to see the house and the cottage, because my family does spend time there. We spend holidays there, and if any of my cousins get married, they're bound to have the wedding there…"

"I get that, Ava, but if we're going to have a romantic getaway, then I want it to be someplace fresh, someplace new. Especially when it's our first time going away together." He stroked a thumb over her knuckles before gently squeezing her hand. "I want to take you someplace that you'll remember because of me, because of us, and no one else. Does that make sense?"

How was she supposed to get her night in the cottage if he refused to go? All sorts of dramatic scenarios played through her mind: running away and having him chase her there, having her car break down on the property so he'd have to come and get her, being kidnapped by Bigfoot and left for dead at the cabin… She almost chuckled out loud at that last one, but if she got desperate enough, she knew she could come up with some way to get him to that cottage.

She noticed that Brian was looking at her expectantly

and realized she never answered him. "Of course it makes sense. I guess I just wanted to share something that is a big part of my life with you. I know the cottage isn't any big deal, but I always wanted to spend the night there and never had anyone to do that with."

"What about Mason?"

"Oh." She waved him off, pulling her hand from his. "Mason hated the mountains and was merely tolerating having the wedding there because it was what I wanted. He didn't want to spend the night there at all." She smiled sadly at Brian. "I guess I wanted to have my moment, my night, with you."

Well hell, how was he supposed to say no to that? Those big sweet eyes were wide as saucers looking at him, and in that moment he knew he'd give her anything she wanted. Even if it meant spending the night in the one place he should be avoiding at all costs.

Chapter 7

LATER THAT NIGHT, AVA LAY IN THE DARK LISTENING to Brian breathing and said a silent prayer of thanks that he didn't out and out refuse her request of going to the cottage. But it worried her that he was still sensitive about Mason. How were they going to overcome this? There was no doubt in her mind that she was completely over Mason and he was over her. The man was getting married; how much more over her could he be?

Maybe she and Brian should consider getting together with Mason and making sure there were no hard feelings. Then maybe Brian would change his mind about the cottage. She turned her head and studied his shadow in the dark and smiled. She said a little prayer that he would soften toward the idea. It was a part of who she was and what she wanted for her happily ever after.

Surely that wasn't asking too much, was it?

—⁓—

Two days later as they were sharing dinner, Ava decided the best course of action was just to throw it out there and hope for the best.

"I think we should get together with Mason."

Brian almost choked on his food. "What?"

"Well, it seems like you maybe have some outstanding issues with him and I thought it would be best if we all sat down together and talked about it. You know, cleared the air."

"Wait a minute," he said, rising from his chair to pace the kitchen. "Are you seriously suggesting we just…go out for drinks or something with him?"

Ava nodded.

"And his fiancée?"

She nodded again.

"Why?"

"You clearly have some major hang-ups about my relationship with Mason and it's becoming an issue with us!"

"*An issue?* You asked me one time to go to one place and I mentioned that I wasn't crazy about the idea and now all of a sudden we have issues because of it? It seems to me that you are the one with the issue, Ava. For whatever reason, you seem to be a little preoccupied with going to this cottage."

"I'm not preoccupied, Brian," she countered as a small amount of panic began to set in. "I enjoy going there and it's been a while since I've been there. I thought it would be romantic, but if it's that big of an *issue* for you, then just forget about it. I'll go to the damn interview by myself. I wouldn't want you to feel uncomfortable or anything." She was steaming mad and started clearing the dinner table even though they'd barely touched their food. Brian stopped her before she dumped their dinner.

"Okay, okay," he said calmly. "Let's take a step back here." He took a deep breath and looked Ava in the eye. "I'll admit your announcement about meeting Mason took me by surprise. I just never considered the possibility of us needing to do this."

Placing the dishes back on the table, she then turned to face him. "I thought I was being helpful. I thought if I could show you that it doesn't bother me to speak to Mason and I'm okay with hanging out with him, then you'd see there is nothing for you to worry about."

Brian placed his hands on her shoulders and pulled her a little bit closer. "I was never worried about you and Mason, Ava. I just don't want to live in the shadow of that relationship. I want us to have a fresh start—go to places that are purely ours and nobody else's."

Trying to mask her disappointment, she nodded in agreement. "I can't help that I love that place, Brian. It's a part of my life, my family, my heritage. I'm never going to *not* want to go there. Can't we just go this one time and start fresh on the next getaway?"

Again, Brian had a hard time denying her anything. "I guess I never felt that kind of connection to a place so it's hard for me to understand your feeling so strongly about a house."

"I want you to understand that I feel the way I do because of good family memories. It has nothing to do with Mason." She snuggled in close to him and hugged him. "So are we okay now?"

Kissing the top of her head, he smiled. "Yeah, we're good." Then he pulled back and looked at her and his smile grew. "Does this mean we can skip going out with Mason?"

Giggling, Ava playfully punched him on the arm as she pulled free of his embrace. "Are you kidding me? I wouldn't miss this for the world!"

The next night, Ava was kicking herself for not backing out when she had the chance. They were seated in a too-small booth in a local hotel bar. It was the four of them—Ava, Brian, Mason, and his new fiancée Melissa. It took all of five minutes for everyone to catch up on their lives before silence fell among them. Ava seriously considered ordering shots for them all just so they'd have something to do, but then, luckily, Mason broke the silence.

"So, Ava tells me the two of you have been dating for about two months now," he said to Brian, who simply nodded.

And they were back to silence again.

"So, Melissa, tell me about the big wedding plans!" Her voice was overly enthusiastic but she was hoping no one else noticed it. Soon she and the young paralegal were engrossed in their own conversation about dresses and caterers and the men were all but forgotten.

Brian finally looked at Mason. "So, seriously," he began, clearing his throat, "are you okay with this? With me and Ava?"

Mason smiled. "I knew probably before you did that you had feelings for her. It just pissed me off that what you were telling me back then was going to mess up my plans. As it turns out, you did me a huge favor." He paused and smiled across the table at Melissa, who beamed a sappy smile right back at him. "I can see now all that was missing from my relationship with Ava. Melissa makes me happy. We both want the same things. I'm sorry it took me so long to realize what you were saying was the truth. Chalk it up to ego, pride, and whatnot."

"I'm glad for you, I really am," Brian admitted, feeling

relaxed for the first time that evening. "And I have to admit, I'm happy, too. She's everything I ever wanted."

"I know," Mason said sincerely. "I don't want things to be awkward between us. You're one of my best friends and I don't want to lose you, man. Believe me, I thought this would be weird. When Ava called me I was a little shocked, but I think everything worked out for the best."

"I have to agree," Brian said, and reached under the table for Ava's hand and squeezed. When she turned her head and smiled at him, Brian felt as if someone had a fist around his heart. She was so beautiful, so amazing, and he didn't think he'd ever get used to knowing that she was his.

That night he took her home with him to his place. There was a sense of urgency, a need to show her exactly how much she meant to him. From the moment he turned the lock on the front door, his seduction began. Without words, he leaned in and kissed her. Wrapped in his arms, Ava let out a sweet sigh that always managed to bring him to his knees. They kissed until they were breathless, and when Brian finally lifted his head, Ava's passion-glazed eyes told him all he needed to know.

He swept Ava up into his arms, wanting nothing more than to love her all night long. When her arms went around him, Brian knew he would never grow tired of this, of her. If anything, his need for her grew stronger every day. Luckily, Ava's need matched his. They moved together as if they were doing a choreographed dance and yet every touch, every sigh, was new. There was a new, heightened level to their intimacy and though not a word had been spoken since they arrived home, he knew they had said more to each other than ever before.

As the sun rose all too soon the next morning, he finally allowed himself to say what he'd been holding back since she'd come back into his life.

"I love you."

Chapter 8

THE NEXT MORNING AVA KNEW SHE'D HEARD HIM; she'd heard his whispered "I love you" and fought the urge to say it back. She felt exactly the same way and she wanted to scream it from the rooftops but quickly reminded herself that she was waiting for the perfect moment. She just had to wait one more week to say it!

As much as she loved the Callahan legend of the cottage and all that went with it, it was a heck of an inconvenience right now when all she wanted to do was greet Brian when he came out of the shower with an "I love you too."

Why was she fighting this so hard? Why was she trying so hard to orchestrate something that others let happen naturally?

Her thoughts immediately went to Ean and Lacey. They had just…known. There was no planning or waiting for the exact right moment; they led with their hearts. Or maybe… She sighed. Maybe it was easy for them because they had been at the cottage. *Any couple who spends the night in the Christmas Cottage shall have love everlasting…*

She wasn't asking for the impossible!

Darn legend! And darn her for being such a slave to tradition! Why did it seem to consume her more than any other member of her family? Ean didn't believe in it and yet he had gotten to experience it for himself with Lacey! Of course, Ean was a guy so maybe that had something to do with it, but all of her aunts and cousins… Well, they had thought it all enchanting, but none of them seemed as consumed with it as Ava was.

Why was that?

She had no time to analyze that before Brian was standing before her wearing nothing but a towel and a grin. "Good morning, beautiful," he murmured as he leaned in and kissed her. "Did you sleep okay?" Her blush said it all. "I've got a ton of appointments today, and I'm meeting Ean later on to discuss his plans for the house again. Now that they're settled in with the baby, he said they're ready to get serious with the extension."

"That's great! Are you meeting him at the house or his office?"

"He's actually coming to my office. He's my final appointment for the day, and we're going to go over some plans and discuss what exactly they want to do and how we can accomplish that without disrupting Lacey and the baby too much."

"Good luck with that," she said lightly, rising from the bed to stretch and then wrap her arms around him. "I haven't had any opportunity to observe the new family at home. Ean's always at work when I stop by, but they seem to be the stereotypical paranoid new parents. If I know my brother, he'll end up renting someplace for them to live while the construction is going on."

Brian's eyes widened. "Seriously?"

Ava nodded. "Unfortunately, yes. Ean is a computer geek who likes to work with little to no noise around him, and Lacey is constantly shushing me if I talk too loud while Olivia is sleeping. Trust me, it would be to your benefit if they moved out for a while."

"It seems a little extreme, don't you think?"

"For normal people, yes. For the two of them? No."

"Wow…thanks for the heads-up. Now I won't look like a deer in the headlights should he bring that up later on."

"My pleasure. Too bad Lacey sold her condo when they got married. It would have been nice if they had a backup for a situation like this."

"Well, be realistic, Ava, who honestly thinks they'll need a backup place to live? I mean, maybe they can stay with you or with your parents during the construction. It wouldn't be for long."

"Believe me, I would love to have them stay with me, but I think it would put a damper on us having any alone time," she said with a sexy grin as she reached up and kissed him again, deeply.

"I certainly don't want to put a damper on us," he whispered as he returned the kiss and slowly eased her back down onto the bed. "That would not be a good thing." He gently kissed her lips, her jaw, her throat, and was rewarded with a purr of delight.

"No, that would be terrible." She sighed and reached for his towel. "Let them find their own place to live."

And that was the last of that conversation for a while.

"So you still haven't told him."

Ava gave an exasperated sigh as she cradled the phone to her ear. "No, Lace, I still haven't told him. Why do you ask?"

"Well, I just figured you would have called me if you did finally say the words, and being that I haven't heard from you in a couple of days I thought I should ask. Inquiring minds and all that…"

"I'm trying to find the perfect time to tell him. I want the first time I say I love you to Brian to be someplace special, someplace perfect."

"Oh, sweetie," Lacey said with a laugh, "enough with the perfect!"

"Not you too," Ava grumbled.

"What? What about me too?"

"Brian is tired of me talking about things being perfect, so we've had to agree to disagree on that topic and now it seems as if the word has been deleted from his vocabulary. I don't see what the big deal is."

"Look, everyone has their idea of how they want their life to go and what they want to accomplish, but you are missing out on so much because you are always trying to stage things so that they're 'perfect'! And while you may have convinced yourself of how perfect they are, the truth is, it's not real."

"How can you say that? When have I ever staged anything?" Ava cried in despair.

"When have you ever…? C'mon, Ava, do you honestly hear yourself?" Lacey laughed again, hoping to soften what she had to say. "Your whole wedding to Mason was staged. You became obsessed with how everything had to be, down to the tiniest detail!"

"That's not staging, Lacey, that was me being detail-oriented."

"That's a load of hooey and you know it. You wanted everything to look like a page out of a bridal magazine."

"There's nothing wrong with that."

"No, normally there's not, but it wasn't because you liked how those things looked, you liked it for what you thought it would represent. That is where the problem lies."

"There is no problem." Ava sighed.

"Okay, let's just say, for the moment, that there is no problem. When do you plan on telling Brian that you love him?"

"Well, we're going up to Asheville on Friday because I have an interview with a university up there, and we're going to spend the weekend at the cottage and I was thinking…"

"I see exactly where this is going. You're going to take Brian up to the cottage—which you will somehow manage to have set up or decorated or whatever to your specifications—so you can tell him you love him and have your night there because you think that's what you need to be happy. Why can't you just let nature take its course and tell Brian that you love him now? Do you honestly need to wait to be up in the mountains to be sure that's how you feel about him?"

"No, but…who wouldn't want a setting like that?"

Lacey let out a soft chuckle. "No one knows better than I do the wondrous effects of a romantic setting, Ava. I'd be lying if I said it didn't play a part in Ean and I getting together. But you have to understand, we were still able to say that we loved each other without being there."

"But it helped," Ava insisted.

"Ava, it's a beautiful place with a romantic history."

"But…"

"But…what's different about being up there from being here, other than geography?"

"Well, it's just that…um…I just wanted…"

"Yes?" Lacey inquired.

"I wanted it to be romantic." Ava thought for sure her statement would bring an end to their argument.

"So you're saying the two of you have done nothing romantic at all since you've been dating?"

"No, that's not it at all, we do plenty of romantic stuff."

"So why wait?"

"Why are you obsessing about this? Did I harass you about telling Ean that you loved him?"

"As a matter of fact, you did! And my reasons for waiting to say it had to do with my fear of commitment and you making me doubt my feelings for him!"

"Me? What did I do?"

"You had me second-guessing my feelings for Ean and wondering if they were true or if I was under some ridiculous spell!"

"It's not ridiculous. Family history has proven…"

"This is so not the time for the reciting of the tale!" Lacey was getting frustrated and if Ava were in front of her right now, she'd slap her on the back of the head. "There was nothing staged about my time with Ean. Nature took its course and it wouldn't have mattered if we'd never gone to the cottage."

"I'm not saying I *need* the cottage…"

"Then don't go," Lacey said flatly. "Tell Brian you love him and don't go to the cottage."

"But I want to," Ava said. "I can't explain it. There is something magical, something wonderful and dreamy, and I want to experience it for myself and then I'll know, finally, what all the fuss was about."

"Look, I will give you that—there is definitely

something magical and…and wonderful about the cottage. It's quaint and lovely and when you're there, it's like you're in your own little world. But…"

"I knew it! I knew you felt it too!"

"You know what, Ava? I'm done. You're not really listening to me and you're going to do what you want to do and there's nothing I can do to stop you. I'm just worried it's like it was with your wedding. All of the signs were right there in front of you but you refused to see them."

"I'm not making a mistake with Brian. I love him."

"That's the thing, Ava, I know that you do. You know that you do. You don't need geography to confirm that."

"Says the woman who was blessed with it," she mumbled.

Suddenly Lacey had a brainstorm. "The saying clearly says that any couple who spends the night in the cottage will have love everlasting. It never says it has to be the place where you proclaim your love for one another for the *first time*."

"But it can't hurt."

Lacey considered banging her own head against the nearest wall. "Okay, let's just agree to disagree and move on, okay? What are you doing on Thursday?"

"Um, nothing. Why?"

"Well, I have a meeting with a potential client all the way in Charlotte. Ean's going to go with me but we need someone to stay with Olivia for the day. I thought that maybe…"

"Done! Look no further, I am totally here for you."

Lacey smiled at the enthusiasm in Ava's voice. "You'll need to be here early because we want to be on the road by eight, and we probably won't get home until dinner so it will be a long day."

"Not a problem. We're leaving for Asheville on Friday morning so I have nothing to do except pack."

And plan, Lacey thought to herself but decided to keep her mouth shut on the subject. "I'll have everything you'll need to know written down for you, and you have both of our cell numbers, and if you needed anything, your mom could always swing by."

"Please, I am so *not* going to need my mom to stop by. Olivia and I are going to be fine. This will be some quality bonding time for us and we'll have a blast."

"You realize she's not even three months old, right? She doesn't know how to have a blast yet."

"She will by the time you get back," Ava said confidently.

"Maybe I should call your mom…"

"Don't you dare! Relax, it's not like I'm going to take her out and get her pierced and tattooed, you know."

"I know, I know, but this will be the first time we're leaving her so I'm just a little twitchy, okay? Someday you'll understand how it feels."

"Any idea on when that will be?" Ava said, only partially joking.

"When the time is right, Ava," Lacey replied. "When the time is right, everything will fall into place for you."

"I hope you're right, Lace. But I've got to be honest, the waiting is killing me."

Lacey laughed. "Me too!"

~~~

Thursday morning dawned sunny and bright and Ava was practically bouncing on her toes when she rang Lacey and Ean's doorbell at seven a.m. Ean opened the door, looking less than excited to be awake. "You're early," he said as he stepped aside to let her in.

"Still not a morning person," she said as she twirled beyond him and went in search of her niece. "I thought it might be easier for the two of you to get ready if I got here early."

It was hard to argue with that. "Thank you," he said grumpily. "We didn't get a whole lot of sleep last night. I think Olivia's cutting a tooth. We took turns getting up with her, but it's hard to sleep when she's crying."

"Oh, my poor princess," Ava said and then laughed at Ean's angry expression. "Not you, you idiot, I'm talking about Olivia! Geez, get a grip. I'm worried about her. Anything I'll need to know for today?"

"Lacey's got the list," he said as he led Ava into the kitchen where coffee was waiting for them.

Sure enough, there on the table was a four-page-long list. There was everything from the pediatrician's phone number to a diagram of the house with everything Olivia could need listed and marked, along with the best fire escapes. Ava rolled her eyes but held her tongue; no need to poke the bear this morning.

Within minutes, Ean was heading up to the master suite to take a shower and get ready while Lacey headed down to the kitchen with a very content-looking Olivia in her arms. At the puzzled look on Ava's face, Lacey spoke. "She was miserable all night, but she's been nothing but smiles all morning. Hopefully that will be the case all day." And then she launched into her whole presentation on how to care for Olivia.

Ava listened to every word—with one ear—because at the same time, she was smiling and making goofy faces that were making Olivia giggle. When she noticed that Lacey had stopped speaking, she looked up to see Lacey staring at her expectantly.

"I got it, every word, I swear. You've got everything written down here and I have your numbers. I'm not an idiot, Lace. I can handle babysitting for the day. Don't worry." With that, she pushed Lacey toward the stairs and ordered her to go get ready. Once she was out of earshot she turned Olivia in her arms and smiled. "You must be exhausted from dealing with your mommy and daddy all day long!"

Olivia cooed in response. And so their day together began.

By two o'clock, Ava was approaching exhaustion. Who knew that caring for one tiny baby could be so much work? While Olivia hadn't been overly fussy, it was the keeping her entertained, cleaned, and fed that had Ava feeling more than a little worn out. Lacey and Ean's home was spacious, and while the bedrooms were all on the second level, they kept a lot of Olivia's supplies on the main level to keep from having to run up and down the stairs.

Having finally put Olivia down for a nap, she decided to call Brian and see how his day was going.

"It's all business as usual here," he said. "But you sound a little tired. How's it going over there?"

Ava told him about her morning—how comical it had been to get the nervous parents out the door and how they checked in with her hourly. They both laughed. "I always knew my brother was going to be like this, but I expected a little more from Lacey."

"I'm sure all new parents act like that. What time did they say they'd be home?"

"Around dinnertime. Why?"

"Well, Ean texted me that he left some papers there in his home office for me to look at. I guess he figured I'd be stopping by to see you."

"That would be great! What time will you be done for the day?"

"I'm hoping to be done by four. Are you sure you won't mind having me stop by? I know we had plans for later and that we're leaving tomorrow for the mountains, but I don't want to intrude on your girl time with Olivia." His tone was light and playful and it just made Ava love him even more.

"Aren't you sweet," she gushed. "But I would love for you to come by and hang out with us. She's such a sweet baby, and as much as it's been a bit tiring trying to keep to Lacey's schedule, it's been a great day."

"Well then, I'll plan on seeing you sometime around four thirty, okay?"

They had no sooner hung up than the home phone rang. Ava didn't need to look at the caller ID to see who was calling. "Oh my God! She's sleeping! She's fine! I haven't burned the house down! Stop calling!" she said in place of a greeting.

Ean chuckled in response. "Well, I'm glad she's been okay for you. After last night we weren't so sure it was a good idea to leave her, but the doctor told us this was all normal. Has she slept for you a whole lot?"

"Actually, she just went down a little while ago so I'm thinking I'll have an hour or two to regroup."

"Exhausting little thing, isn't she?"

"Who knew, right?"

Again he laughed. "Listen, we really appreciate all that you're doing and how you came over to help us out today. It's been great to just get out of the house together, even if it was work related."

"I'm sure Lacey's gotten a little tired of sitting at home. She's too hard of a worker to sit still for so long."

"That's the truth. The thing is, we are both exhausted. Lacey nearly fell asleep while waiting to do her presentation, and I feel a little like the walking dead myself."

"Wait, what are you saying?"

"I'm saying I don't feel up to another three hours of driving. If you're okay with it, we'd love to just sort of crash at a hotel here in Charlotte and head home tomorrow."

"Well, I did have plans with Brian for tonight…"

"You can invite him over! Get some takeout. That's fine with us."

"And we're planning on leaving for Asheville in the morning. I have an interview tomorrow afternoon."

"We'll be home by ten, I promise."

Ava thought about it for a minute and was just about to answer when Ean spoke again. "If you can't, I can call Mom and Dad and have them come over. Honestly, we don't want to inconvenience you, Ava. We're just so darn tired." Ava didn't need to be convinced; she had seen him that morning and could hear it in his voice right now.

"It's no problem, Ean. Go find someplace nice to stay. Order room service and get some sleep. And I mean sleep—no using this as a romantic getaway. The two of you looked way too tired this morning."

"Believe me, romance is the last thing on our minds.

The thought of a full night's sleep is far more tempting than anything else right now." His words were followed by Lacey yelling "*Hey!*" in the background and Ean's cry of pain. "She just punched me on the arm. I can say with great certainty that nothing romantic is going to happen tonight."

Ava wasn't so sure, but she promised to take excellent care of their daughter and hung up after promising to call if there were any problems. It looked as if she were going to get the full babysitting experience. A whole night with an infant. That didn't sound scary at all, did it?

She placed the baby monitor next to her and decided to take advantage of the quiet right now and grab herself a nap. Setting the alarm on her cell phone, she settled on the sofa and dozed off quickly.

All too soon she was awake again and thinking about what else she would need to get done before Olivia woke up. First stop was the kitchen to make sure bottles were made. Check. Next she searched for something to make for dinner but came up with nothing. There was a folder on the kitchen counter with takeout menus, so she decided to follow Ean's advice and just order in. Dinner? Check.

Walking around the house, she made sure things were picked up and put away so when Brian arrived she wouldn't have much to do but spend time with him and Olivia. A glance at the clock told her he'd be there in about thirty minutes. Deciding the only thing that needed freshening up was herself, Ava ran up the stairs and utilized Lacey's master bath. Next she went to the guest room and felt giddy at the thought of her and Brian sleeping there tonight. It would be like this was their home and Olivia was their daughter.

And she sighed.

It was such a pleasant thought and it felt so good, so right, that for a moment, she hoped her brother and his wife would stay away longer. Then she remembered her big plans for the weekend and why they needed to get up to the mountains as soon as possible.

That thought made her smile. She couldn't wait to see the look on Brian's face when she finally told him she loved him too. Would he be surprised? Happy? Ready to start planning their future together?

Her daydream was interrupted by the very loud cry from the very small person in the next room. Ava quickly fled the guest room and went to comfort her distressed niece. "Shh…" she cooed. "It's all okay, Aunt Ava is here for you," she said softly as she lifted Olivia from the crib and proceeded to get her changed and took her back downstairs. She wanted her to look fresh and clean, and most of all happy, when Brian arrived.

Ava settled on the sofa with Olivia, waiting for his arrival. She talked all kinds of gibberish to keep Olivia entertained and seemed to be doing a good job of it. With every silly face and sound, Olivia giggled and kicked her tiny arms and legs. Ava found herself singing nursery rhymes and was totally oblivious to the sound of Brian entering the house.

Walking in and seeing Ava cradling baby Olivia stopped Brian cold. Seeing her sitting there, he suddenly imagined this was their own home, that she was holding their child. The realization that he wanted that vision right now hit him hard. Taking a minute to calm his pounding heart, he had to take a step back and not alert her to his presence just yet.

"Brian? Is that you?"

Damn, he wasn't as quiet as he'd thought. "Yeah, it's me," he said as he walked into the room and smiled, and was rewarded with one of Ava's that looked way more serene than he'd ever seen. "You're looking pretty content there, Ava," he said.

"I'm feeling very content." She sighed, looking down at Olivia. "Isn't she just beautiful? I still can't believe how in love with her I am." She looked back up at Brian. "I just keep touching her little toes and her hands and her cheek and I'm just blown away at how overwhelmed I feel. Is that crazy?"

The glow on her face, the sheer joy he saw there left him speechless. To cover up his own emotion Brian came and knelt beside them to seemingly get a closer view of the baby. The truth was he just wanted to be close to Ava and needed a minute to compose himself. "I don't think it's crazy," he finally said, his voice a little more gruff than he intended. "I think she's pretty amazing, too." They shared a long gaze before Olivia began to fuss.

"She's probably just hungry," Ava said softly as she rose from the sofa and headed toward the kitchen. Brian followed.

"I'll let you get her settled while I look around. Ean said he left some notes on requested materials in his office, so I'll take care of that."

"Sounds like a plan."

"What time are they due back here tonight?" Brian asked.

"Oh, actually, Ean called a little while ago with a change of plans. They're going to take advantage of having a free babysitter and are spending the night in Charlotte. So I'll be staying here tonight." She watched the disappointment creep across Brian's face. "You're more than welcome to join me." When he was about to speak, she said preemptively, "It's okay, Lacey and Ean are more than okay with you staying here with me—they suggested it, actually."

His relief was obvious. Brian nodded in agreement and then headed for Ean's home office to search for the paperwork and to catch his breath a little. Staying here with Ava and Olivia for the night would allow him the opportunity to live the fantasy for a little while longer. He sat down at Ean's desk and picked up the papers, but wasn't really seeing them.

"I'm being ridiculous," he mumbled to himself. "I should not be getting this worked up over spending the night babysitting. What am I, twelve?" He gave himself a snort of derision and tried once again to focus on the paperwork. He heard Olivia cry from the other room, followed by Ava's soothing tone; whatever it was that she said or did must have worked because the baby quieted instantly.

In all of their time together, in all their conversations, Brian realized that they never touched on the subject of the future—weddings, kids, the whole shebang. Why hadn't they? The picture of Ava sitting with Olivia in her arms popped into his head and refused to budge. "Well, that's going to change tonight," Brian vowed. Maybe if they talked about it and put it out there in the open, he'd be able to breathe; he'd be able to focus on his work and not spend so much time in his own head trying to figure out where his life was going.

He felt a moment of panic when he thought about it being too soon; was he rushing things? Would Ava feel pressured if he began talking about wanting to marry her and have babies with her? Maybe she'd just think this was due to them being caretakers tonight for her niece. Maybe she'd think it was fun for them to play house for a night.

Or maybe she'd just think he was completely insane.

If nothing else, Brian wanted Ava to at least start thinking about a future with him. There was nothing wrong with that, was there? Why shouldn't they talk about it? He wasn't ashamed of how he was feeling, and although Ava hadn't said she loved him yet, it was there in her eyes, in her touch, in the way they made love.

Shaking his head, he felt better now that he had a plan. Finally, he was able to focus on the papers in front of him and went about the job he originally came here to do. The sooner he got that done, the sooner he could join Ava and Olivia.

"She looks so small in this crib."

"And so peaceful."

They both looked down at a now-sleeping Olivia and sighed. Together they'd played with her, fed her, changed her, all while Brian looked over Ean's plans and Ava ordered them dinner. They ate while Olivia sat and watched from her infant swing. "Yeah, so peaceful," Ava said, echoing his words.

Brian waited a beat. "How can something so small be so loud?"

"I know, right? That child has some set of lungs on

her." They started to laugh but when Olivia started to stir, Ava put her fingers to her lips to silence them. Brian wrapped his arms around her waist as he stood behind her and pulled her in close. "I think she just missed her mommy and daddy."

"She's too young to miss them."

Ava elbowed him in the ribs. "She is not too young to miss them. Her whole little life has been spent with just the two of them. They've been gone all day, and I think she was fine until the whole bedtime ritual fell apart."

"Ava, I have no idea how to sing 'The Itsy Bitsy Spider.' And who is she to be such a critic?"

She chuckled in response. "All in all I think we did a good job as last-minute replacements."

"Sure, I don't think we scarred her for life or anything."

Ava stiffened in his arms. "That's not possible, is it? Oh God, Lacey will never let me babysit again if I traumatized Olivia."

Turning her in his arms, Brian placed a gentle kiss on the tip of her nose. "Relax, Ava, we didn't traumatize their daughter. She's been fed and cleaned and changed and now she's sleeping like a…well, like a baby. She's fine. Stop worrying."

Standing on tiptoes, Ava kissed Brian on the cheek. "Thank you for helping with her tonight. I had no idea how exhausting one tiny person can be. I have a whole new respect for Lacey."

"I'm sure Ean does his share of the work, too, you know."

Ava took him by the hand and led him out of the room. "I'm sure he does something, but I'm not exactly sure what it is. All I know is that Lacey is the one at home with her every day, and after the day I had—and it was only one—I know I could sleep for a week." They were standing at the door to the guest room.

"So," he began in a husky tone, "speaking of sleeping…"

She looked up at him and smiled. "Olivia still doesn't sleep through the night. Would you be terribly upset if we just…slept?" Her words were said shyly and she actually felt herself blush.

Placing a finger beneath her chin, Brian tipped her face up toward his. "Sweetheart, we don't have to make love every night of the week. I love just sleeping with you in my arms."

He followed that with a kiss that was so soft, so tender, Ava felt like her bones were melting. She tried to deepen the kiss, but Brian slowly pulled away and trailed a finger along her cheek to her neck and finally placed a hand on her shoulder. "Get ready for bed. I'm going to go downstairs and make sure we're all locked up and the alarm is set and everything's put away."

"You don't have to do that, this was my responsibility today and…"

A finger on her lips stopped her. "I know I don't have to, Ava. I want to. Let me help you. Let me take care of you. You spent the whole day caring for Olivia and you deserve some rest. Go," he said and turned her toward the bedroom. "I'll be back in five minutes."

"Okay." She sighed with gratitude. She was in the bed in fewer than five minutes, and by the time Brian returned, she was already half asleep. She watched as he undressed and climbed in the bed beside her, and sighed with contentment as he pulled her in close. "Thank you," she whispered.

"For what?" he asked, settling her head on his shoulder as he gently combed his fingers through her silky blond hair.

"For being you," she said, and then she was asleep.

While he would have liked to spend more time just talking with her, there was something just as wonderful in having her lying in his arms like this. The afternoon and evening had flown by. He had to admit, although it was early by his own standards, he was a bit tired himself. Who knew babies were so much work?

Beside him, Ava sighed and snuggled closer. They did have a lot of fun trying to figure out all of the mysteries of an infant. What made Olivia happy one minute made her cry the next. Maybe Ava was right and Olivia simply missed her parents. It seemed a bit odd to him for a baby to actually miss someone, but Brian guessed the parent/child bond was just that strong.

So many times over the course of the evening he'd looked over at Ava as she held the baby and just felt his gut clench. It was very easy for him to temporarily forget they weren't married and that it wasn't their child she was holding. It fit; it worked. They worked well together tonight with Olivia. True, it was only for a few short hours, but for two people who had never spent time together with a child, they honestly and truly survived it and had fun doing it.

At one point when Olivia had been particularly upset, the look of pure devastation on Ava's face broke his heart. He knew she was hurting for her niece and would do anything to make her feel better. How much more would she be willing to do for a child of her own? Their own?

He wrapped an arm around her a little tighter and sighed with contentment. Soon. They would talk about their future soon. Tonight ended up not being the right night. Ava was focused on caring for the baby and not letting Lacey and Ean down. She needed to put all of her energy into being the caretaker this evening, and he wasn't so selfish that he would try to distract her from her responsibility.

Soon, though, he thought. He wanted a future with Ava and he wanted that future to start as soon as possible.

Chapter 9

OLIVIA HAD ONLY WOKEN UP ONCE IN THE NIGHT AND both Ava and Brian had gotten up to tend to her together. While Ava had changed her and soothed her, Brian had gone down and heated up a bottle for her. Ava sat in the rocking chair in the nursery while Brian then went and made himself a middle-of-the-night snack and was back just as Ava was placing the baby back in the crib. All in all, it was a pretty uneventful evening and before they knew it they were all going back to sleep.

When the alarm went off at seven, Ava felt she'd gotten a pretty decent night's sleep. She took a quick shower while Olivia was still sleeping, and as she got out and got herself ready for the day, Brian hopped into the shower.

Lacey texted at seven thirty that they were on the road. Somewhere near eight, Olivia let out her first sleepy cry. Ava tended to her niece and by the time she had her cleaned up and dressed, Brian was emerging from the guest room looking too delicious for words and as if he was ready to tackle the day.

"I'm going to head back to my place in a few minutes to go pack up for the weekend and I'll meet you back here. What time did Lacey and Ean say they'd be back?"

"Sometime around ten," she replied. "You don't have to come back here if you don't want to, we can just meet up at my place at noon. Most of my stuff is packed, so we'll just need to grab my bags and go."

"What time is the interview?"

"Four, so we'll be under a time crunch."

"No worries. If you dress for the interview, we can go directly there and I'll hang out while you're in your meeting, and then we'll head to your parents' place. What do you think?" He took Olivia from Ava's arms as they prepared to head down the stairs.

"That works for me. So, my place? Noon?"

"I think I'm still going to head back here first. I want to just run a few things by Ean, and then I'll head over to you." He settled Olivia into her swing and set it in motion before turning back to Ava.

"You're a natural with her, you know," Ava said.

"So are you," he replied. "We make a good team." He wanted so badly to say something about how good they would be with their own kids, but didn't want to take a chance of seeming pushy, especially if she wasn't on the same page with him.

"Well, she's my niece, so we've got a bit of a connection. But you? Most guys aren't so at ease around babies. Do you have any nieces or nephews?" It hit Ava just then how little she knew about his family.

"Unfortunately, no. I'm an only child, so the only kids I get to be around belong to friends."

"Well, you are definitely a natural with them. Olivia is completely smitten with you." As if to prove her point, when Brian turned to look down at Olivia, she seemed to blow raspberries at him and then giggled. "See? She's flirting with you."

Brian turned and wrapped Ava in his arms and kissed

her. "She's a little young for me. Besides, the only woman I want flirting with me is her smoking-hot aunt."

"Smoking-hot aunt, huh? I think I like that title."

"I'll have the T-shirt made," he joked and released her. "Let me head out of here before it gets too late. I'll be back in about an hour and a half. Don't do anything to traumatize Olivia," he teased and headed for the door.

"Not funny," she called after him but she was grinning from ear to ear. Looking down at Olivia, she continued to smile. "Okay, little miss, let's get you fed and ready to see your mommy and daddy." With that she lifted her up and together they went to the kitchen in search of breakfast.

Lacey came barreling through the door at exactly ten o'clock. She looked more relaxed than she had the previous morning but had the harried look of a mother who had missed her baby. "Is she awake? Did she go down for a nap yet?"

"Please, like I would put her down before you got home," Ava said with an eye roll. "We were just reading about bunnies and although I, for one, am anxious to hear how the story ends, I don't think Olivia would mind if we waited until next time."

Lacey scooped the baby from Ava's arms and held her tight. "Oh, I cannot believe how much I missed her," she said, her voice catching. "We thought it would be no big deal to be away for one night, but I have to tell you, it was like a giant part of me was missing! I just can't believe how hard it was."

"Well, technically, she is a part of you," Ava

observed. "It's only natural that you'd miss her." She stopped speaking for a moment to watch Olivia place her tiny hands on Lacey's face and thought how much she would love to have a child of her own do that to her. Clearing her throat, she spoke again. "So, how did the meeting go?"

Sitting down on the floor and not taking her eyes from her daughter, Lacey replied, "It all went very well. They're an architectural firm moving their operations here to Raleigh and they wanted to get started on making plans for their new offices. The building's not even done yet, but it's never too soon to start."

"Couldn't your firm send somebody else for the pre-liminaries? I mean, why interrupt your maternity leave for this?"

Lacey finally looked at Ava. "Actually, this is my first step in branching out on my own."

Ava stared at her for a moment in confusion. "Wait, what? What do you mean, branching out on your own? Aren't you going back to work?"

"Oh, I am. I'm just going to be doing it for myself now. I'm starting my own company."

"Wow! I'm so excited for you! I know it's what you always wanted—I just didn't think you were ready yet. You know, because of Olivia."

"I know, I know. But actually, now is kind of the perfect time because I'll be able to make my own hours and have time to spend with her and not have to put her in day care or anything. I didn't say anything about it because I didn't want to jinx it. I figured if the meeting didn't go well, we'd stick to our original plan of my going back to work part time."

"But it did go well," Ava said with a smile.

"It certainly did," Lacey replied, beaming.

"I am so excited for you guys. I think it's great news. We are definitely going to need to celebrate." Then she stopped and thought for a minute. "So this extension on the house is going to also include work space for you, right? That was the new stuff Ean added to the plans?"

Lacey nodded. "Do you think I'm doing the right thing? Am I being completely crazy?"

"I think you are an inspiration, my friend."

"Me? Why?"

"You keep chasing a dream. You went after your man, you got married, had a baby, bought a house, and now you're doing what you always said you would. I'm so proud of you."

"Dammit, Ava, I'm still hormonal. Don't make me cry."

Ava leaned over and hugged her. "It's okay, Supergirl. You're allowed to cry happy tears." She gave her another squeeze. "Okay," Ava said as she rose from the sofa. "I need to get home and finish packing for the weekend. I've got that interview at four and…"

"Is this a position you're interested in?" Lacey asked, coming to her feet as well.

"It's all right, I guess. Nothing has wowed me so far, but I keep hoping."

She looked up as Ean walked into the room and came over to take Olivia into his arms and kiss her hello. The scene was beyond sweet and Ava felt like an intruder watching it all. "I better get going."

Ean turned and looked at her. "Big interview today, huh?"

"Could be, who knows?" she replied.

"Where are you guys staying? That great new resort up there looks amazing. What's it called?"

"We're staying at the cottage," she said, a bit defensively.

Ean couldn't mask his disappointment. "You're kidding, right?"

"What is so wrong with going to the cottage for the weekend?"

"Ava," he said with exasperation. "All I'm saying is please don't turn this weekend into some kind of crazy production and put all kinds of pressure on yourself or Brian, or the cottage for that matter. If you're just looking for a nice getaway, then go and enjoy it. But don't let yourself believe the cottage is the be-all, end-all for your happiness."

"Thanks for the advice," she said flippantly as she headed for the door. "Olivia's had her breakfast and she's clean and changed and ready for the day." She looked over at Lacey. "I'll call you when I get back."

And then she was gone.

"That was your idea of brotherly advice?" Lacey asked him after the door shut.

"You and I both know from personal experience what she was like at this time last year over that cottage."

Lacey had to agree. "Nothing anyone has said to her has changed her mind, though."

"Maybe the wrong person is talking to her," Ean said and kissed his wife on the cheek and then his daughter, and then headed out of the room and into his home office where he thought out what needed to be done.

―〜〜―

Brian arrived back at Lacey and Ean's thirty minutes later and was a little disappointed to see that Ava's car was already gone. He knew he'd be seeing her shortly and then they'd have the whole weekend together, but he found that he missed her already.

Lacey let him in and led him to Ean's office, and then went back to putting Olivia down for her nap. He sat down in the chair Ean gestured to. "The plans look good, Ean," Brian began. "I think the time frame should be something both you and Lacey will be comfortable with."

"That's great. I knew after our meeting the other day that we were on the same page and you understood our situation."

"Are you going to stay someplace else while the construction's going on?"

"I'm keeping my options open at this point. My folks have offered to let us stay with them if we need to. This time of year, they tend to head up to Asheville and spend some time at the house up there." He hesitated a moment as if this was all just coming to him. "Oh, hey, isn't that where you and Ava are heading this weekend?"

Brian nodded. "Personally I was hoping for a five-star resort with room service but she was adamant about going to your folks' place."

"Well, Ava has a little bit of an obsession with that place."

"I've noticed," Brian replied and then took a minute to gather his thoughts. "What…what is it about this place? I've heard Ava talk about it but…you're a little more realistic. Am I missing something?"

Ean couldn't believe he was even going to get this

deeply into it. Running a weary hand down his face, he chose his words carefully. "The cottage has been in our family for generations. It's always been a tradition to have weddings at the ranch and then the bride and groom spend their wedding night at the cottage."

"Okay, I get that, but Ava's determined to just spend any night there."

"Well, it became *legend*"—he rolled his eyes— "that those who got married there were blessed with a strong marriage."

"That's it?"

"It's also said that those who chose not to get married at the ranch and all that, well...their marriages didn't last. And if we're going to get technical, the story—as told by my grandmother—says that any couple who spends the night in the cottage will have love everlasting. She never said it had to be their wedding night. Personally, I think it's kind of implied, but that's only if you want to get someone on a technicality."

"But you're a firmly grounded guy and I know you're not buying into all of that, right?"

Ean shifted some papers around as if looking for something to show Brian. "I was thinking of adding..."

"Wait," Brian interrupted, "do you?"

Ean halted his search for the nonexistent piece of paper and looked at Brian awkwardly. "I should have my man-card revoked for this, but...the place is kind of cool. It's the place that brought Lacey back into my life. For that alone, it's always going to be..." He swallowed hard. "...magical to me."

"And the legend?"

Ean sighed. "Look, it's just a silly myth, or legend,

but I think Ava takes it pretty seriously. Everyone else takes it with a grain of salt. But it's a great place and I'm sure you'll have a good weekend. It's nothing to worry about. I'm sure she's going to be fine with the whole thing."

Brian ran a hand through his hair in frustration. "Dammit, Ean!" he said and then stood. "I knew something was weird about this whole thing."

"Brian, I didn't mean to get you all worked up. So our family cottage has a reputation of being a bit magical and any couple who stays there is supposed to be promised love everlasting." God, he hated saying that out loud! "Personally, I don't think it's the cottage. Our family has had our share of long-lasting marriages, it's true, but we've also had our share of miserable ones. Ava chooses to only pay attention to the long-lasting ones and claims it's because of the cottage."

The wheels were turning in Brian's head as Ean continued to talk.

"She was majorly pissed at me and Lacey last year when we got snowed in at the cottage because she felt we had 'stolen her magic,' and for a while she blamed us for her problems with Mason. Of course, at that point she was still in major denial about how wrong they were for each other. It was a tense couple of weeks."

"So you and Lacey," Brian began as he cleared his throat, "what you guys have…"

"Has nothing to do with the cottage. Lacey had a crush on me before I left for college and I'd always thought she was pretty, but back then she was way too young for me. Then last year I saw her in the grocery store when I first got back for Ava's wedding, only I didn't know it was her, and I was drawn to her like a magnet. What happened between us would have happened whether there was a cottage or not."

Ean watched as Brian warred with his thoughts, and felt a little guilty for throwing all of this at him. He liked Brian and he could tell Brian truly loved Ava, but Ean believed the only way their relationship was going to work was for Ava to deal with reality and stop living in a fantasy world based on a legend.

Looking at his watch absently, Brian said, "I need to get going. We need to be on the road by noon if Ava's going to make her interview." He stretched out his hand to shake Ean's and said good-bye, but his mind was elsewhere.

After he left, Lacey walked into Ean's office. "Well?"

"Just like I thought. It was all new information to him."

"What do you think he'll do?" Lacey asked, concern filling her voice.

"I'm hoping he'll do whatever needs to be done to bring Ava back down to earth so she can finally be happy."

"What if she can't be happy until she goes to the cottage?"

Ean looked up at his wife's sad tone. "I think Brian is the man to show her that she doesn't need the cottage to be happy."

"I hope you're right, Ean," she said as he pulled her into his embrace. "I really hope you're right."

Chapter 10

AVA WAS DRESSED AND WAITING WHEN BRIAN finally knocked at noon. She opened the door with a big smile. "I'm packed and ready to go!"

He walked in and barely looked at her. When he was in the middle of her living room, he finally turned to face her. "Let me ask you something, Ava," he began calmly. "What if I said I would go only if we stayed at a hotel?"

"I'd have to ask why. What changed your mind?"

"Fair enough question," he said, his eyes never leaving hers. "I'm not sure quite yet. Let me ask you something else. How do you feel about me?" He wanted to come right out and ask if she loved him, but he wanted to draw this out a little and see if she would admit to her real reason for wanting to go to the cottage.

"How do I feel about you? What kind of question is that?" she asked nervously, not liking the look on his face. "Brian, you're scaring me. What's going on?"

"It's a simple question, Ava. I've told you I love you and you never seem to tell me how you feel about me. Why is that?"

"I…I'm not good with talking about my feelings," she stammered. "I thought you could tell easily enough how I feel."

"Sometimes a man likes to hear how the woman he loves feels about him."

"This is ridiculous, Brian, and I'm going to be late for my interview!" she cried.

"Then answer my question," he said flatly.

"I care about you, Brian. Deeply. There…are you happy now? Can we leave?"

He simply stood and looked at her. "You care about me," he repeated. "Certainly not words to make my heart race." She reached for one of his hands but he eluded her. He tried a different approach. "How do you feel about your family?"

"I love them," she said simply.

He nodded. "You didn't have to even think about it."

"Brian, please," she pleaded. "We don't have time for this! Let's just get going and we'll talk about this later when we get settled at the cottage."

"We've got an almost four-hour drive ahead of us, sweetheart. Can we talk about it on the drive?"

"I am trying to prepare for an interview. Certainly you can understand and respect that. We have the whole weekend ahead of us to talk."

"I don't want to wait for the weekend. I don't want to wait to get to the cottage. I think I've waited long enough. I want to know where you see this relationship going."

Tears welled in her eyes. "Why are you doing this now? I don't understand why you're pressuring me!"

Her tears were always his undoing. His shoulders sagged and he cursed himself for being so hard on her, but it felt like it was now or never. There was no way he was going to live his life doubting what she felt for him and whether it was real or some fairy tale she created in her mind based on a family legend.

Reaching out, he cupped her face. "Ava," he said,

leaning his forehead against hers, "I've waited a long time for this. Do you love me?" His words were a softly spoken plea. He was certain that now, finally, she'd sense the importance of her answer and how it would affect their future together.

"Brian, I…I…" Ava began and closed her eyes. The words were there on the tip of her tongue, but she couldn't seem to force them out. "You know how I feel about you. Don't force me to say it right now while we're fighting." Her heart beat frantically in her chest and breathing was a chore.

Lifting his head, Brian placed a gentle kiss on her forehead. "Sweetheart, if I have to force you to say it, then you don't really feel it." His voice cracked on the last word and he took a deep breath before he could continue. "Almost a year ago I told you I loved you. I had to step back and wait to see if you'd marry another man or if you'd seek me out. I've had to constantly be the one pursuing you. I can't do it anymore. If you can't stand here and confidently tell me how you feel, then I have to step away." And he did just that; he released her face and took a step away from her, and then another. "A man can only wait so long to know where he stands, Ava."

"Brian, please!" she cried, watching as he backed toward the door.

"When you figure out how you feel, you know where to find me."

"Please don't do this!" she said as she walked toward him, but he held his hand out to stop her. "Forget about the interview, we'll talk on the drive and we'll have the weekend to work this all out." Desperation laced her every word and unfortunately Brian understood that.

"Geography isn't going to change anything, Ava," he said sadly. "There is nothing you can say to me in the mountains that you can't say to me right here, right now."

He was right, Ava knew he was right, but she was beyond rational thinking right now. It was the word "geography" that had done it for her. Lacey had said it to her, and Ean had said it to her, and she had no doubt they were behind this. And somehow, when Brian had returned to their house, the two of them must have talked to him about this situation. Ava did not like being forced into anything and this whole argument had her back up in defense.

If Brian couldn't accept her for who she was and what she believed, then clearly he wasn't the man she thought he was—wasn't the man for her. It saddened her terribly; she couldn't imagine pain any worse than what she felt in the region of her heart at this very moment.

But it was all for the best. She would have given him her heart and all that she had if he had just given her another couple of hours. She'd never criticized him for his choice of timing when he'd first told her he loved her, and yet he was trying to tell her when she should say it. She wasn't going to tolerate that.

Stopping right in front of him, Ava noticed a small glimmer of hope in his eyes. "You're right," she said finally. "Geography won't change anything." And with that she picked up her suitcase, grabbed her purse and keys, and opened the door. "Please lock up when you leave" was all she said as she walked out the door, slamming it closed behind her.

How she made the drive in one piece, she'd never know.

How she made it through the mind-numbingly boring interview, she'd never know.

How she was going to survive the heartbreak of losing Brian, well, Ava didn't think she could. All of her previous relationships combined had never led to pain like this. As she pulled up to her parents' home in Asheville, she gave herself a moment to contemplate whether to stay there or go on to the ranch and see the cottage. Indecision warred within her and the cottage won out, if for no other reason than for her to finally face the one thing that was holding up her whole entire life.

With the car parked just off to the side of it, Ava considered the small house. There was nothing to it. It was cute, sure, but it wasn't something so disarmingly charming that she should be thinking about it so much. Taking a deep breath, she got out of the car and let herself in. Funny how—with all of her planning last year—she hadn't actually come here herself. She'd let Lacey and Ean handle all the setup. All of her planning and her binder full of ideas were based on a place she had built up in her mind.

Stepping inside, she looked around. It was a one-room floor plan. There was a tiny kitchen area, a sitting area in front of the fireplace, and a bed. Her shoulders slumped. This was it? This was the place where all of her hopes and dreams were based? It was a room! Sure, when it was all decorated it was charming, but in the light of day in November? It was still just a room.

Ava turned around and immediately walked back out, locking the door behind her. She drove back down the hill to her parents' house and settled in there. She felt restless and couldn't seem to relax. Knowing she needed some answers that she was finally ready to hear, she reached for the phone and dialed.

At the sound of her mother's voice, Ava nearly began to cry. "Mom?" she said shakily.

"Ava? Are you okay, sweetheart? What's the matter? You sound upset." She told her mother what had happened and how confused she was at the moment. "Oh, Ava, you always seemed to make more out of that cottage than anyone else."

"But the stories… Grandma used to always talk of all of the happily ever afters that happened because of the cottage. Was it all a lie?"

"No, it wasn't all a lie, Ava. It was a bit embellished, though."

"What do you mean?"

"Well, for starters, not everyone in the family got married there, and not everyone had a long-lasting or happy marriage."

"Then why would Grandma tell me all those stories?"

"Because you loved them! There wasn't a book written that kept your attention the way a story about that cottage did," she said, and Ava could hear the smile in her voice. "The two of you would sit for hours and she would spin a yarn about distant relatives and friends who stayed there, and honestly, most of that never happened. She created a lot of that purely for your entertainment."

"But…but…" Ava sobbed. "I've ruined two relationships over those stories and now you're telling me it was all for nothing! Oh God, what a fool I am!"

"No, no, sweetheart, you're not a fool! You believe in love and you believe it can last forever, and that's nothing to be ashamed of."

"It is when I'm basing all that on a bunch of fairy tales!"

"Ava," her mother said sternly, "there is nothing wrong with wanting to have a long-lasting marriage to a man who loves you unconditionally. That is every woman's dream! Your only fault is somehow believing you weren't worthy of that love. Don't you see? You don't need the cottage for you to have true love. All you need is to open your heart and trust your feelings with the man you love."

"I think it's too late for that," she admitted. "I think I made Brian wait too long, and then I walked out on him because of my pride and ego, and I don't think he'll be willing to forgive me."

"If he loves you like he claims he does, Ava, then he'll forgive you."

"I hope you're right, Mom." She sighed. "But for now, I think I'm going to take a few days to be alone and try to come to grips with some things about myself."

"Oh, I hate to think about you all by yourself up there."

"No, I think it's for the best. It's time I grew up and faced the person I truly am."

"There's nothing wrong with the person you are, Ava. You're a pretty amazing woman."

"Thanks, Mom, but you're supposed to say that," she said, feeling better than she had all day.

"Doesn't make it any less true."

Ava hoped that in time she'd be able to believe that.

The weekend turned into a week. Ava had decided she needed the time to get her head on straight and figure out what she wanted to do with her life. It was time to stop procrastinating and start taking action. She'd called the bookstore and told them she needed some personal time, and luckily her boss wasn't upset by it. He did get upset when she gave her two weeks' notice.

Next she finally went through all of her job offers and decided on one. For so long Ava had thought she needed to move away in order to start fresh when all she needed was to give herself a break and then her fresh start could happen anywhere.

By the time she got home the following weekend, her voice mail was full of messages. Most of them from Lacey.

"Ava? Ava, honey, where are you? We're worried. Give me a call."

That was the first one. By her fifth message, she was a little less sympathetic.

"Ava, come on… You've clearly turned off your cell phone and enough is enough. Ean and I want to talk to you. Call us." It wasn't a request.

The twelfth one pretty much said it all.

"Okay, so clearly you're still off pouting or whatever. I'm not going to call you again. When you're ready to talk, give me a call."

In between there were random sales calls and a couple from her friend and coworker Julianne, but none of them were from Brian and that hurt. Not that she expected him to call; she'd pretty much made a grand statement when she'd walked out of here a week ago and he'd told her exactly where he stood. He couldn't wait anymore for her, so she shouldn't be surprised that he hadn't called.

Only, she was.

If he loved her like he said he did, why would he give up so easily? *Easily*? She snorted with disgust at that thought. The man waited eight months to come see her and then pretty much kept showing up in her life until she was ready for him. If anything, she was surprised he hadn't given up sooner. If the tables were turned, Ava was certain she wouldn't wait around that long for any man to return her affections.

Sadly she went about the task of unpacking and making mental notes of what needed to get done in the week ahead. She had finally decided to accept a position as her university's new librarian, but she still had a week left at the bookstore. With her new position, she realized, she would need a new, more professional wardrobe.

She reached for her phone and smiled when Lacey answered.

"So I need to do a major wardrobe rehab for my new job. Are you up for a shopping spree?"

―――∾∾∾―――

All Lacey wanted to do was grill Ava on what had happened with Brian. In the last week she had only heard things secondhand from her mother-in-law and Ean, who had seen and talked to Brian. Only one thing was clear: Ava had left Brian. According to Ean, Brian was taking it pretty hard but was determined to get through it.

Typical guy.

When Ava called, Lacey took it as a lifeline. Rather

than harp on what happened, she decided to take her cues from Ava before opening her mouth. Right now, they were on their third store and all Ava wanted to talk about was the new job and Olivia.

"I still can't believe you didn't bring her," Ava chastised. "I mean, all girls love to shop. We'd be teaching her important life skills."

"Well, I don't think she'd be too interested in them right now. She is definitely cutting a tooth and not happy about it. If I fall asleep in one of the dressing room stalls, please make sure I'm covered and not just slouched there in my underwear."

They laughed and shopped, and it wasn't until they stopped for coffee that Lacey had had enough. "Okay, fabulous new job, you're very excited about it, blah, blah, blah. How are you doing? Have you talked to Brian?"

Ava wanted to be annoyed that she would even ask but had to commend Lacey for her self-control in waiting so long to do so. "No, I haven't and I don't plan to."

"What? Why?"

"I did a lot of soul-searching this last week and I have to tell you, I don't like the person I've been."

"Oh, Ava, there's nothing wrong with you!"

"Yeah, yeah, yeah, Mom said the same thing and I didn't believe her either," she said as she waved Lacey off. "Brian deserves someone who can be open and honest with their feelings. Clearly, I have issues." It hurt her to even say the words.

"But you love him!" Lacey cried. "I know you do! Talk to him. I'm sure the two of you can work this out."

Ava looked at her friend and smiled sadly. "In a perfect world, sure. But I'm being realistic for the first time in my life and I'm trying hard to not be selfish anymore. Brian gave me everything he was, and I held myself back. I'm not proud of myself and I realize now how much I must have hurt him."

"We all make mistakes, Ava. No one in a relationship ever gets off without getting hurt a time or two."

"This was different. This was…I don't know. I can't quite forgive myself for behaving the way I did."

"But Brian would forgive you," Lacey reminded her.

"Maybe I don't deserve it."

"I'm not going to change your mind, am I?" Lacey asked sadly.

"Afraid not."

"Maybe I can," a masculine voice said from behind her. Ava turned around and looked up at Mason.

"Mason, hi. How are you?" Ava was giving serious thought to never coming back to this coffeehouse again. "Care to join us?"

Pulling up a chair beside her, he sat down and stared at her. "So…what's new?"

Lacey looked between the two of them, and made an excuse that she needed to call Ean to check on Olivia and left them alone.

"What's going on, Ava?"

"What do you mean?"

Mason sighed with irritation. "I always hated when you answered a question with a question. I ran into Brian a couple of days ago and he said you two broke up. I thought things were going well."

"They were," she said. "And then they weren't."

He nodded. "I can understand that. Are you doing okay?"

"Honestly? No. I'm trying, but it's a lot harder than I thought it would be."

"Why? Seems to me you were the one who walked away, so you got what you wanted. Why shouldn't you be okay?"

"Is that all he told you? That I walked away?" Again he nodded. "He gave me an ultimatum. I just chose the less-desired option."

"Fancy talk for saying you walked away," Mason stated.

"Don't take that lawyer tone with me, Mason, I hate that," she snapped. "We were going away for the weekend and I had it all planned out to tell him how I felt about him over a romantic dinner, but he couldn't wait. He wanted to force me to say it right then and there, and you know I don't like being forced to do or say anything."

"I thought you might've outgrown that," he said with a grin as he lifted his coffee to his lips.

"Ha, ha, very funny. It was his tone, and I had fought with Ean and Lacey about it, and I guess it all felt very familiar, like when everyone was ganging up on me about our wedding. I just snapped. At the time, walking away seemed like the thing to do."

"And now?"

"Now? I don't know. I know Brian deserves someone who won't walk away from him. He gives so completely and so honestly and knows how to show his love and…" Her eyes filled with tears at the thought of all the ways Brian had shown her how much he loved her. "And I just want him to find someone who can do the same for him so he can be happy."

Mason looked around uncomfortably. Where the

heck was Lacey? "Ava, you can do all of those things. You know that, don't you?"

She shook her head in disbelief as the tears continued to fall.

"Look," Mason continued, "one of the reasons you and I didn't work out was because you give so completely and so passionately, and at the time, that didn't work for me. But you and Brian? You belong together. You work. That night when we went out for drinks, it was beyond obvious how much you were in love with each other."

"Was it? Because Brian claimed he couldn't tell." She sniffled.

"It wasn't that he couldn't tell, Ava, it was that he wanted you to be able to tell him, to say the words to him without needing to set the scene. He just wanted your honesty."

"Well, clearly I blew that, didn't I?"

"Yes, you blew that one opportunity," he said. "Don't blow another one." With that, he stood and said good-bye just as Lacey returned to the table.

"Are you okay?" Lacey asked hesitantly.

Ava turned and waved to Mason as he walked out the door. "You know what? I think I am going to be."

Chapter 11

THE FIRST DAYS OF HER NEW JOB AT THE UNIVERSITY proved to Ava that she had made the right choice for her career. She'd put in an application early in her job search, and with her degree and her experience at the campus bookstore, her interview had gone better than any of her other relatively unexciting prospects. She loved her school and the faculty, and to now be a part of them was like being embraced by loved ones. The current librarian was retiring next year, and was going to train Ava to take over. The president of the university was excited with the plans Ava had for updating some of their systems and the new programs she was gearing up to begin. All in all, she knew she was going to be doing what she loved.

Taking a job so close to home meant she didn't have to move after all, but she was toying with the idea of selling her condo anyway. At the end of her workdays, she came home and searched the real estate ads for homes that might appeal to her. The practical side of her knew there was no good reason to rush, but the new Ava wanted to start fresh in all areas of her life and her condo just held too many memories.

What surprised her more than anything was that her family was letting her be. There was no talk of her running away or that she needed to go after Brian; all in all she found it a little odd and unnerving. Her typically overly vocal family was suddenly very tight-lipped when it came to her personal life.

The work was well under way at Lacey and Ean's, and Ava had been certain she'd be getting some sort of update on Brian through that endeavor. But again, Lacey was suspiciously silent on that topic. Ava thought about bringing it up herself but then thought better of it; why open that can of worms?

As fall gave way to winter, Ava was saddened at the loss of the leaves on the trees and the beauty of her drive to work. The fall foliage made her think of the mountains, and for the first time in possibly her whole life, the thought of the mountains didn't lead to thoughts of the cottage and how she was going to get her turn there. She'd learned her lesson; she only wished she had learned it well before she lost the greatest love of her life.

Thanksgiving was days away and Lacey was in a particularly melancholy mood. They were having coffee when Ava finally asked why.

"Well, we hoped the house would be done and we'd be able to host dinner this year. With it being Olivia's first Thanksgiving, we thought it would be extra special to be the ones hosting it. But I guess we were being unrealistic." She sighed and rested her head in the palm of her hand.

"Okay, so you'll miss being the Thanksgiving host this year, that's not a big deal. You know your mom always loves having everyone by her. You'll do Christmas, that's all," Ava said optimistically. "Besides, that is going to be way more fun to watch Olivia celebrate. All of the presents, the tree…it will be more exciting for her at Christmas than at Thanksgiving."

"I guess you're right. I just had it all worked out in my mind and if we had started on the darn project sooner…"

"Oh, stop it. You had to wait until you were ready and I'm sure it's going to look beautiful when it's all done. It's got to be close to completion, right?" It was on the tip of her tongue to ask about Brian, but she prided herself on all the progress she'd made in her life in the past weeks and did not want to take a step backward. Clearly, if Brian had wanted to get in touch with her, he would have called by now.

The silence from her phone was a daily reminder of how much she'd screwed up.

"It's coming along beautifully and we are both very pleased. We were able to move out of your parents' house this week and finally come home."

"How'd that feel?"

"It was like returning from a very stressful vacation," Lacey said. "I mean, you know I love your parents to death, but all of us in that house was just too much 'together time.'"

"Sorry about that. I thought they would have gone up to Asheville for some of the time so you'd have a little space."

"We did too, but they were having too much fun with Olivia. The extra help was great—it was basically like having an in-home babysitter 24-7—but there were times when it was just a little…"

"Overwhelming?" Ava supplied and laughed at Lacey's enthusiastic nod of agreement. "I can only imagine. She's the first grandchild and she's still tiny and new. Someday the novelty will wear off."

"Sure. When *you* have one."

Ava's gaze snapped to Lacey's, her eyes filled with devastation. Though she tried to mask it quickly, she knew Lacey saw it. "Right, like that's going to happen anytime soon. Sorry, Lace, keeping them in grandchildren is your job. When are you planning on having the next one?"

"Very funny." Lacey smiled and then turned serious. "I didn't mean to upset you. It was a thoughtless comment and I'm sorry."

"Nothing to forgive, we've been joking about this since forever. There's no reason for you to stop now."

"I know, but it's just that after you and Br—"

"Don't, okay? Just please…don't," Ava interrupted. She wanted to say more but her throat clogged with tears. *Dang it*, she cursed herself. All the progress she'd made was about to come undone.

Lacey reached across the table and grabbed Ava's hand. "Sometimes I just don't know when to shut up!" she cried. "Please don't cry, Ava. Everything's going to be okay, I know it will. You've got a great new job and you were telling me how well everything's been going with that. Focus on that, sweetie, please!"

Wiping the tears from her eyes, Ava lifted her head and looked at her best friend. "I do. Every day I get up and focus on that, but you know what? At the end of the day, I'm still alone. I can work at a fabulous job, I can sell my condo and buy a beautiful new place, but I'm still alone." She took a moment to compose herself a little more and just when she thought there were no more tears, one last one fell as she admitted, "And I miss him."

"I know you do," Lacey said softly. "I wish there was

something I could do that would make you feel better. I hate to see you hurting like this."

"It's my own doing, so I'm trying to live with that."

A sad smile crossed Lacey's face. "You don't have to be so brave, you know. I'm sure if you just…"

Ava waved her words away. "No. For the first time in my life I am trying not to be so selfish. Brian deserves better. I want him to find someone who puts him first and makes him happy."

"You made him happy."

"I wasn't honest with him, Lace. I was playing a silly game he didn't deserve."

"You're being too hard on yourself. There's no need to be a martyr, Ava. We all do stupid things in our relationships. But you learn from them and move on, you don't need to just quit!"

"I love you so much, Lacey, but this is something I need to do. It's time to move forward and that's what I'm doing. I'm taking baby steps, but each day it gets a little bit easier."

"I still think it doesn't have to be this way."

"Well, I think it does. Can we leave it at that?"

Reluctantly Lacey agreed. She knew when to push and when to pull back, and right now there was no reason to keep pushing. When the time was right, everything would fall into place.

Thanksgiving morning found Ava finishing some last-minute pie baking, thanks to her procrastination. While she loved the aroma of her freshly baked goodies, her kitchen looked as if a team of mad bakers had been at work. She wasn't due at Lacey's parents' house for another couple of hours but even that didn't make her feel any more enthusiastic about the cleanup.

Well, that's the beauty of living on your own, she reminded herself. *There's no one here to get mad at me if I decide to leave the cleanup until later.* With that, she went about getting herself ready while watching the parade on TV, which always made her happy.

By noon, she was getting all the pies loaded into her car when her cell phone rang.

"Okay, don't hate me," Lacey said by way of greeting.

"I'll try," Ava said. "What's going on?"

"Well, we're here at my parents' house and I'm helping with the cooking and Olivia is napping and Ean's down with a migraine."

"Oh, sorry. Wow, he hasn't had one of those in years!" While all of this was clearly upsetting to Lacey, Ava had no idea what it had to do with her.

"In our rush to get out of the house earlier, I left the sweet potato casserole in the fridge and I just can't leave to go get it right now. It's chaos over here. Could you please run by the house and grab it for me? You have a spare key, right?"

"I do, I do," Ava said. "I'm sure nobody would even notice if there wasn't a casserole, Lace. I mean, your family puts out way too much food every year. Why stress about it?"

"Because I made it and it's Ean's favorite and I hate that I couldn't even remember to bring it because we were loaded down with so much baby paraphernalia! Honestly, it's like we're moving every time we leave the house! And with Ean not feeling well I just want him to have what he likes and…"

She could tell Lacey was stressed and decided to cut her a break. "Okay, okay, I'll get it. My share of the meal is dessert, so it's not like I'm needed there right now anyway. So stop worrying and I'll get there as soon as I can."

"Thanks, Ava. You're a lifesaver," Lacey said and then hung up.

It wasn't a big deal to go over to Lacey and Ean's; it was on her way to the Quinns' home. It was just that, it was there that she had last been happy, truly happy, and Brian had still been in love with her. She'd been dying to see the extension but hadn't allowed herself to go over to see it just in case he was there. *Thanksgiving should be safe, right?* she thought. *No one works on the holidays.*

With a better frame of mind, Ava got in her car and headed over to grab the casserole and face her demons.

———

Easier said than done.

Ava stood outside the house for a solid ten minutes before she forced herself to go inside. Once she let herself in, it all came rushing back to her—their time here together, taking care of Olivia as if they were a real family—and her heart sank. When would this heartache go away?

Shaking off her sadness as much as she could, Ava walked back toward the new addition and gasped in awe. It was beautiful. There was a large sitting area with a stone fireplace, and off to either side were his-and-her offices. The work seemed to be near completion and she found herself walking around, touching the built-in bookshelves and staring into the fireplace as if she could imagine a cozy fire blazing in it. The room was perfect.

As if she'd conjured it up herself, the fireplace lit on its own and she shrieked.

"It's a gas fireplace," a masculine voice said from behind her. "All you need to do is flip a switch and voilà, instant fire."

She was afraid to turn around. Her heart was beating madly in her chest as Mason's final words played out in her head. *Yes, you blew that one opportunity. Don't blow another one.* Taking a deep breath to steady her nerves, she faced Brian.

"It looks beautiful in here. I had no idea what they were planning, but this is perfect for them. You did a wonderful job." It was a safe topic.

"Thank you," he said formally, all businesslike. "They seem pleased." And then he just drank in the sight of her. It had been weeks, but it might have been years, so starved was he of the need to be near her. "So, how've you been?"

Oh God, she really didn't want to have this conversation. If only she hadn't stood in the driveway for so long, she would've been gone by now! She wasn't ready for this…this confrontation, this final, civil good-bye! Why today? Why now? Of all days for Lacey to flake out, why did it have to be now?

"Good," she said levelly, congratulating herself on the steadiness of her voice. "I started a new job at the university. I'm being trained to take over for the retiring librarian."

He nodded. "That was one of your best offers. Good for you. Are you enjoying it?"

If she'd said it once, she'd said it a million times: she hated small talk. What was the point? It was a waste of time and all she wanted to do was grab the stupid casserole and leave! But then Ava looked at Brian and realized that wasn't what she wanted to do at all. No, if she were completely honest with herself, she'd admit that what she wanted most right now was to throw herself into his arms and beg his forgiveness.

Only then she remembered the whole not-being-selfish thing.

"I am," she said softly. "I don't know why I fought it for so long."

"You were searching for something perfect," he said. "You just didn't think it could possibly be something that was right in front of you."

Boy, does that ring true on multiple levels, she thought. Nodding, she said, "You're right. I guess I wasn't paying attention very well. Lesson learned."

"Is it?" he asked, taking a step into the room before stopping himself.

"Is it what?"

"Learned," he replied.

"It is," she said with a little more strength.

"That's good. It would be a shame for you to keep missing out on what could be an amazing opportunity because you were searching for something that maybe didn't exist."

She couldn't speak; he knew her too well. She knew they were no longer talking about a job or anything else. This was about them. "I'm done looking for perfect," she admitted. "I'm very happy with the things I have. The things I want, well, they may not be perfect, but neither am I." Tears sprang to her eyes and she looked down before Brian noticed them.

She wasn't fast enough.

When she looked up again, Brian was standing directly in front of her. Without asking permission, he reached up and wiped her tears away as he cupped her face. "You're the closest thing to perfect I've ever seen," he said fiercely just before he lowered his head and kissed her with all of the pent-up longing he'd been feeling. When she sighed and wrapped her arms around him, he deepened the kiss. "I've missed you," he said gruffly between kisses.

"I missed you too," she whispered, seeking his mouth again and again. "I'm so sorry, Brian! I'm so sorry for not being honest with you." Ava was going to say more, but he stopped her because he was too hungry for her. It had been too long and he knew there would be plenty of time to talk later. Right now all that mattered was the two of them and this moment.

Scooping Ava up into his arms, Brian walked out of the room and brought her into the living room where there was furniture, a sofa they could sit on. Gently, he laid her down and then followed beside her, unable to keep from touching her, kissing her; having her near him was more than he had hoped for.

Pulling back, he gazed down into her face and smiled. "I didn't understand," he said after a moment. "I think I was so consumed with the fact that the cottage was someplace you almost went to with Mason that I was blind to everything else." He rested his forehead against hers. "But I get it now. It's not about geography and it's not about the actual structure—it's about family. It's about tradition. I'm sorry I didn't get it. I'm sorry I was so unwilling to compromise for you."

Ava shook her head. "No… Brian, I'm the one who's sorry. I was so focused on one thing—so single-minded about it—that I lost sight of what was really important." Her eyes met his and held. "You. You're what's important. I shouldn't have let myself get distracted from that."

His smile grew before he lowered his head and claimed her lips again and seemingly melted into her.

Ava pulled back and softly ran her fingers across his face. "I love you, Brian," she said honestly. "I have from the beginning and I'm so sorry I didn't tell you."

"I shouldn't have pushed you," he admitted. "I wasn't honest with you either. I wanted to start planning a future for us, but I kept it to myself. So I was making plans in my head and not sharing them with you when I should have."

"You wanted a future with me?"

"I *want* a future with you," he corrected. "Ava, I love you. I don't want to be without you ever again."

"I thought maybe you wouldn't want…"

He placed a finger across her lips to quiet her. "Shh… don't. I will always want you. I'm always going to love you." Brian kissed her softly and pulled back. "What I want more than anything, Ava, is to give you your happily ever after. What do you think?"

No words had ever sounded sweeter.

"I think I'd like that very much." She sighed and snuggled in closer to him.

"And if that means spending one night or a dozen nights in the cottage, then that's what we'll do."

"I know now that it's not necessary. I would love for

us to go there, but I finally understand that I don't need to have it. As long as I have you, I know I'm going to have my everlasting love."

"I love you so much, Ava. I can't wait for us to start our lives together."

"You are my every hope, my every dream. You are my knight in shining armor and I can't think of anyone else I'd rather live my fairy tale with than you." Kissing him again because she couldn't seem to stop herself, Ava felt content for the first time in her life.

She'd been searching for her ever after for so long, who knew it would come and find her first?

Epilogue

One year later

"SO THERE NEVER WAS A SWEET POTATO CASSEROLE."

"Nope."

"And Ean's migraine…?"

"Hasn't had one since he was fifteen."

Ava sighed dramatically. "You know, it's like I don't even know who you are anymore, Lace. Basically you've just turned into one big lying liar." The words would have been harsh had they not been said with a grin.

"That's me," Lacey sang. "But like it or not, you owe all of your happiness to a sweet potato casserole."

"Oh please, I am not saying thank you to a fictitious casserole. That's just ridiculous."

Lacey shrugged. "Hey, you're the superstitious one. All I'm saying is that if it weren't for me being forgetful…"

"But you weren't forgetful! There wasn't a casserole to be found in your house!"

"See! I had forgotten that I didn't forget it, but look at how great it all worked out! The holidays are here again and look at you! You are positively stunning."

Ava turned and looked at herself in the mirror for possibly the tenth time. This was it; she was marrying Brian McCabe. The wedding was a very different affair from what Ava had ever dreamed of for herself. For starters, they were skipping the Callahan tradition of having the wedding on Christmas Eve up in Asheville, and the bride and groom were not spending their wedding night in the infamous cottage.

"Are you sure I look okay?" Ava asked nervously.

"Fishing for compliments?"

Ava grinned. "No...yes...maybe. I don't know. Gosh, I'm so nervous! Why am I so darn nervous?"

"Because it's your wedding day! You've been planning this for a year and now it's finally arrived!"

"Do you think Brian's nervous?"

Lacey shook her head. "I think he is just anxious to get this all over with, and I for one can't blame him."

"This was a lot of work," Ava admitted. "I mean, I didn't use a binder or anything this time, but just the whole process of getting here was a little exhausting."

"Yes, I'm sure picking up the phone and screaming *'We're going to Hawaii!'* had to wear you out," Lacey deadpanned.

"You know, it was harder than it sounds. There were flights to coordinate, and then trying to find sunscreen in North Carolina in the winter... I'm telling you, it wasn't easy."

"Personally, I think it's great. Having the resort's event planner handle the major details was a smart way to go. Believe me. When you gave me and Ean your wedding two years ago, at first I was disappointed that I didn't get to really plan anything, but in the end, we enjoyed ourselves so much more! We were able to relax and celebrate and have fun."

"I know this isn't the wedding that anyone ever thought I would have..."

Lacey waved her off. "Don't worry about that. I don't think anyone's going to complain about being someplace tropical for your wedding."

"No, I know, but Brian and I tossed around so many ideas, and when he mentioned us having a destination wedding so that I'd finally get to travel someplace I'd never been… Well, if I wasn't in love with him already that would have sealed the deal."

Lacey couldn't help but smile.

"What? What are you smiling about?"

"I just… I love that he gets you. I mean, I know you've always wanted to travel but it's not something you talk about all the time, and the fact that he remembered that and put it out there as an option?" She placed a hand over her heart and smiled. "I think I'm a little bit in love with Brian too."

"Well…back off." Ava laughed. "You're only supposed to have eyes for my brother."

"Oh, I do, believe me. It's just wonderful to see a man being so in tune with the woman he loves and how he just wants to make her happy. It's very romantic."

Now it was Ava's turn to smile. "It really is, isn't it?"

"Definitely." Sitting down in one of the oversized chairs in the bridal suite, Lacey watched as Ava checked her reflection in the full-length mirror. "I have to admit, your dress is not what I had imagined at all."

"Surprised you, didn't I?"

"Absolutely. So…what happened to the big princess dress with all the crystals and beading and the mile-long train that we shopped for and—last I saw it—was hanging in your closet?"

"Well, I did some extensive research…"

"You had your final fitting two days ago," Lacey reminded her.

"After extensive research!" Ava cried. "Now hush up and let me talk! Anyway, it didn't feel right to have something so big and so formal for our ceremony on the beach." She twirled around in her sarong-style white gown. "This is so much more comfortable and I'm going to be barefoot and enjoy the sand between my toes."

"Okay, fine, you're a rebel." At that moment, Olivia toddled over and lifted her arms up to her mother. "And I hate to be a spoilsport because I appreciate that you wanted Olivia to be a part of this, but it took a little bit of the fun out of it for me and Ean. We were hoping for a second honeymoon of our own."

"Too bad," Ava said as she checked her reflection one last time and fixed her lipstick. "You already got more out of my last wedding than I did. This time it's all about me, baby."

"I can't even argue with that," Lacey said as she picked up her daughter, who was dressed in a frilly pastel blue dress that matched her eyes. "So where exactly is the ceremony going to be? You've been pretty quiet about it."

"That's because I haven't felt the need to oversee everything. The event coordinator told us exactly what we were going to have—it's one of their most popular packages—and I've found that delegating is very freeing. All we need to do is wait here until she comes and gets us and then we'll be escorted down to the beach when the sun starts to go down."

They had opted for a small ceremony with only Lacey, Ean, and Olivia and their parents in attendance.

Neither felt the need for an over-the-top reception, and Brian knew it was important to Ava to somewhat keep with the Callahan tradition of family-oriented weddings. Brian didn't care where he married Ava; only the fact that they were finally getting married mattered.

Ava's tummy was full of butterflies when the coordinator stepped into the room and announced that it was time. She anxiously looked to Lacey. "I'm nervous! I shouldn't be nervous! This is what I want, what I've been dreaming of."

Lacey reached over and grabbed one of Ava's hands. "It's natural. I knew I loved Ean and couldn't wait to be his wife, and yet that walk down the aisle was nerve-wracking." She smiled. "C'mon, let's go have a wedding!"

Jack Callahan was waiting outside the door and simply beamed at the sight of his daughter. "Ready, sweetheart?"

"More than, Dad," she said and took a steadying breath as she linked her arm through his. They emerged from the resort and were escorted down a path laid with white carpet that led them to an area where several short rows of white chairs and a flower-laden arbor were set up. Ava could see her mother and Brian's parents, their smiles bright. Just beyond them she spotted the pastor and Ean and finally…Brian.

The wedding coordinator stopped Ava about fifty feet from Brian and cued Lacey and Olivia to walk ahead of her. There was a harpist off to the left, and Ean stood beside Brian, both looking so handsome in their tuxedos.

When Lacey made it to the pastor's side, Ava and

her father were cued to begin their walk. The closer she got, the calmer she felt. Her dress flowed slightly in the ocean breeze, and all around her she could see nature at its finest—the waves crashing on the shore as the sun began its glorious descent.

As she finally came face-to-face with the man who would soon be her husband, she felt nothing but peace. Her whole life had led to this very moment. There were no more yesterdays, only the promise of tomorrow and the wonderful future they were going to share.

The pastor spoke briefly, and then it was their turn to speak their vows.

"Ava," Brian began softly. "You came into my life in a most unusual way, and I knew from our first meeting that you were the woman for me. I knew the timing wasn't right for us just then, but I also knew I would wait an eternity for you. You are my love and my life. You are my everything. I promise to love you all the days of my life." He placed the ring on her finger.

Taking a deep breath, Ava took her turn. "Brian, nothing could have surprised me more than your declaration of love. It was the most amazing thing that ever happened to me. I wanted to be perfect for you, but you taught me that I don't need to be. I just need to be me. Thank you for encouraging me to be myself and to live, love, and laugh—mostly at myself," she said cheekily. "You are my strength. You make me believe that anything is possible." And then she quoted the words she once said to him. "You are my every hope, my every dream. You are my knight in shining armor and I can't think of anyone else I'd rather live my fairy tale with than you. I promise to love you all the days of my life." And she placed the ring on his finger.

"By the power vested in me by the state of Hawaii, I hereby pronounce you man and wife," the pastor declared. "You may now kiss your bride."

And Brian did just that. It was a kiss that sealed a promise, and it went on and on until Ean discreetly cleared his throat to get their attention.

Olivia had taken to picking the wildflowers from the arbor and the photographer had sort of wandered off and followed her while the bride and groom continued to kiss. When they finally broke apart, they turned to look at their friends and family, who were beaming at them. Hands were shaken, hugs were exchanged, and soon they were escorted back up the covered path and headed back to their hotel for a celebratory dinner.

Later that night, when it was just the two of them, Ava wrapped herself tightly next to Brian and kissed his cheek. "Thank you," she whispered.

"For what?"

"For not giving up on me," she said simply.

"You were worth waiting for."

She smiled and sighed. "It took us a long time to get here. I'm sorry I made you wait."

Brian pulled her in tighter. "I'm not. I think this day was perfect. We made it our own, and not about other people's expectations or traditions."

Raising her head, she smiled at him. "All my life I thought a specific place held the key to my happily ever after, but it didn't."

Taking one of her hands, Brian placed it on his chest over his heart. "Yes it did, Ava. Do you feel my heart?

That's the place that holds the key to our ever after."
And with that he gently pulled her down for another
kiss, thankful for the start of their new life and the promise of their happy ending.

KEEP READING FOR AN EXCERPT FROM

Made *for* Us

IN THE SHAUGHNESSY BROTHERS SERIES

WHY WERE PEOPLE SO INCOMPETENT? IT WAS A question Aidan Shaughnessy asked himself far too many times a day. How difficult was it to follow instructions? How hard was it to read the damn directions?

"Clearly, it's beyond anyone's comprehension," he muttered to himself as he walked through the model home of the new subdivision his company was working on.

The trim was crooked, the ceiling looked wavy, and the paint job was horrendous. Not only that, but when he reached the master bedroom, he saw the paint colors were completely wrong. Pulling out his phone, Aidan called his assistant and left her a message to get the designer on the job to meet him first thing Monday morning. It was already after seven at night, so Aidan knew no one would be around to clean up the mess now.

With a weary sigh, he shut off all the lights and was locking up the house when his phone rang. Looking at the screen on his smartphone, Aidan felt some of the tension ease from his body.

"Hey, Dad," Aidan said into the phone. "I'm running a little bit behind but I promise to have the pizza there by the time the game starts." He smiled at the thought of having a couple of hours just to unwind and relax with his family. Most men would cringe at spending a Friday night at home with their father and teenage sister, but it was something Aidan looked forward to.

"See that you do," his father said with a chuckle. "Darcy is having a fit that you're not here yet. She's threatening to eat all the brownies herself before you get here!"

That made Aidan laugh because although his seventeen-year-old sister loved to bake, she loved taunting her brothers with her delicious creations even more. "Tell her if she does that, I'll make sure neither of the pizzas have pepperoni. I'll load them with mushrooms and anchovies before I let her take away my dessert!"

Ian Shaughnessy laughed hard. He loved that the age difference between his youngest child and his oldest didn't deter them from bantering with and teasing one another. "Oh, I'll tell her, but be prepared for her wrath if you are one minute late."

"Deal," Aidan said and then called in their order to the local pizzeria.

"Hey, Aidan," Tony said as he answered the phone. "Your usual?"

Shaking his head, Aidan couldn't help but laugh. Small-town living. "Hey, Tony," he said with a smile. "What do you think?"

"Two large pies, one with extra cheese and pepperoni and the other with sausage. Gimme twenty minutes, okay?"

"You got it, Tony. Thanks." Disconnecting, Aidan turned and looked at the house he had just locked up. At least it was beautiful from the outside. Between the stonework, the colors, and the craftsman style, it made for a very appealing home. Aidan had spared no expense on the materials for the model. Everything was top of the line, and he used every upgrade available inside and out to dazzle potential buyers.

Taking a couple of steps back, he admired the landscaping. The grounds looked ready for a *Home and Garden* photo spread. Everything was perfectly manicured, and all the greenery was acclimating to its new soil and cooperating by staying green and in bloom.

If only the inside were up to the same caliber...

"Okay, I have *got* to let that go for tonight," he reminded himself as he walked over to his truck and climbed in. "Dad will have my hide if I spend the night complaining about work."

You would think that at age thirty-four, parental disappointment wouldn't faze a man, but Aidan was different. His father had been through so much in his life, had struggled so much after Aidan's mother had died unexpectedly, that Aidan swore he would never do anything to cause his father any extra grief.

He left that to his siblings.

And they were good at it.

In the years following his mother's death, Aidan had wanted to do more to help his family out. The day after the funeral, Aidan told his father he wanted to quit college and come home, but Ian had put his foot down. Aidan knew his mother wouldn't have wanted him to leave college, but at the time, he'd felt so helpless.

When he blew out his knee in his junior year, it officially ended any dreams of a career in the NFL. But he wasn't disappointed about that now; his life was exactly where it was supposed to be. He had a construction business he had built up all on his own, and he was surrounded—for the most part—by his family.

Some of his brothers had moved away from their small North Carolina town, but Aidan didn't resent them for it. Quite the opposite, he encouraged them to follow their dreams because that was exactly what their mother would have done. With their father preoccupied with raising a teenage girl after a houseful of boys, Aidan had taken it upon himself to be "the encourager" in the family.

Did he date? Sometimes.

Was he looking to settle down? Maybe.

Were there any prospects on the horizon? No.

Maybe he should do something about that, he thought as he drove through town to pick up dinner. The streets were crowded, but that was nothing new. It was Friday night and everyone was out and about. As his truck crept along Main Street with the windows down, Aidan was able to smile and wave to many familiar faces. This was what he did, who he was. But for some reason, tonight it bothered him.

Why wasn't he walking along the street holding hands with a woman? When exactly was the last time he had done that? Searching his memory, he couldn't even remember when. Was it with Amber or Kelly? Hell, he couldn't even remember their names or their faces. That was a surefire clue it had been too long.

"Nothing I can do about it tonight," Aidan muttered and pulled into the last spot in front of the Italian restaurant. There was a line out the door and Aidan was relieved for the side entrance reserved for takeout orders. As he walked in, he was greeted by the same faces he saw in there every Friday night. But by the time Aidan had paid and was walking back out to his truck with the pizzas, he was feeling a little down for some reason.

Aidan had had too long a day to puzzle out the source of this sudden depression, however; for tonight, he vowed to enjoy himself. He loved catching up with what Darcy was up to and hearing about how she was doing in school. And even though Aidan and his dad saw each other on a daily basis because Ian Shaughnessy was in charge of all of the electrical inspections on new construction in the county, Aidan knew his dad always just liked having him around.

Ian was dedicated to his children, and it didn't matter how old they got or how far away they moved: Ian Shaughnessy wanted nothing more than to see his children be happy.

Just as Lillian would have wanted.

Pulling up to his childhood home, Aidan felt a lot of the tension leave his body. This was his haven. No matter what was going on in his life, he still enjoyed coming back here and spending time. Not to mention that right now, the scent of hot pizza was practically making him drool and he had no doubt his little sister was pacing the floor waiting for him to get inside and feed her.

His suspicions were confirmed as soon as he walked through the door.

"It's about time, Aidan!" his sister cried, grabbing the pizza boxes from his hands. "Honestly, a person could die of starvation waiting for you."

"Ex*cuse* me, Duchess," he said with a chuckle, "but some of us have to work for a living. We can't all have food delivered on our every whim."

She rolled her eyes at him as she placed the pizza on the kitchen table. "I would love to have a job, big Brother. But you and Dad and the rest of the Shaughnessy bullies won't let me."

"Bullies?" he asked with a laugh, washing his hands and winking at his father as he walked in from the living room where the pregame bantering was on. "There are Shaughnessy bullies? Why wasn't I told of this?"

"Oh." Darcy swatted his arm playfully. "You're the captain of the bully squad."

"Now we're a squad?"

"Aidan!" she huffed, and plopped down into her seat at the table. "You know darn well you have been the biggest voice in keeping me from getting a job. If you would—"

"Darce, we've been over this before. You don't *need* to work right now. You need to focus on your school-work so you can get into a good college."

Darcy looked from her father to her brother and back again. "A good college? Don't you really mean one that's close to home?" This wasn't a new argument, but Darcy was hoping she'd wear them down eventually.

"There are plenty of colleges close to home," Aidan said evasively, reaching for a slice of the fast-cooling pizza.

"But I don't want to go to any of them."

"Can we please have one meal without an argument?" Ian finally chimed in.

"I'm not arguing, Dad," Darcy countered. "I'm

simply stating that there are plenty of great colleges that aren't within a ten-mile radius of our house."

"So in answer to your question, Dad," Aidan said with a smile, "no. We cannot have one meal without an argument." Normally that was all it took to get Darcy to back down, but tonight she slammed her palms on the table.

"Why won't anyone take this seriously?" she snapped, looking at her father. "Everyone else was allowed to pick where they wanted to go to college. Why can't I?"

"Come on, Darce," Aidan interrupted. "It's been a crappy day. Can't we just enjoy dinner?"

If there was one thing Darcy had learned to perfect in her seventeen years, it was the art of the argument. She had even been on the debate team since her sophomore year, bringing home a trophy or two, and learning some skills that had come in very useful with her siblings. She thought of it as a form of mental self-defense. Unfortunately, she just didn't have it in her tonight. Being the only female in a male-dominated household, there were so many things about her life that didn't seem fair, but she had learned to accept most of them.

Out of her five brothers, she was probably closest to Aidan, even though he was the oldest. He was one of the few siblings who still lived in the area, so she saw him the most and she enjoyed spending time with him. Lately, she could tell something was up with him even though Aidan seemed unwilling to admit it.

Darcy could think of a million reasons why Aidan's day had been crappy. All he did was work and go home alone and spend Friday nights having pizza with her and their father. *Bor-ing*. She wished he'd find someone and go out on a date. Have a social life. She supposed he was good-looking, but if he didn't go out and find a girl soon, he was going to be old and gray and no one was going to want him. Probably not the best time to bring up the old and gray thing.

"Fine," she grumbled. "Why was your day crappy?"

Finishing his slice of pizza, Aidan went to the refrigerator and grabbed himself the one beer he allowed himself every Friday night. "Oh, you know, it's the same old thing. No one reads the instructions on the job site, things aren't getting done the way I want them, my assistant is asking for an assistant. Nothing new."

"Everything was looking good when I was on site on Tuesday," Ian said. "What changed?"

"The paint job is crap, there's some trim that's messed up, and the decorator got all the color tones wrong. I did a walk-through tonight before I left, which is why I was late getting dinner, and I just couldn't believe my eyes. It was as if I had never said a word about anything. I mean, how difficult is it to follow a set of plans?"

"So what are you going to do?" Ian asked, knowing his son was a perfectionist by nature and wouldn't rest until everything was up to his standards.

"I'm bringing in a new painting crew, and I've put a call in to meet the decorator on Monday morning." He shook his head. "Tired of wasting my time."

"Ever think maybe you're looking a little too closely at things?" Darcy asked, and then instantly regretted her comment when her brother aimed an angry glare in her direction.

"I look at things the way they are meant to be looked at," he said defensively. "The craftsmanship I put out there is what makes Shaughnessy Construction stand out. If I relax my standards, then what?"

"Sorry," she mumbled and reached for another slice of pizza.

"Aidan, don't take it out on Darcy. All she's saying is that you have a craftsman's eye. The typical home owner and buyer won't notice the things you see."

"So that makes it right? That makes it okay to just put a crappy product out there? I can't believe you would suggest such a thing."

"I'm not suggesting anything of the sort, Son," Ian said. "I'm just suggesting that you relax a bit." He looked at Darcy slouching in her seat, staring at her plate, then back at Aidan, who looked ready to turn the table upside down. "Who's up for a game of bowling?"

Darcy and Aidan looked up at him incredulously.

"Bowling?" Darcy repeated. "I'm not going to the bowling alley with my dad and brother on a Friday night. Forget about it."

Now it was Ian's turn to roll his eyes. "*Wii* bowling," Ian pulled Darcy out of her seat and then turned to his son. "Don't make me pull you up too. C'mon. Family bowling in the living room. Now. Let's go!"

It was the last thing Aidan wanted to do, but he knew it would make his father happy so he didn't argue. Five minutes later, the three of them were standing in the middle of the living room choosing their order of play. Ten minutes later, it was as if the earlier tension had never even happened.

And that was what was most important to Aidan—his family's happiness.

About the Author

New York Times and *USA Today* bestselling author Samantha Chase released her debut novel, *Jordan's Return*, in November 2011. Although she waited until she was in her forties to publish for the first time, writing has been a lifelong passion. Teaching creative writing to students from elementary through high school and encouraging those students to follow their writing dreams motivated Samantha to take that step as well. When she's not working on a new story, Samantha spends her time reading contemporary romances, blogging, playing Scrabble on Facebook, and spending time with her husband of more than twenty years and their two sons in North Carolina. For more information, visit her website, www.chasing-romance.com, or find her on Twitter @SamanthaChase3 or on Facebook at www.facebook.com/SamanthaChaseFanClub.